Readers love

MARY CALMES

Mine

"*Mine* has drama, sizzling sex, danger, excitement, and a riveting storyline that will grab you and hold you till the end."

—A Joyfully Recommended Read, Joyfully Reviewed

Again

"(An) incredibly romantic and sweet story with just the right side of drama."

—The Romance Studio

Sinnerman

"...packed full of intrigue, romance, excitement and hot steamy sex!"

—Dark Divas Reviews

After the Sunset

"There's just something about this well-developed and believable couple that pulls as the heartstrings."

—Literary Nymphs

Change of Heart

"*Change of Heart* will hold a special place in my TBR list for those occasions when I need to true love in all its many forms."

—Coffee Time Romance and More

By MARY CALMES

NOVELS
Change of Heart
Honored Vow
Trusted Bond

A Matter of Time, Vol. 1 & 2
Bulletproof

Acrobat
The Guardian
Mine
Timing

NOVELLAS
After the Sunset
Again
Any Closer
Frog
Romanus
The Servant
What Can Be

THE WARDER SERIES
His Hearth
Tooth and Nail
Heart in Hand
Sinnerman
Nexus
Cherish Your Name

Published by DREAMSPINNER PRESS
http://www.dreamspinnerpress.com

Acrobat

MARY CALMES

Published by
Dreamspinner Press
382 NE 191st Street #88329
Miami, FL 33179-3899, USA
http://www.dreamspinnerpress.com/

Acrobat

Cover Art by Anne Cain annecain.art@gmail.com
Cover Design by Mara McKennen

ISBN: 978-1-61372-500-9

Printed in the United States of America
First Edition
May 2012

eBook edition available
eBook ISBN: 978-1-61372-501-6

The idea for *Acrobat* was inspired by a painting of Steve Walker's called *Parallel Dreams*. I saw it on his website and was moved to try and capture what led to the moment in the relationship of the two men, one of aching tenderness and trust. My version has its flaws, his artwork has none. When I finished the book, I asked if the picture might possibly be used for the cover and only then was informed that he had passed away. He will be missed, and I for one cannot thank him enough for all the wonderful ideas he gave me.

—Mary Calmes

The allure of the figure has been immortalized in painting and sculpture for centuries, yet few artists capture the quiet grace and vulnerability underlying the voluptuous musculature and sinewy lines of the idealized male nude. Through light and color, Steve Walker created warm, living, *real* men of beauty and emotion on the canvas, imbuing his figures with the subtle tenderness of shared love and quiet moments of reflection. As an artist, I cannot express how much his artistic voice has influenced my own, helping me to ground the idealized male physique in a language that conveys the sincerity of true emotion. The body of work he leaves behind in the wake of his short life is a treasure—not only for us in the art community, but for all who understand that underneath the chiseled physique of a Greek god is the warm, beating heart of a human soul.

While I can never compare myself to your mastery, Steve, the cover art for *Acrobat* is a small token of thanks for what you've given us. You will be missed and loved, always.

—Anne Cain

I would also like to say a special thank you to Ariel for her words on wine. I needed her desperately since I am woefully uneducated there. And to Lidia who was my Italian translator and understood exactly what I needed.

—Mary Calmes

ONE

THERE was just no way.

"You won't know unless you try."

I turned to look at my ex-wife, who was still my best friend in the world. "Are you kidding? It's hopeless."

"It's actually kind of cute."

"Oh God," I groaned and buried my face in my folded arms.

We were having lunch on a Sunday at a bistro she liked that I, of course, had never heard of. But to say that she knew things about fine dining or even "chic" dining that I did not was the understatement of the century. She was more chateaubriand, and I was steak and potatoes.

"Sweetie, there's nothing wrong with it."

"I think there's a code or something."

"What code?"

"Thou shalt not covet your ex-students."

She laughed. "I think you made that one up."

"Oh God, it even sounds disgusting."

"It does not."

"Like you would know."

"Don't be an ass just because you're having a crisis."

I groaned louder.

"You said you had him in class fourteen years ago? Is that right?"

"I bet he doesn't even know who Duran Duran is."

She started laughing. "So that makes him, what, thirty-two now? Thirty-three?"

"Or a Rubik's Cube."

The laughing got harder. "Even thirty-two is perfectly respectable for a man of forty-five."

"Oh God."

"You're so ridiculous."

"That's a thirteen-year age difference, Mel. I could be his father."

She was lost in a fit of giggles.

"I could!"

She just shook her head, wiping at her eyes. Christ, it wasn't that funny.

"Jared is closer to his age than mine."

"True." She shivered slightly in the crisp November air.

It made more sense for the man I had a very immature crush on to date my twenty-seven-year-old son. I was too old for him.

"But your son isn't gay, and Sean is, and so are you, my darling."

I lifted up my head, raked my fingers through my thick dirty-blond hair, and looked at her. "Do you mean to not help?"

"Love," she chuckled, "twenty-eight years ago me and my best friend got drunk off our asses, and because he was hot—still is, I might add—I jumped his bones when I had the chance and got knocked up just like the nuns said I would."

"Thank you for the recap." I grunted, leaning back, looking at her.

Her hand went to my knee. "And lo and behold, nine months later you did the right thing and made an honest woman of me because you loved me and fell madly in love with your kid the second you saw him."

"He was cute." I sighed in memory.

"He looked like an undercooked slab of meatloaf."

"That's disgusting."

"But true," she added brightly. "And that cute little blob grew up to be a wonderful young man."

"Who will make an excellent wildlife biologist very soon." I smiled at her.

She made a noise that was not nice.

"Oh c'mon, Mel, everyone takes a semester off when they're getting their doctorate," I defended my wayward kid. "It's a lot of studying to do all in one shot."

She waved her hand dismissively. "Whatever. We're not discussing Jare; we're discussing you."

"Let's not." I exhaled sharply, picking up my menu. "What're we eating?"

She snatched the leather-bound piece from my hands, which should have been my first clue that I was out of my depth in the "bistro," and smacked me with it.

"Owww," I complained loudly.

She banged it back down on the table. "I want to talk about Sean."

"I don't. I'm not ready anyway."

"No-no-no, you will not hide behind your dead relationship with Duncan anymore. It's been over a year and a half, Nate. It's time to dive back in."

"I have," I assured her. "I've been on some dates."

"Who have you slept with?"

"How is that your business?"

"Nate, you need to get laid."

"Ohmygod, could you speak up, please," I said sarcastically. "The people one street over didn't hear you."

She tried not to smile.

"Jesus, woman," I scolded her.

"It's time to get back on the horse."

"Mel—"

"Or back in the saddle, which is it?"

I dropped my voice an octave. "Listen to me—"

"Oh no, you did not just try and use your teacher voice on me."

I rolled my eyes at her.

"How dare you."

"Can we just—"

"You didn't love him anyway."

Again with the same argument—she was like a broken record. "I did."

"You cared for him, but you didn't love him. Someday, I hope, you'll understand the difference."

"There isn't anything to get," I argued. "Caring for someone, being in love with them, it's the same thing. You're arguing semantics."

"I'm not."

"You're so stubborn."

"And you're in denial."

I shook my head. "I don't see the difference."

"I know, and that's the problem."

"Being in love the way you're talking about is nothing but trouble."

"Spoken like a man who's never been head over heels in love."

"Thank God. Have you read *Romeo and Juliet*?"

She growled.

"I cared for Duncan deeply."

She gave me a look.

"Listen, what does it matter what it was called? I was invested in the man's happiness. How is that not love?"

"I hate it when you do that!"

"Do what?"

"You're equating love and caring again, and we both know that love is more than caring, so therefore they cannot mean the same thing."

"I love you, I love Jare, hell, I even love Ben. I know what—"

"I'm not talking about loving me because I'm your best friend and the mother of your child, and I'm not talking about loving your kid because you're his father or the love you feel for your friends. I'm talking about romance."

"Fine. I had a romance with Duncan Stiel that unfortunately came to an end."

She huffed out a sharp breath.

"You don't like that description either?"

"Listen, one of these days, you are going to fall madly in love with someone, and I pray to God I'm there to see it so I can point at you and yell 'ah-hah' at the top of my lungs."

"That's very mature."

"Whatever," she said dismissively. "All I know is it's time for you to start dating again with a chance of it getting serious, and the handsome young doctor would be someone nice to start back up with."

"I've been on dates since Duncan," I said again.

"But you haven't gotten laid. That's the part that's missing."

"How do you know?"

Her eyes lit up. "You got laid? When? Who was it?"

I was not about to discuss my sex life with her. "What are you, living vicariously through me?"

She gave me a dismissive wave. "Instead of talking someone to death, have sex instead."

"You want me to be a manwhore?"

"I want you to begin a new physical relationship with another man."

But that wasn't just something I could jump into, at least not long term. One night stands were another area all together. "There has to be a deeper connection than dinner and a movie," I told her.

"Like love."

"Like caring," I corrected her. "Like things in common, goals."

She rolled her eyes.

"I'm sorry, who's the romantic here?"

"Nate—"

"I saw him coming out of a bathhouse, did I tell you?"

"Who?"

"Duncan. God. Try and follow the conversation."

"Why do I care about Duncan Stiel anymore?"

"Because he was coming out of a bathhouse!" I was indignant.

"I hardly cared about him while you two were together. What makes you think I give a crap about him now?"

"You are completely missing the point."

Her sigh was long and exasperated. "And what were you doing there?"

"Where?"

"Now who's not keeping up?"

"Oh, you mean at the bathhouse."

She widened her eyes and gave me the exasperated waggle of her head.

"I wasn't at a bathhouse; I was across the street buying porn."

"Are you sure?"

"That I was buying porn?"

The snort of laughter was not ladylike at all.

"Shit."

She made a rolling motion with her hand for me to go on.

"I can promise you, I no longer frequent bathhouses." I smiled at her. "They're gross."

"You're a prude," she pronounced.

"I don't want to catch a disease."

"That's what condoms are for."

I squinted at her. "Who are you?"

"Just—keep going."

"That's it. I saw him there, my ex at a bathhouse."

"Oooh, was he carrying his badge and his gun? Was it a bust?"

"No, it wasn't a bust; you're completely missing the point."

"I'm not." She cleared her throat. "I get it, and I'm sorry."

"It's fine. It's just, you know, he can't move in with me, he can't be seen in public even holding my hand, but he can apparently fuck hundreds of nameless, faceless guys in bathhouses and clubs with impunity."

"In all fairness," she said softly, "you knew the man was in the closet when you started up with him. He was very up-front and honest."

"Please don't remind of the huge-ass hypocrite I am."

"That's not what I meant to do. It's just that if he can't be in a loving, committed, grown-up relationship with another man since he's in the closet because of work, he still has needs. What are his options, really, besides screwing in bathhouses and clubs? You have to think about it logically."

"True, it's just that when I saw him leaving with that boy a couple weeks ago, I thought about how old I was, you know?"

"Ohmygod, Nate, you're not old!"

"But I'm older than the guy he was with, and I was so way up on my moral high horse at that moment, and now look at me in the same boat, lusting after some twink who probably bottoms like a—"

"Not a twink at all," she championed Sean Cooper, the man in question. "I met him, you'll remember."

This was why she was badgering me; she had been with me when I ducked down the produce aisle a week ago, running around like an idiot because I had seen him first.

"And I think the man's a top, actually."

I put my head back at the futility of the situation. The young man who had made me tongue-tied in English 101 all those years ago was, in my opinion, absolute perfection.

Sean Cooper was six feet two inches of heaven. He ran, he swam—had been, in fact, on the water polo team when he was in college—and was in possession of the most beautifully carved physique I had ever seen. The lines of him defeated me, but more than that was his kindness.

He remembered everything anyone ever said, as evidenced when he caught me and Melissa in the wine aisle fifteen minutes after I had sought to evade him.

"Doctor Qells." He had smiled, and the light-blue eyes had glowed warmly.

"Sean." I sighed because the jig was up and I was caught.

"Still hunting for the perfect merlot?"

Fifteen years I hadn't seen him, but he could still recall a small, insignificant detail from me fooling around in class with my students. It was heady stuff. The man was thoughtful and funny and sarcastic and smart. He was, he told me, an attending at the county hospital, having just moved back to Chicago from the West Coast, from California. He was going into pediatrics—he wanted kids. And that brought up a whole laundry list of other concerns, because I was forty-five and….

"Forget it." I shook my head. "It's useless anyway. If I wanted to ask him out, I should have done it right then, when he was looking at me and…. But now what am I going to do, call him up out of the blue, ask to take him out? Really?"

"Why not? All he can say is no."

"You know, why do women not get the whole horror of asking someone out on a date only to be shot down? Why? If I live to be a thousand, I will never get the whole quick shrug thing like it's nothing. It is physically painful to be told no. Do you get that at all?"

"Don't be ridiculous." She lifted her hand to wave at her husband, who was coming up the sidewalk to meet us for lunch.

"Don't tell Ben," I muttered before he got there.

"Don't tell Ben what?" the man in question said as he leaned over, kissed his wife's cheek, and then came around the table as I stood up.

He hugged me tight and was back taking a seat beside his wife seconds later. He looked at me expectantly.

"What?" I asked.

"I don't know. How the hell *should* I know? You're the one who said 'Don't tell Ben.'"

"How did you even hear that?"

"I've got good ears."

The man had bat ears, apparently.

"So give."

"Just never mind."

"Are you guys having an affair?"

I squinted at him, and he burst into laughter.

"Sorry, that was stupid."

"Hey," Melissa Qells Ortiz scolded her husband. "I could be having an affair."

"Not with a gay man." He snickered, turning to look up at the waitress hovering over our table. "Ice tea, and we'll be ready to order when you get back. Thank you, dear."

And the waitress puddled into goo under his big warm brown eyes and sexy smile. Melissa and I were silent as he turned back to us.

"What?"

"I dunno." I shrugged. "Are you done flirting with our waitress?"

"I—what?"

Melissa lifted one golden eyebrow.

"Oh c'mon, I get to take a goddess home, why would I want anything else?"

"Nice save," I grumbled as his wife, my ex-wife, leaned forward and kissed his cheek. They were a great couple. I was glad when we divorced, when Jared was ten, that she had then found the love of her life. She was a great stepmother to Ben's three kids, and they adored her. Ben was a wonderful stepfather to Jared, and they got along well. Not as well as he and I, but I was kind of secretly happy about that.

My son had grown up understanding that his father was gay. He recognized that this was the reason we were getting a divorce. When Melissa and I had sat him down at ten, he was too young to understand the specifics, but he knew I loved men. It had never been a secret. I was thrilled when she remarried, and because I was, Jared was. I had worried as he got older that perhaps he would turn away from me and toward his stepfather, as they had the love of women in common. But as it turned out, a lifetime of love and devotion actually counted for something. My kid, rowdy and rude at eleven, rebellious and full of angst at thirteen, even apathetic and snarling at sixteen and undecided about what he was going to do with his life at eighteen, still never lost the ability to laugh at himself or love his parents. Even now, at twenty-seven, the first thing I got when I met him at the airport was a big hug followed by a sloppy kiss on the cheek. And at home, on the couch, he would still stretch out, put his head in my lap, and fall asleep. It turned out that who I slept with didn't matter in the least. When he was a teenager, I had been called a douche, but my sexual orientation had nothing to do with that, only my rules. I was his father, and him believing I was antiquated and unfair was the only factor in our arguments. Our shouting matches never included what I did in my bedroom.

When my ex had walked out of my life a year and a half ago, the first thing my son did was whoop for joy over the phone. Just like everyone else, he had not liked Duncan Stiel. The second thing he did was suggest I find someone new. But I doubted he would want that someone in his father's bed to be just a little bit older than him.

"So what are you going to do?"

I came out of my thoughts to find both Melissa and Ben staring at me. They really did make a nice couple, her with her mane of blonde hair pulled up into a french twist, diamond studs in her ears, classic and elegant and radiant. Ben was tall and dark and handsome, dashing in his dark charcoal-gray suit and black turtleneck. They were a matching set. Me in my jeans with a Henley over a long-sleeve T-shirt and hiking boots, I definitely looked out of place.

"I'm going to go buy a bottle of wine, drown myself, and try and think of something interesting to say about Shakespeare tomorrow."

"Seriously." Ben squinted at both of us. "What are we talking about?"

"Never—"

"Nate has a little crush."

"Really? Finally." He sighed. "Enough with moping around over Duncan Stiel already."

"I haven't been—"

"Yes, you have," they both said at the same time.

"Oh jinx." Melissa laughed, and her husband rolled his eyes at her.

"You guys wear me out."

Ben smiled. "How many girls, would you say, fall in love with you every quarter?"

"What does—"

"And they have no idea you're gay, do they?"

It took me a minute. "What are you talking about?"

"The girls all go nuts for you because you look the same now as you did when I met you at twenty-eight. And while once you were a struggling grad student working three jobs to support himself, help pay child support, and actually eat on occasion, now you're a tenured professor with a doctorate in English literature—"

"And I'm still poor," I cut him off.

"I actually kind of like your loft in Lincoln Park," Melissa assured me. "It's much less fussy than my house that I have to have a maid to clean."

"Excuse me?" Ben asked her, sounding just slightly put out.

"She didn't mean it," I chimed in, kicking her under the table.

"Owww, you shit," Ben grumbled, which sent Melissa into peals of laughter.

I couldn't help laughing when she did; her laughter was infectious, just like my kid's.

"I just meant to say—" Melissa chuckled, blowing her nose on a napkin. "—that your loft is warm and homey and I love it."

"It is nice," Ben grumped as the waitress returned to take our order.

When she left us with bread, I sat there in the chilly November air and wondered what my life would look like to a thirty-two-year-old man.

"You're a catch, Qells."

I turned back to look at Ben.

"You are. You have great friends, and I don't just mean us. Your kid loves you—hell, my kids love you—you have a really nice home, a wonderful job, and hair that any man would die to have. You're in possibly the best shape of your life, and your interests are so varied I can't even keep up with you. I had no idea you could change the oil filter on your own car."

“This is not something to put on your résumé,” I assured him.

“Yes, but I can’t do it,” he told me. “I can’t do crap with my own car, and I’m the CEO of my own company, for crissakes.”

“You have people to do it for you.”

“Yes, but the point is that you can go to the ballet with me or a baseball game or a concert and wherever is fine. You’re like the Swiss army knife friend; you have an attachment for everything.”

I did a slow pan to Melissa. “Did that sound filthy, or was it just me?”

“Oh no, that was filthy,” she assured me, her eyebrows lifting as she surveyed her husband.

“Wait.” He thought about it. “I just meant—”

“Thanks, buddy.” I smiled, reaching out to pat his shoulder.

“Just call Sean,” Melissa ordered me. “Don’t let the whole thing squick you—”

“Squick? I’m sorry, I’m not familiar with this word.”

“You know, freak you out, weird you out, gross you out—squick?”

“How old are you again?”

She smacked me really heard, and when I looked at Ben for help, he just shook his head.

“No hitting,” he told his wife.

She swatted him next.

“What the hell?”

“Oh, I know.” She brightened. “Why don’t you just call Jare and ask him how the kids ask each other out these days?”

“Oh God. Kids.”

“You know what I meant.”

Great idea. Call my son and ask him for advice with asking out a younger man. That was brilliant.

“It couldn’t hurt.”

Good God.

Chapter TWO

BEING a hero should have been less painful. I was thinking that as I sat on the small hospital bed on Monday night, waiting to see a doctor. I had saved a woman from getting mugged or worse—she had been more worried about the "worse" than the contents of her designer handbag—but I had succeeded in getting smashed in the face and then, when I was down, kicked in the ribs. Suzie Rais was very appreciative—so was her husband, when he met her at the hospital—and they told that to my friend Douglas Kearney, whom I had called instead of Melissa or Ben. Doug would be cool about it. Melissa and Ben would blow it way out of proportion.

"You might look like a superhero," Doug said from the chair by the door, "but you're not, buddy. Take it easy."

"Just sit there and get ready to take me home."

"In like ten hours." He yawned, getting up. "You know that time stops when you're in the emergency room just like when you're watching a basketball game."

I grunted my agreement.

"You want something from downstairs? I need a soda or something."

"No, I'll buy you dinner after this."

"A steak?" He sounded hopeful.

"Yes, if we must."

"Oh yes, we must."

"I'm thinking I wanna go bowling or something this weekend. Maybe we can—"

"No." He shook his head. "Me and Dave and Jackie are hitting the clubs this weekend."

I narrowed my eyes. "Did my invitation get lost in the mail?"

He looked at me like I was nuts.

"What?"

"For starters, you never pick up anyone at the club, you just talk everybody to death, and second, I don't feel like looking like chopped liver standing next to you."

"What are you talking about?"

"Dr. Qells?"

We both turned toward the voice, and there, standing in the doorway, was Sean Cooper. Dr. Sean Cooper, MD. The smile I was getting was really nice.

"Yeah, that's what I'm talking about," Doug said drolly, rolling his eyes.

I quickly returned my eyes to the vision in front of me. The long, thick golden eyelashes were just beautiful, but the eyes were an even bigger thrill. Really, what did you call that color, brilliant summer sky? With his big blue eyes and golden honey-blond hair, the man looked good enough to eat.

"I thought it was you," he breathed out, crossing the room to stand in front of me, his eyes everywhere before they met mine and stayed. "When I saw your name on the board, I got here as fast as I could."

"Well, that was really nice of you to worry about your ex-English professor," I observed.

He squinted, pressed his lips together, and then excused himself for a moment.

Doug cleared his throat, walked over to me, and punched me in the arm.

"Shit, I'm hurt, you know," I groused, rubbing my bicep. "I might have a concussion."

"You obviously have a brain tumor, you idiot," he snapped, slapping me on the back of the head.

"I will seriously beat the crap outta you." I shoved him off me.

"For crissakes, Nate," he growled. "That fuckin' gorgeous-ass doctor is dyin' to get his hands on you, and you go and bring up the fact that you used to be his teacher? What the hell?"

"He—"

"Nate"—his eyes got big—"try not to be a total imbecile right now, okay? Christ, I'm outta here."

I sighed. "I'll see ya in a bit."

"No." He shook his head, gesturing to the clipboard sitting beside me. "Have the good doctor take you home."

"What are you—oh, you're back." I smiled at Sean as he walked back into the room. "This is my buddy Doug Kearney—Doug, Sean; Sean, Doug."

They shook hands, and Doug explained how he had to go and he was sure I would be well enough to take a cab home. He was gone before I could say another word.

"Your friend bailed fast, huh?"

"Yeah." I forced a smile. "So you think I'll live?"

"I need to look at you first."

"I… uhm—" I cleared my throat. "—thought you worked at County."

"I do. We're doing a trade this week, cross-training in different conditions. They do it a lot since Mercy Glen and County are partners."

I nodded. "Got it."

"Why?"

"Why what?"

"Did you not want to run into me?"

"No," I blurted out, "just the opposite."

"Opposite?"

Shit.

He was waiting, stepping closer so that the white hospital coat brushed my knees.

"Dr. Qells?"

"You're the doctor."

"So are you," he assured me, and I couldn't help but notice the breath he took.

"Sean, I…."

"Yes?"

He stepped closer, between my legs, and his hands—those finely boned, long-fingered hands of his—rested on either side of me on the bed. I swallowed hard.

"I kept thinking," he said, one hand reaching up, and the first touch of his fingertips to my jaw made me shudder, "when I saw you the other night at the grocery store that if I kept running into you, then maybe you'd eventually invite me over for dinner. I've been going there every night since."

Dear God in heaven.

"I had the biggest crush on you when I had you for freshman English, Dr. Qells, but you knew that, didn't you?"

"No," I said and smiled at him. "Not at all."

"No?" He seemed surprised. "Christ, I must be the shittiest flirt ever."

"I'm sure you're very smooth," I teased. "But you were very young."

"I wasn't that young." His eyes narrowed. "I was legal."

I laughed softly. "Just barely."

"Well, I'm all grown up now."

And suddenly I wasn't laughing anymore.

"Are you seeing anyone?" he asked pointedly.

"No." I tried to breathe around the lump in my throat.

"Why not?"

"What do you mean?"

"I mean," he said with a shrug, "why not? A man like you, why aren't you dating anyone?"

"A man like me?"

"You're a catch, Dr. Qells; you don't need me to tell you that."

I peered at him. "I wasn't fishing."

"No, I know, I can tell. You were actually interested in my answer."

I cleared my throat as one of his hands settled on my knee.

"So," he prodded, "why isn't there anyone special?"

"I just got out of a relationship."

"How long ago?"

And it was going to sound stupid. "Year and a half ago," I confessed.

He didn't laugh or snicker or even smile, and I was surprised. "And it took you a while to get over it."

"Yes, it did."

"But now?"

"Now I'm all fixed up."

He nodded. "So you've had the rebound guy, huh?"

I cleared my throat. "I'm sorry?"

"You've had a guy since him, right?"

In what context?

"Right?" he pressed me.

Why would I play games and not just answer? "Are you asking me if I've been with anyone since my ex?"

"Yessir, that's what I'm asking." He grinned.

"Well, the answer is yes, Sean, I have."

The gorgeous blue eyes sparkled. "That's good."

"Why?"

"Because, Dr. Qells, I would love to take you home with me, but I do not plan on being the one-night stand rebound guy. I plan on being the guy who gets to take you out."

All the air was sucked from my lungs.

His eyes followed his fingers as they traced over my jaw. "I know this is sudden for you, and maybe I'm freaking you out just a little, but Dr.—"

"Nate," I corrected him.

"Nate," he repeated. "Like I said, I know to you this is coming out of right field, but… I've been carrying this torch for close to fifteen years, and before I fall into something else, or you do, I would really like to have a shot at seeing you. I figure us bumping into each other at the store last week and now here… maybe I'm supposed to be paying attention."

I was concentrating on breathing.

"And at least if nothing else, would you come home with me and get in my bed?"

"I thought that wasn't what you wanted?" I teased.

"What?" He had stopped listening to me, too intent on my mouth.

I chuckled because he was very good for my ego.

"I'm usually better at this," he coughed out, "but you're kind of short-circuiting my brain."

Me? He was the walking, talking wet dream come to life. "Sean—"

"Please." He licked his lips. "Let me see you."

"Sean."

He made a noise in the back of his throat, and only then did I get that the overwhelming reaction I was having to him, he was having to me. God, he really liked me.

I tipped my head, squinting at him. "It used to be hard for me to keep my train of thought when you asked me questions. I always got caught up looking at your beautiful eyes."

His breath caught, and it was adorable. "You're kidding, right? All of us—the boys, the girls—we all had it so bad. The first day when you were up there talking nonstop about Milton and you were all into it, smiling and laughing, I kept thinking, Jesus Christ, I won't learn a damn thing from this man if I get a boner every class."

I chuckled and his smile widened, heated.

"Could you just let me take you out to dinner? This is me begging."

"The begging's not necessary. I would love that," I told him. "When?"

"Tonight would be great, but I'm on shift until eleven. Would tomorrow night work? Tuesday night? You probably have plans, but—"

"I have no plans."

He nodded. "How 'bout I pick you up at seven. Would that work?"

"That would work."

"Can I get your number so I can call and get directions?"

"Sure," I said, pulling my phone from my pocket. "And I'll get yours, but I could wait."

"Wait?"

I looked up. "It's a little after nine now. I could wait and we could have dinner tonight."

"And tomorrow?"

It was impossible for me to stop staring. "What about tomorrow?"

"I want to pick you up and take you someplace great."

"Okay." I smiled. "Tonight it's my treat, tomorrow it's yours."

"Perfect."

"You know, I wasn't thinking. Maybe you're tired or—"

"I'll meet you downstairs in front of the reception desk," he said quickly, eyes wide suddenly. "Don't ditch me, you understand?"

I squinted at him, watching as he pulled the drape around me closed.

"What are you—"

"I gotta find you a doctor," he told me.

"I thought you were my doctor."

"I'm a surgeon, actually, and besides, that would be unethical." He grinned evilly before he left. "And I'm all about the ethics."

"But—"

"Wait for me!" he yelled from the other side of the ugly khaki-green drape.

I sat there a minute and was just about to get up and peek around the curtain when it was yanked open and a very pretty doctor looked in at me. Her eyes were large almond-shaped perfection, and her skin was actually that smooth mocha that you read about in romance novels but never saw in real life.

"Hello there." She beamed. "I'm Dr. Vargas, and I'll be taking care of you tonight."

"It's a pleasure." I smiled at her.

"Oh he's right, you are cute."

Christ.

Almost two hours later, I was in reception, waiting for my date and wondering as each minute ticked by why I had opened my mouth. Things were going so well. Why had I suggested dinner after he got off his shift as well?

"Hey, Nate."

Turning, I saw Michael Fiore walking toward me. He was my next-door neighbor, all of sixteen, living with his uncle instead of with his mother because she had died four years ago in a car accident. She had only been thirty at the time.

"What are you doing here?" I smiled as he took a seat beside me.

"Oh shit." He winced, looking me over. "What happened to you?"

"I saved a lady from getting mugged and got beat up a little."

He was squinting, not liking seeing me hurt but trying for bored and casual with his tone. It was his body language that was giving him away.

"So," I said, swiping the knit beanie from his head and shoving it at him. "What are you doing here?"

He rolled his eyes, knowing he was supposed to take it off inside, his uncle forever telling him to do that. "My grandma's here, and Dreo wants me to see her."

"You don't want to see her?"

He shrugged. "She was never close to me and Mom, and then when Mom died, she wanted me to go live with her and Papa, but my Mom made it so if anything happened to her I went with Dreo."

I nodded even though I really didn't understand his mother's thinking. Andreo Fiore seemed cold to me, not the kind of man who should be raising a child. I had never once seen the man smile, and I had lived next door to him and his nephew for the last four years.

Dreo came and went at all hours. I knew he carried a gun because I had seen it on more than one occasion, and my best guess was that he was mob muscle. Of course, maybe he was an accountant for all I knew. I had never asked him or Michael, but I seriously doubted it. The thing was, I didn't really know the man at all. It was his nephew I knew. Michael was the one who knocked on my door at night when he was alone, watched TV on my couch while I graded papers, and listened to me bitch about the underwhelming sentence structure of college juniors. He would laugh as he listened to me spew and would eventually offer to make me some tea. I had gotten him addicted to chamomile before bed.

Sometimes he would fall asleep and I'd be up writing—it was publish or perish, after all—or reading, and then Dreo would be at my door to collect him.

He was taller than my own six one, and I had to tip my head back to meet a gaze that was so dark brown it looked black. He had thick brows, so the effect together with the deep-set eyes was altogether dangerous. He shared glossy black hair and olive skin with his nephew, but whereas Michael was handsome, Andreo was scary. The clothes, his heavy black leather jacket over a sweater or dress shirt, always somehow reminded me of all the mafia movies I had ever seen. It was probably simply that he was Italian, spoke Italian, and came and went with a posse of other men. I had seen too many Pacino movies, and I could own that.

Whenever he came to my door to fetch his nephew, Andreo Fiore was always appreciative that I had kept the young man company. The first time he'd ever come to collect him, about a week or so after they moved in, he had started peeling twenties off a wad he had retrieved from his pocket.

"What are you doing?" I asked, squinting.

He looked confused. "You took care of him for me."

"Which I enjoyed," I explained, gesturing at a picture of me and my son Jared on the table where I dropped my keys when I came home every night. "My boy's all grown up, but I remember what it was like to help with homework and talk about girls."

He nodded, and I smiled.

"So it's fine, I enjoyed his company. He can come over if he wants."

"*Grazie*," he said.

And those had been our only spoken words for another six months. I saw Michael, I talked to Michael, and we got to be friends. He actually knew more about Chaucer and Milton and Shakespeare than a lot of my students and laughed on the rare occasions when he helped me read essay questions. Some nights he'd come by, and we'd have dinner and watch *Monday Night Football* or we'd walk to get dinner—Chinese, my favorite, or burgers, which was his. Sometimes we would even see Andreo out, and when Michael tugged me after him—I never wanted to intrude—we'd say hello. Everyone with him, men and women, were always nice, but Andreo always sort of got rid of us, politely but firmly.

Now, when I passed him in the hall, I got a head tip, no words then, but he always thanked me when he picked up Michael. Sometimes after the exchange of pleasantries, he would ask me a question about work, what my plans were for the weekend or for whatever holiday we were closest to, or he'd compliment my home. It turned out that he was a fan of my hardwood floors, the exposed pipes in the ceiling, and my overstuffed, welcoming-looking furniture. I wondered about him, about how a twenty-eight-year-old man made enough to support himself and his nephew, living somewhere I never could have afforded at that age. The lofts in Lincoln Park were upscale, our building had a security system with a key fob and intercom to buzz you in, and even though I wanted to ask, it was more curiosity than a burning desire.

"Nate?"

"Sorry." I smiled at Michael. "I hope your grandmother will be okay."

He reached up and touched my jaw with light fingers. "This looks kind of bad. Did a doctor look at you?"

"I'm fine," I assured him, taking his hand in both of mine and holding it tight for a moment. "So hey, tomorrow I'm having dinner with someone, but Wednesday night I have tickets to the opera, and I want you to come with me, all right? It will be a little shot of culture for you, and Mrs. Chang said she'd give you extra credit if you wrote up your experience."

"What?"

"You heard me."

"When did you talk to Mrs. Chang?" He scowled.

"I ran into her at the ballet last week."

"You did?"

"I did." I smirked.

"Shit, I knew I should have never introduced you guys at the school carnival last month. God, what a nightmare," he groaned.

"You need the extra credit."

"Whatever."

"You have to dress up."

He groaned louder.

"So do you want to go?"

"Do I have a choice?"

"Always."

"Fine, I'll go."

I chuckled over his disgust, like he was doing me a favor instead of the other way around. "So you have to ask your uncle if it's okay."

"Ask me if what's okay?"

We looked up and Andreo Fiore was there, towering over both of us, all six four of him, broad-shouldered, muscular, and V-shaped, making me look small by comparison and Michael absolutely puny.

"Nate's gonna take me to the opera on Wednesday night." He gagged.

"If it's okay with you." I smiled, standing up, feeling better when I was closer to his height.

"Are you sure?"

"Course." I leaned over and tousled Michael's thick hair. "I'll see you then. Come around six and we'll eat first, all right?"

He nodded, beaming up at me. "Thanks, Nate."

"Sure."

"Nate."

I turned to look at Dreo and into his amazing eyes. They were really something, hot and wet, deep and dark.

He tipped his head at me. "What happened to you?"

"He saved a lady from gettin' mugged," Michael answered for me.

"Oh?"

Dreo Fiore's brown-black eyes were not like any others I had ever seen, and sometimes, just for a second, I got lost there.

"Nate?"

"Oh, yeah." I smiled. "You know, close by that park down off Pearson?"

He nodded.

"Some guys had her against that chain-link fence by the vacant lot."

"What guys?"

"Those same guys that are always there." I sighed. "They always yell stuff and—"

"They yell at you?"

"They yell at everybody." I chuckled. "But I never thought they actually moved, you know? I thought they were all bark, but I guess not."

His eyes slid over me. "How many?"

"Like three, but one ran when I got there."

"I see. So did the police pick anybody up?"

"I have no idea."

"You walk that same way every day, huh?"

"Most of the time, and it's really lucky I did today." I smiled. "But let me let you guys go. It's a school night, and Michael needs to get home, get in bed."

"*Sì*," Dreo agreed.

"Nate?"

I turned, and there was Sean smiling at me, topcoat on, laptop bag hanging at his side.

"You ready to eat?"

"Yeah." I sighed, lifting my arm for him.

He came forward, moving into the embrace, and I introduced him. "Sean Cooper, I'd like you to meet my friends Andreo Fiore and his nephew, Michael."

"Pleasure." He smiled at them both, shaking each hand in turn.

I watched Sean take in Dreo and not like what he saw.

"Let's go," Dreo snapped at Michael, grabbing his arm, steering him toward the elevators.

We watched them leave.

"Spooky guy." Sean grinned, leaning closer.

I realized I'd been right and not imagining things. Sean had been intimidated, or maybe even scared, by Dreo Fiore. "Really? Michael scared you?" I teased, wanting to soothe whatever concern he had.

"Funny." He chuckled, slipping an arm around my waist. "Now come on, I'm starving. You promised to feed me."

"Yes, I did. Tell me where you live."

"In Lakeview, you?"

"Lincoln Park."

"Okay, so we can eat somewhere in the middle," he said as he tightened his arm around me. "Or you can just take me home with you."

Oh, the man was very good for my ego.

THE diner had good home-cooked food, and I had pot roast and he had swiss steak. It was nice, talking to him, and as I listened, I found myself completely charmed. His family, friends, his career, all of it was interesting and fun. By the time we finished off our meal with coffee and pie, it was late. Since I had to teach in the morning and he had to be back on call at nine, we decided to call it a night.

It was raining outside, and as we stood under the canvas awning in the downpour, he told me that he'd really had a great time.

"So where are we going tomorrow?" I asked.

"I'm going to wine you and dine you," he promised, and I watched as he caught his breath as he stared at me. "And then take you home."

"Oh," I teased. "I was hoping for more."

"To my home," he told me, laughing. "God, you're an ass."

I reached for him, took his face in my hands, and bent him toward me. The way his eyes closed, the long, thick lashes brushing his cheek, the sigh that came out of him… man, I was blind.

When my lips closed over his, he parted them instantly and my tongue met his in a wicked, wanton tangle. The whimper in the back of his throat was very sexy, and when I deepened the kiss, I felt him jolt against me, his hands fisted in my sweater.

I mauled his sweet mouth and understood at that moment how wrong my dear friend had been. The man wanted desperately to submit to me. There was no top in him in at all.

"Jesus," he gasped, breaking the kiss to breathe, staring at me with heavy-lidded eyes. "Forget what I said, Nate, just come home with me now."

But I didn't want rushed, I wanted real, so I leaned back in and told him so in his ear before I kissed him again. I put him in a cab a minute later. When my phone rang as I was in a cab traveling in the opposite direction, I smiled before answering.

"Not sick of me yet?"

"Nate," he breathed out my name. "Why didn't you put me over your desk when I used to come by your office when I was your student?"

"Because that would have been unethical," I teased. "And you're all about the ethics, right?"

He laughed, and it was a good sound.

"So I'll see you tomorrow, right?"

"Definitely. I'll be the guy on your front stoop at seven sharp."

"I can't wait," I assured him.

"Thank you for saying that. The honesty is really nice."

"Same here."

"God, I really don't want to say goodnight."

"Then say you'll see me later, since you will."

"Okay." He took a breath. "I'll see you later."

"Good."

I couldn't stop smiling even after I hung up.

THREE

THE auditorium was a sea of blank stares. I had to make them understand, because only my grad student, Ashton Cross, seemed to be following what I was talking about, as was evidenced by the eye rolling.

"Okay," I told the room, "so we're talking about just switching out two characters from two of Shakespeare's plays and then writing either about what the plays would look like with those new protagonists in place or writing them into one pivotal scene."

Nothing.

A girl in the back raised her hand.

"Yes?"

"Is this going to be on the test?"

Dear. God. "An exercise like this, yes."

Middle of the second row.

"Yes?"

"Is there an example we can reference?"

"No, I want to see what you come up with. Have fun with it."

"So there's no reference, then?"

"Correct"

Front row on the left.

"Yes?"

"How will we know if it's right?"

"It's open to interpretation."

Ten hands up at once.

I looked over at Ashton, snarky beast that he was, small and blond and perfect, the kind of man that both women and men dreamed about at night. His expression held nothing but disdain for them and sympathy for me.

I picked one of the many hands in the air. “Yes?”

“Are we supposed to have read more than the plays you had us read?”

I wanted to say, “As lit majors, I would hope so,” but I refrained because being a sarcastic asshole was no help to anyone. “It would have been helpful” was what I said instead.

He looked distraught.

After class Ashton was venting about how most of the papers he’d just read didn’t even reference other sources.

“You realize that most of these kids haven’t read Virgil or Plato or even Homer, for crissakes. I mean, Jesus, Nate, you need to flunk them all. How can they understand what they’re reading if they don’t get the mythology behind it, or the history?”

“You’re very scary,” I assured him. “They’re only juniors.”

“When I was a sophomore, I was already taking your tragedy class, and—”

“I pity the kids that take classes from you when you’re a professor.”

“Novelist,” he enunciated for me. “I’m going to write books, not teach idiots all day like you do. God, I’d have to start doing drugs again.”

“Shakespeare while high?” I chuckled. “Really?”

He growled.

“Just take deep breaths.”

His gorgeous cobalt-blue eyes narrowed. “You’ve got a date.”

“That’s impressive, actually. How do you know that?”

“You’re all shiny and happy today.”

I smiled, stuffing books into my courier bag.

"Congratulations, by the way."

My eyes flicked to him. "For going on a date?"

"No," he snapped. "I saw that your paper on Marlowe got into the *Cambridge Quarterly*. Very impressive."

I waggled my eyebrows.

"You shit."

"Don't be jealous, kitten."

"I'm not jealous, you know that. You deserve everything you—" He took a breath, cutting himself off. "I finished my book. Will you read it?"

"Of course I'll read it."

"And you won't be nice. I don't need nice, Nate."

"I'm never nice," I said, closing my bag. "According to you."

He sighed heavily. "I e-mailed it to your personal one, okay?"

"I'll read it before the weekend. I promise."

"Thank you."

"C'mon, coffee's on me."

And he walked with me and put his hand on my shoulder and was basically the guy he never was with anybody else but his mother and his boyfriend, Levi Stone.

The day got better after that. The lower-level classes were fun, as I was teaching Shakespeare's comedies, and in Chaucer we were writing as though the writer were speaking to the character and what he would say. My office hours went by quickly with a lot of students just coming by to visit. When I was on my way out that afternoon, leaving my office in Walker Hall and passing the office of our department chair, Richard Hampton, Gail Chase, our chair's secretary, popped out of her office.

"Hey, you." She smiled.

"Hey back." I stopped, pleased to see that she had returned to work. "How are you feeling?"

"Better, thank you," she said, her eyes soft as she looked at me. "And thank you so much for sending over all the groceries, Nate, that helped so much. Being a single mom and recovering from gallbladder surgery at the same time was a little rougher than I thought it was going to be."

I reached out and squeezed her shoulder, and she patted my hand.

"But that's not why I stopped you." She smirked.

"Did you get my flowers?" I smiled big and hopeful.

"Oooh, you're very cute, but it's not gonna help. Greg wants you to help Vaughn with the Medieval Feast, and that's all there is to it."

"But he wanted to do it by himself." I almost whined for her benefit, even giving her a little foot stomp to complete the picture of petulance.

"Nate." She giggled.

"Oh, Gail, you should've seen him: he stood up in the middle of our staff meeting and said that"—I deepened my voice—"someone else should be allowed to put their stamp on one of the only black-tie events that the English department hosts."

"Nate," she repeated, trying really hard to stop laughing and look serious.

"You were on leave, you don't know. I—" I heard voices in the hall and saw two of my colleagues. "Rox, Paul!"

Dr. Roxanne Chaney and Dr. Paul Valdez both came when I called them, both smiling, happy to see me.

"Tell her." I pointed at Gail.

"Tell her what?" Roxanne asked, smiling, offering me a bite of the apple she had just started.

I took the Granny Smith from her. "Tell her what Vaughn said."

"Oh," Paul said as I bit into the apple, more than happy to chime in before Rox. "So Gail, he stands up in the middle of the meeting, scares the crap out of Richard 'cause he's napping, right, and—"

"Henry is, like, what the ef," Roxanne interrupted, cackling. "I mean he's trying to have his regular meeting with Toni knitting and Crosby texting and Greg dozing and frickin' Vaughn is like"—her voice dropped an octave just like mine had, all of us ready to mimic how serious the man always was—"I don't see why Nate coordinates the Medieval Feast every year and no one else ever gets to take a turn."

Gail looked at me, and I waggled my eyebrows at her to confirm the story as I ate more of the apple. I was hungrier than I thought I was.

"And he goes on to say that it's not fair that just one faculty member is involved and that we should all be involved, and Peter's like, screw that, he doesn't want to be involved. It's Nate's baby, and this way all he has to do is bring a damn date."

She started laughing again.

"I mean, come on." Roxanne chuckled, turning back to me. "Gimme that."

I shook my head at her, taking more bites.

"It has my spit on it."

"I like your spit." I grinned at her with apple in my mouth.

"When are you going to rid of this beard and this mustache?" She sighed. "You would look so much better with it gone."

"I look distinguished this way."

"You're too young for it," she assured me, running her fingers along my jaw, "and much too handsome."

"Oh yes, he's very pretty," Paul teased me, pinching my cheek. "And this year he doesn't have to be the host in the monkey suit working the room at the Medieval Feast."

I gave him a high five for that.

"You know why?" Paul chuckled, turning back to Gail. "Because Sanderson Vaughn is a complete douche who finally stuck his foot in it this time."

Gail coughed to stop laughing. "The department chair, your boss, my boss, the fabulous Richard Hampton, wants you to cohost with Vaughn," she told me. "Apparently when he asked Sandy—"

"Sandy," Paul scoffed. "Really? That's a grown-up's name?"

"Stop it," she warned him and then looked back at me. "Today he asked for status, I mean the damn thing's just eight weeks away, and *Sandy*"—she glared at Paul, daring him to say another word about the man's name—"hasn't even booked the hotel yet or planned a menu or given us a guest list so we can start on the invitations."

I sighed deeply. "I would really love to help," I told her.

"Liar," Roxanne coughed into her hand.

My smile could not be stifled even though I was still chewing. "But I already promised my students a Yule masque at my place."

"A what?" Paul was interested.

I swallowed fast. "Everyone has to come as a character from Shakespeare, Chaucer, or Milton and be ready to explain everything about themselves. And you can't drop it all night long. Them's the rules."

"And you've got kids who are going to willingly do this."

"Sure." I nodded, confused.

"Jesus, Qells, how?"

"The eyes," Roxanne assured him, "and the smile."

"It's his ass," Ashton said as he strutted by, from where I had no idea.

"That's crude," I said, turning to Gail, pointing after Ashton. "You should tell Richard and have that kid kicked out of school."

She rolled her eyes before she grabbed my bicep and pulled me after her.

I shoved the apple core back at Roxanne.

"Eww," she griped.

"Can I come to the Yule thing?" Paul called after me.

"No," Gail barked back. "You're coming to the Medieval Feast."

"But why do I have to go if Nate doesn't have to go?"

She growled before she opened the door to her office and shoved me through.

"You know, you're really strong for a sweet, delicate little—"

"I'm going to kill you," she threatened me, pointing at Richard's open office door.

Walking to the doorframe, I leaned in and saw the chair of the Department of English Language and Literature, Richard Hampton, assistant professor Sanderson Vaughn, Gina Tzu, the Director of Graduate Studies, and a man I had never seen before in my life.

"Hey," I said, smiling. "Didn't want to interrupt, but Gail insisted I poke my head in."

"Oh thank God," Richard groaned, gesturing me in. "I need you."

I opened my mouth, but Gina's eyes got huge at the same instant, and I exhaled before I crossed the room to stand beside her.

"Nate, this is Daniel Kramer from Butler Davenport."

I had no clue what that was.

"Mr. Kramer is here on behalf of one of our former students, Gregory Butler, and—"

"Greg." I scowled, remembering. "He was one of the worst students I ever had."

Daniel Kramer smiled wide and stood, moving around the chairs to reach me.

I took the hand he offered me.

"Gregory is now the new CEO of Butler Davenport, and one of the things on his to do list is to make a sizable donation to this department."

"That's very good of him," I said, releasing the hand of the very handsome man who was still looking at me.

"He wants to also sponsor this year's Medieval Feast, Dr. Qells."

"Nice." I looked over at Sanderson. "Sounds like you lucked out on the budget, huh?"

He smirked.

"Dr. Qells."

I looked back at Mr. Kramer.

"Mr. Butler was very disappointed to learn that you were not in charge of the event this year."

"Oh, well." I shrugged one shoulder. "The department felt that it was time that the torch was passed, and Mr. Vaughn's enthusiasm and drive have been—"

"You're not hearing me, Dr. Qells."

I turned to look at Gina and found her looking right through me. She was about a million times scarier than Richard ever thought of being. I whined softly in the back of my throat.

She made the tiniest *uh-uh* noise, and I looked back at Mr. Kramer.

"Perhaps I could co-host with Professor Vaughn."

He nodded. "That would be best."

"And will Greg be gracing us with his presence?" I asked snidely.

"He will."

"Super."

"Apparently, before you, Dr. Qells, he never had a professor threaten to flunk him."

"He was lazy," I informed him.

"So he says," he told me. "But I, for one, have never seen it."

I nodded.

"So the event itself will be contracted through an agency. The event planner will only need to coordinate with you for the night itself."

"And Professor Vaughn."

"Of course."

"Okay, so we'll all be hearing from you, then."

"Yes, you will, Dr. Qells."

I looked over at Gina. "I have to go."

She grunted, and I turned and shook Mr. Kramer's hand again before walking out of the office. I threatened Gail with bodily harm on the way out, and she threw a highlighter at me. Out in the hall, Paul and Roxanne were still there.

"Oh, you're not going to believe this."

As the three of us left the building both Paul and Roxanne were confused.

"Didn't you flunk that kid?" Roxanne asked me. "'Cause I think if you didn't, I did."

"I gave him a low C, but he worked damn hard for it. He was such a slacker."

"Huh."

"On the other hand, Sanderson can kiss your ass, huh?"

"Yeah, but I never gave a crap either way."

"Which makes it more ironic than anything else." Paul shrugged.

"So now you have the Medieval Feast and your Yule party?"

"Yeah, but it sounds like I don't actually have to do anything for the feast except show up. There's some agency coordinating the event."

"Oooh, it's going to be fancy, then," Roxanne told me.

"Sounds like it, yeah."

"When is it? The week after New Year's like normal?"

"I have no idea. You'll probably get an embossed invitation, though."

"Cool."

But it sounded fussy to me, which was what I told Melissa on the train on the way home when I called her to tell her about my date with Sean.

"How was dinner last night?"

I told her about the kiss, and she was swooning as I got off at the platform and started down the stairs. It was always fun to talk to her, and I made her promise that she and Ben would attend the Medieval Feast with me.

"Oh yeah, do I get to dress up?"

"Yes, dear."

There was clapping on her end.

I told her I loved her and hung up as I made the turn for home.

It was still early, not six yet, so when I was walking down the hall toward my apartment, I was surprised to see Michael's bike leaning against the front door. It was strange for him to be home since he normally had basketball practice right after school.

After I dropped off my laptop and books, I was going to jump in the shower, but I went back out into the hall and knocked on the door to see if he wanted a snack while I got ready for my date. Maybe he was home because he was sick.

No answer.

I knocked again.

"Who is it?" The voice came through the door.

What was going on? Since when did he check first? "Who do you think it is?" I teased.

When he opened the door, he was smiling. And the fact was, he never smiled at me, not at first. Maybe after we talked for a minute or if he thought up some wiseass thing to say to me, but never just big smile, frozen in place, just for me.

Uh-huh.

And he was leaning on the door like that maneuver was new, as though I had never seen it before. Apparently he had forgotten that I was neither stupid nor new to the teenage boy game. Not only had I been one, but I had already raised one, as well. I knew gamesmanship when I encountered it.

"Who's in there with you?" I asked flatly, taking in his flushed face, the red spot on his throat, and the Calvin Klein undershirt telling me exactly what size it was because it was not only turned inside out but on the wrong way as well. "Huh, Mr. Fiore?"

"What? I—what?"

I rolled my eyes and pushed by him, and there, on the couch, brown hair tousled, lips swollen, and her sweater on inside out, was the cutest girl I had ever seen. Her big emerald-green eyes looked like they were going to pop right out of her head. She was terrified.

"Who's this?" I asked my friend Casanova.

"Nothing happened."

"Not what I asked." Something had obviously happened. "Who's this?" I asked for the second time.

"This is Danielle Tulia."

"And?" I waited.

"Nate, nothing happened."

I gestured at her.

"No, I mean, something did happen, but not what you think."

I crossed the room and sat down next to Danielle. "Hi."

She looked like she was going to throw up.

I took her hand and she looked at me, those limpid eyes all over my face.

"Not here to judge, just want to talk, okay?"

She nodded; it was all she seemed capable of.

"Sweetheart, maybe you should go to the bathroom and wash your face and take the sweater off and put it back on so I'm not looking at the seams and your deodorant smudges."

She gasped and fled.

I looked over at Michael.

"Nate—"

"Sit; I want to talk to you about my best friend Melissa and I."

"Oh God," he groaned as he flopped down onto the couch.

When Danielle got back from the bathroom, chin quivering, bottom lip doing the same, her eyes now swollen from crying, I took her hand again and held it while I continued to tell the story of how my best friend and I made a baby when I was seventeen and she was eighteen. We were new parents nine months later at eighteen and nineteen.

The longer I talked, the better Danielle got and the more interested Michael became in the discussion. I explained to them that they were, in my opinion, too young to have sex.

"Physically you're ready," I said gently, "but emotionally? Mentally?"

They both stared at me.

"Fine, I'm just a stupid adult." I shrugged. "So who brought the condom?"

"Dani's on the pill."

I nodded and looked back at Danielle. "But what if he's got the clap or something?"

She caught her breath.

"I don't have it! I don't have anything!" He swore to her before turning to growl at me. "Nate! How could you even say that?"

"It was a question," I said, turning back to Danielle. "But you need to be much more careful than you're being, love."

And I suddenly had my arms full of Danielle Tulia.

Michael's face showed all his irritation.

"So you ditched basketball practice?" I asked.

He nodded.

I leaned Danielle back, my hands on her face. "And where do your folks think you are, sweetheart?"

"Studying with my friend Aurora." She took a breath. "But I thought you were my father when you knocked on the door."

It was a security building; someone would have had to let her old man up, or he would have had to wait downstairs until someone came in. The possibility that it could be her father was small; what wasn't was her guilt.

"Maybe you guys need to rethink this a little, huh?"

Michael was staring at me.

"What if it had been Dreo coming through the door?"

He went white with just the idea of that, and I understood that he hadn't even thought that far ahead.

I took them both to my apartment and made grilled cheese and tomato soup, and we talked a little more after I called Sean and moved our date back an hour. He chuckled when I explained.

"So you're a guardian angel now?"

"I guess."

"You're a good man, Nate Qells; I can't wait to be the one you care about."

He really knew all the right things to say.

When we were done, the three of us went downstairs, and I was on my way to get my car so Michael and I could drive Danielle home when an enormous SUV came to a lurching, squealing-tire stop in the middle of the street.

"Oh shit, it's my dad," Danielle had enough time to squeak out before the huge man came barreling around the vehicle he'd just gotten out of and on up the sidewalk.

Maybe Mr. Tulia wouldn't have hit Michael—he was probably looking for an adult to pummel was my guess—but I wasn't taking any chances. My tall, skinny friend was much too slight to absorb even a tap from the bear of a man, so I was glad I was there to intercede and take the punishment for him. I didn't go down—the angle was wrong, and Mr. Tulia was just a little too close to me when he swung, the punch clipping my jaw instead of landing solid.

"Ohmygod, Dad, what are you doing?" Danielle screamed.

"Dani!" I heard a woman scream.

"Mom, Dad hit Nate!"

"Nate!" Michael yelled.

"Who the fuck is Nate?" Mr. Tulia roared.

It was sort of funny if you forgot the part where I had been hit twice in a twenty-four-hour period and was starting to feel a little like a punching bag. My hands went up to fend the man off, and both Michael and Danielle jumped in front of me, which made Mr. Tulia, from the look on his face, feel like a total ass.

"Awww, shit," he groaned.

Michael sucked in his breath, and I could tell he was scared.

"It's fine," I told him as my eyes started to water. "We're fine."

"Shit," Mr. Tulia swore again. "Siddown before you fall."

It was good advice.

I ended up sitting on the stairs with him beside me on the stoop, leaning forward, elbows on his knees. He had finally calmed enough to address his daughter.

"You were supposed to be with Aurora, but when we went by to get you, you weren't there."

"No, I know, I'm so sorry."

"Aurora said you were studying with Michael, but since I don't know any Michael and I don't know his family or who's at home with him while you're there, I came over here to see what was what."

"And you brought Mom?"

"I insisted," Mrs. Tulia chimed in. "I didn't want your father to kill anybody."

Seemed reasonable, I thought, even as I cleared my throat. "They were alone for a bit, Mr. Tulia, I won't lie, but I get home every day around five, so I was there soon after, and they had soup and sandwiches."

Mrs. Tulia wanted to know what kind of soup, and I said tomato and then told her about the grilled cheese without being asked.

"That combination is always good." She smiled.

"I think so," I agreed.

"I'm sorry I hit ya."

"Thanks." I grinned, turning to Mr. Tulia. The way he had almost snapped out the apology told me it was sincere. He was mad at himself; it was there in his voice.

"So you're Michael's father?"

"You're up," I told my friend the lothario.

Michael explained that I was his friend and that he actually lived with his uncle.

"Who's your uncle?"

"It's not a big deal, Mr. Tulia."

"Michael?" Danielle looked at him oddly. "What?"

"Just—"

"His uncle's name is Andreo. Andreo Fiore." Danielle smiled at her father.

The gasp from Mrs. Tulia surprised me, as did the hand she clasped over her mouth.

"What?" Danielle asked.

Mr. Tulia swore under his breath, and I turned to peer at him.

He took a shuddering breath before he turned to me, his jaw set, unable to hide how scared he suddenly was but ready to face the firing squad. "When do you expect Mr. Fiore?"

I shook my head slowly. "We don't expect him. He'll be home whenever, I guess, but this is between us, Mr. Tulia. Michael's a good boy, and I appreciate you letting Dani come by. I promise you that he'll be a gentleman at your house and that when Dani comes over here in the future that either Dreo or—"

"You can vouch for him, can you? You know Michael well enough?"

I looked up at the long, lanky boy with the lopsided grin and dark brown-black eyes who always carried around just a hint of sadness in the set of his shoulders. "Yes."

"Nate?"

I returned my eyes to the older man.

"You have kids?"

"A son."

"Okay, so you get it, that you need to know where they are, who they're with."

"Course."

"Fine."

But it didn't sound like it was. "Mr. Tulia?"

He took a breath. "I can't have my girl over here in Dreo Fiore's house, Nate."

"What?"

"I have no problem with Mr. Fiore or Mr. Romelli."

"I don't know Mr. Romelli."

"That's Dreo's boss," Michael told me.

"Oh, okay." I smiled at Mr. Tulia. "Well, if you're not comfortable with Danielle—"

"Michael can come by our house, all right, Nate?"

"Oh." I was both surprised and happy. "Thank you," I said, because the rest of it was lost on me, but I knew Michael wanted to be allowed to see the girl who made him breathless and twitchy with anticipation.

He nodded. "How do you know Dreo Fiore, Nate?"

"We're neighbors," I told him, thinking of something. "Mr. Tulia, Michael and I are going to the opera tomorrow night; would you allow Danielle to go with us?"

"You're going to the opera?" Mrs. Tulia asked me, finding her voice finally.

"Yes, we are," I said, standing and putting an arm around Michael's shoulders. "And Michael and I will be in our suits, so—"

"Yes." Mrs. Tulia nodded. "Danielle can go."

My smile was big because I saw it in her face—she trusted me with her kid.

"What is it you do, Nate?"

I explained that I was an English professor at the University of Chicago and what kind of classes I taught, and the longer I talked, the more the Tulias' eyes started to glaze over, just like everyone's always did, because I was going on and on about Chaucer and Milton and Jesus God could I please just frickin' stop?

It was just so ordinary and benign, and Danielle was nodding because she really liked Michael, and the more I spoke and bored the hell out of her folks, the more everything seemed like it had swung back over to normal.

Michael had his hand on the back of my topcoat, and I could feel the weight of it as he held on. And it was doubtful that he was even registering that he was touching me, but I understood because Jared used to do that as well. In Michael's head, I was the adult, he was the kid, and so, just for a moment, he sought comfort.

Mr. Tulia listened to me, looked at Michael, and watched his daughter.

Mrs. Tulia took my hand, nodded, and apologized for her husband's temper.

As I looked at them, I had to smile. They were such stereotypical parents, him all glowering and protective and his wife trying to inject the gentleness and warmth after the flaring of anger. I liked them both already even though the man had left another bruise on my face.

"You understand, Nate; this *is* the man's daughter that we were over here to check on."

"Yes, ma'am. I never had a girl, so I don't know exactly what that's like, but I did raise a boy, so I get the frustration over an adult not being home. I mean, that was the problem, right? Where the hell was I? What the hell kind of chaperone am I?"

"Yes," Mr. Tulia said like finally I got it.

"Come with us," Mrs. Tulia said suddenly. "Our son Johnny has a restaurant off Clybourn. You'll love it."

But I had a date.

Michael's hands were like a vise on my bicep. Danielle's hand slipped into mine. Both of them were screwing with my love life with the pleading puppy dog looks on their faces.

"Sure," I said with a sigh. "But you guys get to ride with me and listen to my music."

Michael groaned loudly. "Fine, just no Hall and Oates, okay?"

I cackled, and Mr. Tulia laughed too.

"Let me go get my phone," I told the small assembly, and I was excused to return to my apartment to retrieve it.

I had missed five calls, and they were all from Sean.

"Nate?"

"Yeah," I said as I took the elevator back down. "I'm so sorry; I forgot my phone when I left my apartment to take Michael—"

"It's okay, and I'm sorry to cut you off, but I have to go to work right now."

"Oh." I was disappointed, and it was stupid because I would have been canceling on him anyway, but the idea that he was blowing me off was sort of depressing.

"No-no-no, please don't think that I'm not ready to beg you to reschedule. It's just that I want to be a pediatric surgeon, and we have this case that—"

"It's okay, you don't have to explain."

"Nate, listen. There's this amazing surgeon operating, and he asked for two other doctors to assist, and my chief, he suggested me. It's a huge deal, and if I don't take him up on it I just feel like that would be like the worst idea ever, you know?"

"I do know."

"But I don't want you to get the wrong impression. I want you to let me take you out tomorrow instead, please."

"Tomorrow I'm taking a couple of kids to the opera. How about Thursday?"

"Really?" He sounded very happy.

I smiled into the phone. "Yes, really."

"Just like that? No begging, no game playing?"

"We're being honest, right?" I asked. "I mean, you really do want us to have dinner, don't you?"

"More than you can imagine."

"And I was looking forward to it all day, but it sounds like Thursday would be better for both of us."

"It would."

"Okay, so then why would I second-guess you?"

"Jesus, Nate, I don't know what I'm going to do with all this honesty. It's so rare."

I chuckled. "So Thursday for sure, same time? Seven?"

"Absolutely. I'll be there."

"See you then. I hope everything goes well for you and even better for your patient."

There was a pause. "Thank you," he said oddly.

"You're welcome."

I hung up, and when I got downstairs, everyone was waiting on me. I told Michael I was going to sing in the car.

His groan of disgust was loud.

FOUR

THE restaurant was amazing. Tucchetti's was small and warm, and the chicken tetrazzini I had was really good and just a little spicy. I watched the kids lean close and whisper to one another, and listened to the Tulias talk to their son Johnny, who came to the booth to sit down. As the older brother, he gave Michael the requisite crap about taking out his sister. Like how they would never find his body if she missed curfew.

I nodded, and Johnny leaned sideways and gave me a hug.

"See, he knows," Mr. Tulia, Ray now, pointed at me. "I bet your boy Jared always brings his dates home on time."

Well, now he had a girlfriend that he lived with, but I took the compliment for what it was. Mrs. Tulia, Carmen, wanted to know more about Michael, and so I explained about the basketball and how he and I went to the homeless shelter on Dearborn one Saturday a month and that he was a lazy student but that we were working on it.

"You take good care of him." Carmen smiled.

"Dreo takes good care of him; I just try and polish him up a little, make him fit for company."

She laughed, and I saw the way her husband and son looked, the warmth in their eyes, the smiles for me.

"My mother," Danielle told me later as we were having oranges in marsala sauce for dessert, "she has cancer."

"Oh." I caught my breath because it was hard news to hear.

"No." She shook her head. "She's in remission now, and we're all okay right this second, you know?"

I took her hand, and she leaned sideways into me.

"But when you sit here and make her laugh, well… we're gonna look at you like that, okay?"

"Okay."

Something was said rapidly in Italian, and when I looked back at Carmen, she was shooing someone away from the table before she retook her seat across from me.

"What was that about?" I asked her, looking at the very attractive blonde woman sashaying away.

"My niece, Angelique, she thought you were very handsome when you came in, Nate, but I told her no, you are gay, so she has no chance to have your baby to get a ring."

So many things at once. "First, how'd you know I was gay?"

"Michael told us when you were in the bathroom. I asked where your wife was, such a handsome man, and he said you were gay but that you and your best friend made a child together."

It had been a lot if information for him convey in a matter of minutes. "Thank you."

"For?"

"Thinking I'm cute," I teased her.

"I said handsome, and you are."

"And your niece?"

"Is a whore." She smiled. "And even if you liked girls, I would not let you near her."

I nodded, and she reached out and put a hand on my cheek.

"This is for what?"

"What are we talking about?"

"This beard, this mustache, why do you hide?"

"Makes me look scholarly, don't you think?"

"I think it's time to get rid of it. You have a good face; we should see it."

I grunted.

"So like a man."

I took her hand in mine, and her smile was dazzling. It was easy to understand why her family wanted to see more of it. "I was actually thinking of getting rid of it, but shaving every day is a pain in the you-know-what."

She shrugged. "Tell me, how did you get the bruises on your face?"

I pointed at her husband.

Her laughter was there again, and her husband leaned forward to look at me.

"What happened really?"

It was fun to explain about the night before and the mugging I had stopped.

"Now I feel worse," Ray told me.

"Good." I smirked. "'Cause I think I need some Tylenol or something."

"Or another cappuccino?" Johnny offered.

"Both, please."

As I watched his son leave, I saw Ray's smile. He liked me. His whole family liked me, and feeling Michael's knee wedged next to mine under the table, I knew my being there had helped.

"So, Casanova," I said, smiling, "what did we learn?"

"Not to skip basketball practice when you're trying to get laid?" he said under his breath, having leaned close to my ear.

"You're a riot."

He bumped my shoulder, and I asked how his grandmother was when he saw her the night before.

"She's fine. She's getting out today."

"What was it?"

"They had to put a stent in her heart."

"But she's okay."

"Yeah, they said she could go home."

“How is your uncle?”

“He’s okay; he was sort of weird last night after, but I think that’s your fault.”

“My fault?”

“He was really upset you got hurt.”

I shook my head. “You’re mistaken.”

“I don’t think so.”

“Michael, who’s your uncle?” Johnny asked.

“His uncle is Andreo Fiore,” his father told him.

“*Figlio di puttana*,” Johnny said under his breath.

“Johnny!” Carmen yelled at her son.

“I’m guessing that was bad?” I smiled at Michael.

When we left after lots of hugging and goodbye kisses from Carmen and Danielle, with a doggy bag that looked more like we had been shopping at Walmart, I asked Michael in the car what it was that Dreo actually did.

“He works for Vincent Romelli.”

“I still don’t know who that is,” I assured him, turning at a light, “but I’m guessing from everyone’s reaction that Mr. Romelli is some scary guy.”

“Yeah, I think he’s a scary guy, and so most people think Dreo is too. I don’t know; I don’t ask. Dreo carries a gun, and he’s never left it at home, even when he goes out on dates. I am never, ever, allowed in his room, but for all I know that’s because he’s got a shitload of porn in there. He’s a really good guy, but I can’t vouch for what he doesn’t tell me.”

Which made sense.

Once we were back, he followed me to my door, and when I told him to go home, he laughed and said that he was going to take a shower and come do homework at my house. It was fine, I didn’t care, and I told him the door would be open because I had to take a shower myself. I needed to get the day off me.

When I emerged, Michael’s books were spread out all over my coffee table. He had poured himself a glass of apple juice, and he was watching some hockey game on ESPN at the same time. I went to my kitchen table, deciding to work out there instead of in my office to keep him company, and we sat in companionable silence except for the game. It was in the third period when the doorbell rang.

Answering it, I found Dreo there in the hall, brows furrowed, looking upset and concerned at the same time.

"Come in," I offered, stepping aside.

He wasn't alone, and when he didn't move, I wasn't sure what he was waiting for.

"Did your friends want to come in too?"

"Just for a minute."

"Sure."

Five men, not counting Dreo, walked into my living room, but when I moved to shut the door, he stopped me.

"They're not gonna stay. I just wanted them to meet you."

It was strange, but I plastered on a smile and offered the first man my hand. "Nate Qells."

They all shook my hand, and I met an Anthony and a Gianni and a Frank and a Paul and a Sal.

"I always wanted to meet a Sal." I grinned and was surprised when he smiled back, even giving me a hard pat on the arm.

"You got hurt there, huh, Professor?"

Funny that they knew what I did. I wouldn't have thought that bit of information important enough for Dreo to share with them.

"Some guys by the park yesterday," I told him.

"Yeah, we heard about that." Sal nodded. "But maybe when you walk by there tomorrow, you won't see those guys no more."

"No," I assured him, "they're always there."

He shrugged. "Maybe not."

But it was doubtful.

"We heard something else happened tonight too, huh?"

I chuckled. "You mean Mr. Tulia?"

"Yeah." Dreo coughed softly, his deep dark eyes flicking to Anthony. "Tulia."

"That was just a misunderstanding," I soothed. "But we've got it all figured out now. No need for you to even get involved."

"Hey," Michael called from the couch, not moving.

Dreo gave him a head tip, and then his eyes, dark and bottomless, were back on me. "So this man, he hit you?"

"Just a love tap. He fed us."

"Fed who?"

"Me and Michael. We have leftovers."

"The good kind of leftovers!" Michael vouched for them from the couch.

"Are you hungry? Any of you?"

"Oh, no, Professor," Frank, I thought, said to me, smiling. "We're gonna go. Thanks, though, that's real good of you to ask. I'll bring you by some of my mother's carbonara tomorrow."

"Friday," I told him.

"What?"

"Carbonara is a favorite of mine, and I bet your mom's is fantastic, so I would love to take you up on your offer, but tomorrow I'm taking Michael to the opera, and Thursday I have a date. So Friday, if that's okay?"

He nodded. "You're on for Friday. What opera?"

"*La Bohème*."

"Nice. Give the kid some culture, huh?"

"That's the plan. Plus he needs the extra credit."

"Okay." He smiled at me, turning to look at Dreo. "We're good here. We'll see you tomorrow."

Dreo nodded, and all five men said good night to me and then left. Dreo locked the door behind them and then turned back to me, eyes locked on my face.

"Are you okay?"

"Fine," he said flatly.

"Okay. Are you hungry?"

He shook his head.

"If you want to just go home and relax, I can send him later."

"No, it's nice over here."

And I knew he liked it, as many times as he'd given me compliments.

"What you've done to this place… the hardwood floors and the ceiling all exposed with the pipes, all the stone by the fireplace." He shrugged. "It beats the hell outta mine."

"All right, then, take off your coat and sit down."

I started back across the room.

"It smells good in here too."

"Oh yeah?" I teased, walking ahead of him. "Does it smell like the grilled cheese that I made earlier?"

"No," he said, and I felt his hand on my shoulder, so I stopped and turned to look at him. "It smells like fire and vanilla and something else."

"Is that good?"

"*Sì*," he said softly, and I saw those melting eyes of his narrow in half.

After a minute of his scrutiny, I smiled. "I think he wants to talk to you," I told him, and he understood that I meant Michael.

I watched as he pulled off the trench coat he was wearing and the suit jacket underneath and laid them both on my love seat, loosening his tie as he walked to the couch. He cleared a space before he sat down on my coffee table across from his sprawled nephew.

The red-and-blue print tie was pulled off and folded and put down beside him as he leaned forward to look at Michael.

"What can I get you?" I asked.

He shook his head.

"Come on, leftovers? Grilled cheese?"

"The grilled cheese was the best thing I had today," Michael said softly, turning to look at me over his shoulder.

"Better than Johnny's ravioli with the spicy marinara?"

"Yeah." He nodded. "It reminded me of when my mom used to make it."

I really hoped that was a good thing.

"God, I can see everything you're thinking right on your face." He smiled. "Yeah, Nate, it's a good thing."

I shrugged before looking back at Dreo. "Apparently my grilled cheese is good? Tell me what you want."

"I don't wanna be no trouble."

"I really want to feed you," I told him.

He sighed deeply. "I don't want you to cook, but if you wanna heat something up for me, I'd appreciate it."

"Coming right up."

After a few minutes, he joined me in the kitchen, leaning on the counter while I moved around.

"I think this is the most we've ever said to each other at one time," I commented.

"I know," he groaned. "It's because I never know what to say."

"You could just talk. I don't bite."

"Yeah, but you're real smart."

I scoffed. "Yeah, I'm brilliant all right."

He shrugged. "Smarter than me."

"Hardly," I assured him. "But we should talk more. I mean, we've got that kid in common and all."

He nodded. "Yeah, we do."

"I've known you a long time."

"Yes, you have."

"So?" I pressed him.

"Fine," he grumbled. "We'll talk already."

I chuckled. "Don't make me twist your arm or anything."

"You're kind of a smartass."

"Which you would have never known if you weren't chatting me up."

He grunted.

"Can I pour you a glass of wine?"

"Red?"

"With marinara?" I teased. "Of course red. You want a Chianti or… oh, I have a really good Côte de Beaune as well."

"The Chianti."

"Coming right up."

I made his plate, filled a glass for him, and carried both to the table where I was sitting. He was still standing in the kitchen when I turned.

"What are you doing? Come sit down."

He levered off the counter and crossed the room, sitting down next to my laptop.

I passed him the napkin and the fork and told him to go for it.

The look I got when he tilted his head back was lost. If it hadn't been, if he had thanked me or smirked or done anything else, things might have been different. But his gaze, full of need, like he was hurting a little, slammed into me hard.

"Jesus, what's wrong?" I said, hand in his hair, pulling the heavy glossy black mane back from his face.

He tensed, and I realized what I'd done. "Shit, sorry." I dropped my hand and took a step back from him.

His fingers curled around my wrist fast, and his grip so tight, he'd leave marks. "I'm not a little boy."

I squinted at him but didn't try and tug free. "I know that."

"You don't need to take care of me like you do Michael."

"I wouldn't dream of it."

He stared up into my face.

"Could you let go?"

He said something, but I didn't get it.

"What?"

His eyes lifted to me. "*Ho una gran voglia di baciarti.*"

The words had almost been whispered. "I don't know what you said."

Quiet grunt from him as he let go and went back to eating.

"Dreo, I—"

"No," he cut me off, shaking his head before he looked back up. "I'm sorry, I was an ass. I overreacted."

"Okay."

"Sit down and talk to me, tell me everything that happened."

"Fine, but you have to give Michael a pass on the lecture. I already did that."

Heavy sigh. "*Sì.*"

"I like that."

"What?"

"When you go back and forth between Italian and English."

"Do you?"

"It's pretty." I nodded before walking to the kitchen to get my own glass of wine. "It must drive the women wild, huh?"

He didn't say anything, but when I turned, he was studying me.

"Just tell me," I said playfully as I returned.

"Perhaps."

"I knew it." I exhaled, sitting down, elbow on the table, head on my hand to look at him. I explained about Michael ditching basketball practice and bringing Danielle home with him. By the time I got to where we were on our way to take her home, he was shaking his head. "So Mr. Tulia hit me, as any father probably would have, because if I was home, I should have called him and his wife to make sure it was all right that their daughter was with Michael."

"What?"

"That's just parental courtesy."

"Why?"

"Just something you do, check up, make sure, and with them even more so, because she's a girl and he's a boy," I said with a smile.

"So this girl should have had her parents' permission to be in my apartment?"

"Yes."

He shook his head. "That's ridiculous."

I gave him a quick pat on the arm. "It's precautionary."

"It's old-fashioned."

"Parents should know where their kids are. It's important."

"Michael isn't your son."

"No, but Mr. Tulia didn't know that when he got out of the car."

He shrugged. "Thank you for taking care of Michael. Ever since he moved in with me…. I realized today that I count on you to watch out for him all the time, whether I'm here or not."

"Of course."

"It means a lot."

I nodded. "Tell me, who told you Mr. Tulia hit me?"

"Michael called and told me. He said it was his fault."

"It wasn't."

"It was. If he hadn't had that girl over at our house, you—"

"He's sixteen, Dreo. What were you like at sixteen?"

"I was careful," he said quietly.

"Of not getting caught," I teased.

"Perhaps."

"Well, he's a great kid, and you know that." I chuckled.

"Yeah, I know that." He sighed.

I realized how exhausted he looked. "Why don't you just go home and go to bed. I'll send him over once he's done."

"The wine is good," he told me, sipping it, ignoring my comment. "But my mother cooks better than this."

"Mothers always cook better than restaurants." I smiled. "And Michael said yours was feeling better. I'm glad. He said she had a stent put in her heart?"

"Which sounds a lot scarier than it was," he said, leaning back in his chair, looking at me. He had unbuttoned his dress shirt, and I could see the rose gold cross on the white T-shirt he was wearing underneath. It was somehow endearing, the sign of faith on the man.

"So she's okay?"

"She's fine."

"I'm glad. Maybe now he can work on getting closer to her."

"How do you mean?"

"He seems to think she wants to take him away from you, so that's what's holding him back from liking her."

"It is?"

I nodded.

"Shit, I had no idea. I'll talk to him."

"She doesn't want to take him away from you?"

"She never wanted to take him away; she wanted me to move home. It makes sense if you think about it."

And it did. "Sounds like you're right, like maybe you should talk to him."

"Yeah."

When I looked up from my wine glass, his eyes were locked on me. "What?"

"Thank you for giving a shit about him. Thank you for being there today—thanks for all of it."

I nodded. "You're welcome."

"He reminds you of your son?"

"A little. He's nicer than mine was at this age, but I suspect that's because mine always had his parents and Michael's learned hard lessons about loss already. He's very lucky to have you."

He scoffed. "I don't know. I haven't been doing a very good job of taking care of him here lately. He'd rather be here with you than home with me."

"But you're working to support him. He understands that and he loves you."

"We hardly say two words to each other most days."

I shrugged. "That'll change. Mine was an angsty piece of crap too for a while."

He leaned forward, and I noticed that his wine glass was empty.

"You want some more?"

"*Sì.*"

I got up and went to the kitchen, but when I turned to go back to him, I realized he was there, right behind me, so that when I pivoted with the bottle, my knuckles brushed over his shirtfront. My head tipped up so I could look at his face.

His hand came down on the counter, on one side of me, and I stepped back as he leaned in closer.

I took a breath. "The Tulias were scared shitless when they found out that Michael was related to you."

He nodded, studying my face, his eyes finally coming to rest on my mouth. "And you thought what about that?"

"It made no sense to me; I mean, I have bunny slippers scarier than you."

A beat of time passed and then another until, wonder of wonders, the man smiled.

In four years, at no time ever had I even seen a grin. His lips never lifted in the corner, they didn't twitch, mirth didn't hit his eyes… nothing. But I was suddenly and without warning looking at a smile that made my breath catch, my heart still, and my mouth go dry.

God, his whole face changed when he smiled. Everything softened, his eyes, his mouth, hard edges smoothed, and he was simply breathtaking. How had I missed that he was so pretty the whole time I'd known him?

He made a noise, maybe a half chuckle, a happy grunt, and then let his head drop forward as he let out a deep breath.

I had no idea what to do, but doing nothing when I was being offered a gift, a chink in the armor, was a mistake. He trusted me with it, with the smile, with the lowering of the wall, so I put down the bottle of wine and put my hands on his face and lifted.

The thick black hair was just as silky as Michael's, just as thick, but whereas Michael's was rail straight, Dreo's had curl to it, so my fingers were tangled fast.

"I just want you to know that I'm not afraid, all right? And Michael and I both think you're pretty great."

"I do nothing… for either of you."

"You make a home for him, and because of that, I get to have my kid fix," I said, dropping my hands, tipping my head for him to move. "Now go home already before you pass out in my kitchen."

He grunted his agreement and stepped back.

I took a breath, a ridiculous breath that I shouldn't have had to take, because if Sean Cooper was too young for me, twenty-eight-year-old Dreo Fiore was jailbait. And he was potentially dangerous, plus he was the guardian of the kid I was kind of attached to. It was just a bad idea all the way around. Not to mention, of course, that the man was straight.

"Nate?"

He was Italian, and Italian men were just a whole touchy-feely group. He probably didn't even know how close to me he was.

"*Tesoro*."

I looked back at him. "Sorry?"

"That you answer to." Second smile of the night, this one sort of bemused. "I'm going. Thank you… again."

"Hey, remember he and I are going to the opera tomorrow. We're taking Danielle with us."

"Who?"

"The girl I'm not going to let him get pregnant."

"You think you're funny?" he said with a slight frown.

I smiled and nodded.

His grunt was filled with disgust that just made me smile bigger.

The scowl I got next was even better. He was really kind of nice to look at.

"So what time are you guys going?"

I liked the strong line of his jaw, how wide his shoulders were, and the inky black of his hair.

"Nate?"

"Sorry, the show starts at eight, so we'll leave here at six, since we're going to eat first."

"You and Michael and Danielle."

"Right."

"So where did the third ticket come from?"

I shrugged. "I got it for you because I thought you might want to go, but then I figured an outing with me might be weird for you, so—"

"I know you're gay, Nate."

"Yeah, I know you know," I said. "But still, being cool with it here at home and being cool with it out in the world are two completely different things."

"I would agree."

"But it worked out perfect because we got to take Danielle."

He nodded. "So you have a date on Thursday?"

I laughed. "Yeah, you heard me tell Sal that."

"With who?"

"With the doctor you met last night. I was supposed to go tonight, but—"

"But you had to be me instead."

"I had to be there for Michael," I corrected.

He nodded. "Okay. Thanks for dinner, and the wine and the company."

"Anytime."

He walked across the room back to Michael, who, between texting on his phone, watching the hockey game, and doing his homework, was completely engrossed. Bending forward, Dreo put a hand on his nephew's shoulder, said something, and then kissed his cheek. Italian men—had to love them.

I enjoyed watching the man walk, the fluidity of it, seeing the muscles bunch and flex under his shirt, the material pulled across broad shoulders, muscular biceps, triceps, and the power evident in his frame, in his every movement. The pants that encased his heavy thighs, legs, his ass, hugged every rippling curve, and I found that breathing was hard just for a second. When he turned back to look at me, I forced a quick smile.

"*Alla prossima.*"

"Me too." I chuckled, having no idea what he'd said.

He left then, closing the door gently after him, and I returned to the table where his plate still was.

Michael was there a second later, picking it up and taking it to the sink.

"That's okay, I can do it."

"The man's a pig." He shook his head, smiling. "He probably thinks because it's your house that you're supposed to do the dishes."

"I do have to do them."

"He should have, but he's just used to me taking care of him."

"That's nice, huh?"

"For him, yeah," he groused. "But for me it's annoying as shit; I'm supposed to be the slob, not him."

I chuckled as he went to wash the dishes.

He grunted.

"Thank you."

"Can I have a glass of wine?" he asked, looking at me over his shoulder.

"You can have a Pepsi."

He made a noise like I was just so irritating, and I smiled as I checked my e-mail.

"Hey."

I turned to look at him.

"*Alla prossima* is like see you again, or see you later."

"Oh. It sounds better in Italian."

"Everything sounds better in Italian."

I couldn't very well argue.

FIVE

MICHAEL saw him first, so there was no way to ignore it or pretend I hadn't as well.

"What the hell?" he growled, freezing there in the middle of the sidewalk. "Isn't that your doctor?"

Sean Cooper was obviously on a date, as evidenced by his presence in the restaurant. But it had nothing to do with me, and I knew that. The sixteen-year-old with me, as well as his date, didn't get it. So there we were, the three of us—me, Michael, and Danielle—lurking at the entrance to an alley across the street from a very upscale restaurant close to the Miracle Mile.

"You guys just don't get it." I chuckled, arm around each of them, turning them to walk out to the curb to get a cab.

"No," Danielle insisted, fighting me, her eyes huge. "I wanna see who this guy's out on a date with the night before he's supposed to be out on a date with you."

"I'm gonna kick his ass," Michael assured me.

"Yeah," Danielle agreed. "Kick his ass."

Their righteous indignation over me was adorable. I started laughing. "Guys, this is not high school." I tried to stop chuckling. "In the real world, people don't date just one person; they date many and finally decide to give it a go with one."

Two sets of eyes looking at me like I was nuts.

"You don't just go steady in the real world."

"Who goes steady?" Danielle glanced at me. "Most of my friends hook up."

"Please don't tell me these things," I told her.

"Oh come on," she snapped. "This ain't Mayberry, Professor."

"How do you know about—"

"I used to watch Nick at Nite."

Of course she had. "Let's just go or you guys aren't getting any des—"

"Shouldn't he at least be waiting to see if it works with you or not before he dates the next guy?"

"It doesn't work like that."

"I think it should," she told me.

"This isn't a Disney movie," Michael told her.

She smacked him hard. "I know all about how gay men hook up. My Aunt Susan has *Queer As Folk* on DVD."

I couldn't help laughing. She was indignant, he was scowling, and they were both very cute. They actually complemented each other really well.

"Guys, we're going out tomorrow, not today," I told them again. "What he's doing tonight has nothing to do with me. Now let's go."

"I just wanna see," Michael said, and with that, in his suit and tie and cashmere overcoat, he dashed across the street.

"Awesome," Danielle said, grabbing my hand, tugging me forward toward the curb. "C'mon, Professor, now we gotta go with him."

"You guys need to go to bed."

She turned and looked at me, her black-lined eyes huge.

"Not together, idiot." I rolled my eyes at her. "You need to go home and go to bed. It's a school night."

"Professor, I am up until midnight every night and close to two or three on the weekends. I dunno where you got the idea that teenagers go to bed at ten, but I promise you it ain't like it is on TV, ya know?"

I sighed deeply.

"Oh, he's comin' back," she almost squealed.

I waited as the world's worst spy came loping back to us.

"And?" she asked excitedly, really into it.

"And"—he squinted at me—"I don't think I like that doctor, Nate."

"Why?"

"He's kissing some guy in there."

"That's because it's a date," I assured him.

"There's, like, a lot of people with them. I think they're celebrating something."

"Well—"

"Nate!"

We all turned, and there, across the street, standing on the opposite curb, was Sean Cooper. He looked both ways before he bolted across and ran up the street to reach us.

"Oh, hey," I greeted. "I'm sorry, I can ex—"

"I thought you were going to the opera?"

"We were. We did," I told him. "We're done already. I brought them down here for dessert, and then we're headed home."

He nodded, smiling, and I heard Danielle sigh. Simple to understand—the man was very easy on the eyes.

"Well, I saw your minion here and knew you had to be somewhere close." He smiled, taking hold of my elbow and drawing me away from the kids. "Hold up one second, okay, guys?"

I looked at his face, at his perfect profile and chiseled lips, as he walked me a little way down the street. The man was just gorgeous.

"So what you said last night, about wishing me good luck for not just me but my patient too… that really made me think," he said, rounding on me, staring into my eyes. "Because all I was doing was obsessing about me and what I wanted, not about what the surgery would mean for the girl and her family, so I wanted to tell you that and thank you."

"Oh, well, I… you didn't have to."

"No, I know, but it was important, and I really wanted to see you and tell you that, and we're out celebrating, and I wanted to invite you, but you said you already had plans and—"

"It's fine." I smiled and nodded. "You're allowed to go on a date, especially to celebrate something wonderful. I didn't mean to interrupt."

His eyes were all over my face before he reached out and took hold of my trench coat. "Are you going home now?"

"After I get them dessert, like I said."

"Could I come along?"

"You're celebrating with your friends," I reminded him. "And aren't you with someone?"

"I am," he admitted, his hand fisting tighter. "But I really wanted to take you out tonight, and I'm afraid I'm using both my friends and my date as poor substitutes."

"That's very flattering." But it was also a little disconcerting. The idea that he would just ditch someone and abandon his friends didn't speak that well of him. And yes, we all ditched our pals for dates, but that was normally bailing on them beforehand, not when we were already out with a hot guy and our friends.

"I wanted to ask if I could come and see you after the opera, but I thought you might think that was weird or—"

"No games, Sean. I wouldn't have thought it was weird as long as you weren't on a date."

"Yeah, but it doesn't matter." He dismissed my concern.

Maybe I was overthinking it, which I did sometimes.

He took a breath. "Okay, so how 'bout this. How about I say goodnight to my date and my friends, grab a bottle of wine, and come over in an hour and sit with you and tell you all about the kid I saved so you can look at me like I'm a god, and then we can make out on your couch. How would that be?"

"And what would we do tomorrow?" I teased him because it was *so* not going to happen. I would not be the cause of someone else getting dumped when it had been me so often in the past. Once, when I told a guy laughingly that I didn't put out on the first date, he had simply got up and left me at the restaurant he had driven me to.

"Tomorrow I'll feed you, take you home to my house, and we can make out some more and then maybe you can fuck my brains out in my bed."

"Maybe you can fuck my brains out," I said, fishing, because even though I could do both, being on the bottom was what got me off most, best, every time. I didn't mind topping, but I had a definite preference.

He let out a huff of air. "I have this headboard on my bed—" He swallowed hard. "—that I would really, really like to hold onto while you fill my ass."

"Been thinking about that, have you?"

"Since I saw you at the store that first day." He nodded, his eyes clouded. "Yeah."

I looked at him, and all I saw was heat and desire and a forced stillness, like he was ready to grab me but was holding himself in check. "I think you should stay here and have a good time and be on time tomorrow to pick me up."

He whimpered in the back of his throat. "I really don't want to do that, and for the record, the date is insignificant. Only the celebration and my friends are important."

"But you're still going to take that guy back to your place," I said knowingly.

"If you tell me I can come and see you instead, just to talk to, just to sit with… I won't."

He would pass up getting laid to come and sit on my couch with me. It was nice, but again, almost irritating at the same time. I was made differently. If I was interested in someone, no one else would do until I had exhausted every possibility with my crush. Obviously, he was more of an opportunist than I was, and I wasn't sure how I felt about that.

"Nate?"

But it was very judgmental of me and probably why I had not been laid in a while. There had been a couple of guys after Duncan that

I had not told Melissa about, some one-night stands that I was not proud of, but on the whole, my friends were right: I was much too serious when it came to actual dating and potential partners. I talked too much, I wanted to know things—I didn't want to waste my time if there was no future. I didn't want to just sleep around. I wanted to find a man I cared for who would want to be a part of my life. I wanted that committed monogamous relationship, but no one else seemed to want to be in one with me. My friends said I should lighten up and just enjoy dating, but if dating equaled sleeping around…. As always I was right back to square one.

"Nate?" Softer the second time.

"Sorry." I shook my head. "You should get back."

"I'd rather—God, do you have any clue how hot you are, or is it just completely lost on you?"

But I wasn't. I was very average, and the compliment, the timing of it, was out of place. It felt like he got caught and was trying to make amends. And he didn't have to. He liked what he saw because he knew me, and that was all. "I grow on people."

"Jesus, Nate, for a smart guy, you have no idea what you're talking about."

But I did. I was not the *GQ* model; I was the other guy, the English professor you liked and waved to at Starbucks and, if I was straight, introduced to your newly divorced mother. "So, tomorrow, then?"

"I guess," he grumbled.

"I'll be looking forward to it."

"I hope so," he said softly, leaning forward but stopping himself. There were teenagers present, after all. "I'll see you at seven."

"Seven," I agreed.

He left without another word, and when I turned back to Michael and Danielle, she was making the *oh* face and biting her bottom lip and Michael looked like he was ready to hurl.

"Well?"

"Awww," she cooed. "He totally leaned right then. He wanted to kiss you so bad."

Michael gagged.

I TOOK them to a great place where the owner made baklava and tiramisu and crème brûlée and many other desserts from scratch. I had bread pudding and coffee and watched the kids share strawberry shortcake with each other. When Michael fed Danielle, I gagged for him.

"Nate!" She squealed, leaning forward to smack my arm.

Michael chuckled, knowing that I was doing it on purpose, smiling in appreciation of that. "Girls are icky, right?"

"That's right." I shivered. "Girl cooties."

Danielle got to pretend to be scandalized as I sipped my coffee with chicory in it. I liked the taste, but a lot of people didn't.

As we were walking back to where I had parked my car, Danielle slipped one arm in mine and the other in Michael's.

"Aren't I the lucky one." She sighed. "I get taken out by two gorgeous men."

"He's too old for you," Michael muttered, but I could hear the sheepish happiness in his voice.

"Too gay too," she agreed, tightening her grip on both of us. "But that doesn't mean I don't feel good struttin' my stuff between the two of you."

I patted her hand. "Just make sure you tell your father how much of a gentleman Michael was. He won't let you go to the Winter Ball with him if he wasn't."

She sucked in her breath and turned to him. "You want to take me to the Winter Ball?"

"I—I would," he stammered, recovering his bravado in seconds. "If you want," he finished with a shrug, like it was no big deal either way. Like he wouldn't die just a little right then and there if she said no.

"I'd love to." She sighed and let go of me to wrap both arms around his one.

They were so adorable together. Really, they should have gone on postcards for young love. I felt like Cupid.

They sat in the back of my Honda Accord, and when we stopped at her house, Danielle leaned forward and kissed my cheek before getting out of the car. Michael followed right behind her, patting my shoulder as he got out.

"Wait for me, driver," he couldn't help adding.

"You know what you can do with your—"

"Quiet or you won't get a tip."

I growled as he got out, scrambling after the girl, slamming the door before following her to the porch. There was talking, and then the light went on, so he leaned and kissed her, which would have been fast, but she grabbed hold of the lapels of his topcoat and held on as she kissed the hell out of the boy.

That was how her father found them, lip-locked on the porch. I was amused, Mr. Tulia was amused, Danielle was in floaty-happy heaven, and Michael was terrified. When he got back to the car, this time sliding into the passenger seat, I asked if he saw his life flash before his eyes.

"I did, yeah."

I chuckled. "Hey, where's my thank you?"

"I know, right?" He turned and beamed. "Shit, Nate, you're fuckin' brilliant. I'm taking Danielle Tulia to the Winter Ball. How can I ever repay you?"

"I want to see what you're going to write about *La Bohème* for Mrs. Chang."

"Oh crap, that's right."

It was fun to listen to him grouse about it all the way home.

We parted at his door, and I walked to my apartment more tired than I realized. I wanted to just pull the suit off and fall into bed, but there was still Ashton's book to finish reading, and it was already Wednesday night. I'd promised it to him by Saturday, and I was not about to let the snippy little man down. And a book about Keats was right up my alley.

The pounding on my door once I was settled in bed with a cup of oolong tea and my laptop was surprising. But I padded across my wooden floor in heavy wool socks that my sister had knit for me, sweats, and a long-sleeved cotton T-shirt to open the door. Michael was there looking terrified, and I reached for him without thinking.

He stepped out of my reach. "No, you gotta come look at Dreo."

I closed my door and followed him, feeling like a little kid just out in socks in the tiled hallway. It was dark inside their apartment, and in it, Dreo was standing, fully dressed, beside the fireplace, hand on the mantel, still as a statue.

I turned to Michael. "I made a pot of tea. Go back to my place and pour a cup for Dreo and bring it back."

He looked from his uncle to me and back again before he left. I moved around, turning on low lights, finally making my way back to him.

"What happened?"

His head snapped up to me, and his eyes, which were normally so alive, were dead.

"Tell me."

When he turned, I understood. He was wearing some kind of orange jumpsuit under his trench coat, but that was not the giveaway. The blood—in his hair, small smears on his face, on his neck—that was what told me that something terrible had happened.

"Dreo."

He trembled slightly. "Men came into the club this afternoon; I've been with the cops all this time. Just me and Tony and Sal… and Joey…. No one else made it out."

So his friends that I had just met, they were all gone except Sal. "Mr. Romelli?"

"Dead. They're all dead."

"And they took your clothes, your suit—" I looked down at the strange black sort of slippers on his feet. "—your shoes."

"Had to compare the blood and the tread on my shoes, and they did one of those tests on my hands where they check for gunpowder, but of course there's gonna be residue, since I was shooting back. I had to give them my gun too."

He was rambling because he was in shock, probably had been all day, and nobody had cared one bit since he was supposed to be a big tough scary guy.

"Some fuckin' bodyguard I turned out to be." He laughed, and it sounded bad, too high, unhinged and fractured.

"Dreo—"

"I was supposed to be moving up and—do you have a job if your employer just got blown away with a shotgun?"

"Dreo—"

"Not that I care about the job, about being more. I really don't, I mean, I was getting out anyway… and he knew, Mr. Romelli did, 'cause I told him, but still… what should I have done?"

"Okay." I took a breath. "Here's what we're going to do. First we're gonna get these clothes off you and throw them away, and then we're going to get you into the shower."

He trembled hard. "There was nothing I could do. It happened so fast."

"When's the funeral?"

"Saturday," he said, and I didn't move, didn't comment, just let him reach out and put a hand on the side of my face and then slide it up into my hair. "I need you to come with me and Michael and stand there at the grave."

The reason didn't matter. He wanted me there, and I'd be there. "Of course," I agreed as his strong, big-knuckled hand cradled my head.

"Nate," he barely got out, his voice fractured and full of aching.

"You will be okay," I said, smiling up into his face. "Can I—is it all right?"

"I'm gross, there's blood in my hair and—"

"I think you need it."

His eyes fluttered closed, and I took that as a yes and moved, sliding my arms beneath the trench coat and over the ugly orange polyester jumpsuit and stepping into him. I felt the shudder tear through him, felt him lean, give me his weight, and then both arms wrapped around me tight, and he breathed for the first time since I got there.

He smelled like sweat and musk and wool, which was the coat, and just a little like rain. I heard Michael come back, and I told him to turn on the heater because the stupid apartment was freezing.

"It's nice over in yours," he told me and left his words hanging there, waiting for me.

I knew what he wanted.

"Why don't you take a long hot shower," I said into the side of Dreo's neck, "and then both of you come over to my place? Michael, bring your laptop. We'll work on the table together and Dreo can pass out."

He tried to let go of me, but I was not some girl he was used to hugging. The man only had three inches on me, more muscle, yes, but not enough to make me do anything without a fight. And I didn't want him to let go. Holding him felt right for more reasons than I cared to concern myself with, but more importantly, he needed to be held. He was barely keeping it together, and the solid, grounded presence I was offering was necessary.

"Listen." I squeezed tighter, talking into the hollow of his throat. "Just do what I say, all right? Take a shower and then walk over to my place with Michael."

When he eased back, I let him. His closed eyes leaked tears, and when I brushed them away, he leaned into my palm.

It took every drop of restraint I had not to grab him. His need for comfort instantly filled me with a desire to have him naked in my bed. Making love to me would remind him that he was alive. Sex trumped death—the throb of yearning to show him he was still very much among the living, washed through me.

"Please tell me what the hell." Michael's voice was on the edge of cracking too.

I turned to look at him. "Your uncle was almost killed today, and his friends and Mr. Romelli were. So the funeral's on Saturday, and we're all going to go, all right?"

He nodded, absorbing the news, obviously more concerned for Dreo than anything else.

"So, I still have reading to do. You have something to write. You can do it with me, okay?"

He nodded before he started out of the room. "I'm gonna change. I'll be right back."

"Nate."

I turned back to Dreo, his dark, wet eyes open and fixed on me as he put a hand flat on my chest.

"You don't have to babysit us."

"I do." I smiled. "It's actually written into the friend code."

His hand pressed hard and then fisted in my T-shirt. "You and Michael are friends, not me and you."

"No? Are you sure?"

He took a shuddering breath, and I studied the man's face, the chiseled features, his lush mouth, the long, straight Roman nose and square jaw. He was all sharp angles, and that, paired with the dark eyes, thick black brows, and long lashes, made him seem like a study in shadow. I wanted to brighten him and make him smile again. I had been treated to the gleaming eyes once and found that in that instant, I had grown addicted.

"Did you eat?"

His laugh was sharp, high, slightly unhinged. "Fuck, you remind me of him, of Mr. Romelli, always wanting us to fuckin' eat!"

I put my hand over his, which was still fisted in my T-shirt, and slowly, he loosened his grip and let his hand drop away. When Michael returned, Dreo left the room without a word.

"Bring him with you; don't let him stay here alone."

"I won't," Michael promised.

"I'll make more tea," I offered.

"Make chamomile." Michael made a face. "That oolong crap smells like sweat socks."

"Okay," I said, tousling his hair as I passed by. Much to my surprise, he grabbed my hand and stopped me from leaving.

"What's wrong?"

"Just—you do a shitload for me, Nate, and I want you to know that it means a whole lot, ya know? I mean, you know that, right?"

"Of course."

"I've known you since I was twelve years old, and you've been just as constant as my family, as Dreo. You've been around, and it means a lot. Whatever you do, like when you talked to that guy tonight… I don't care. I was just screwin' with you."

"I know that," I told him, turning to face him.

It was awkward because he was sixteen, but when I lifted my arms, he was there, filling them, smashing into me so hard that it hurt just a little. I put his head down in my shoulder and rubbed gently, soothing him, petting him.

"I don't care who you sleep with."

Weird thing for him to say. "I know."

"I hate funerals."

"Me too," I admitted. "But it'll be all right."

He nodded into my shoulder, and then he pulled free because he was done. I left fast, crossing the hall and returning to my loft.

It had gotten slightly chilly in the room, as by the second week in November, the air was cool outside and in. I had started a fire so that the flames were just beginning to flicker on the Duraflame log and the plain wood beneath it when someone knocked fifteen minutes later. The lights were low; there was very quiet John Coltrane on, and I was making the chamomile for Michael.

The younger Fiore was in sweats and socks and a threadbare T-shirt with an open sweat-jacket on over it. Dreo had on the same thing, except that he had a heavy zippered cardigan on over a T-shirt that fit snug, clinging to his sculpted chest, showing the definition in the hard pecs and washboard abdomen. Of course the man would be covered in rippling muscle. That just followed since he was gorgeous everywhere else. Not that I had ever noticed before the last two days. And now he was grieving, so it was tacky to even see him in any other light but simply needing company.

They walked by, stopped, and then stood, waiting for me.

"What are you doing?" I snapped at Michael. "Go put your crap down, get the laptop open, let's go."

He made a noise in the back of his throat and walked by, leaving me close to the door with Dreo.

"Anything I can get you? Are you hungry? Thirsty?"

He shook his head.

"Come on."

He followed after me, and I led him down the short hall—past my office, the guest bathroom, my bedroom—until we finally reached the guest bedroom. It was a warm room done in mahogany and wine and umber.

"Lie down." I pointed at the bed. "Yell if you need anything."

He shook his head. "I don't—I'd be better in my own bed."

"Dreo—"

"This was stupid," he said under his breath, turning and charging away down the hall.

I caught him before he passed my bedroom, grabbed his arm, and shoved him through the door. He corrected fast, whirled on me angrily, and stood there scowling when I flicked on the light.

My room, with the ivory walls and traces of brown and hunter green, the mission-style bed, the armoire, the wingback chair and ottoman, and the dark-brown flokati rug, was probably the most inviting space in the loft. The bed was turned down since I'd been in it, but in that instant I knew that I would not be the one back under the covers.

"Get in bed," I ordered him.

He glowered.

"Now."

Heavy sigh before I saw him visibly give up.

The man was exhausted and wrung out and weary down to his bones. He pulled off the cardigan, let it drop to the floor, and staggered over to my bed and crawled in. He collapsed, and his eyes were closed the minute he hit the pillow, my pillow, which he tucked an arm under and pulled tight. I heard him inhale deep, and then nothing. There was no other sound or movement after that.

I went and picked up his sweater, draped it over the end of the bed, and then flipped off the light but left the door open so he could hear Michael and me if he woke up. When I returned to the kitchen, Michael was making tea.

"And?"

"He passed out in my bed."

"So you're gonna sleep in the guest room?"

"I'll sleep on the couch; you've got the guest room."

"That ain't fair. You should have a bed."

"I like my couch," I insisted. "I chose the fabric just for sleeping, since Jare always brings home a friend from college for the holidays."

"Is he coming this year?"

"No." I sighed. "This year he's going to his girlfriend's parents' place in Connecticut."

"I'm sorry," he said and then perked up. "You can come over and have Christmas with us."

"We'll see," I assured him since I already had offers from Melissa and Ben, people from work, my sister Becky and my sister Rachel. Not to mention the fact that we were all supposed to fly to Phoenix to have Christmas with my parents. My sister Rachel had said, "Over my dead body," because she really wanted to have us all to her place in Denver. Becky and I had both laughed at her when my mother started with the world-class guilt trip and she was the first to cave, her plans flying right out the window.

"So do you have that play thing?" Michael asked me.

"It's called a playbill, and yes, I have it. Do you want to look at the program too?"

"Yeah."

I pointed toward the table by the front door where it sat with my keys, wallet, loose change, and receipt from dinner. When I sat down at my kitchen table, he joined me, laptop beside mine, the two of us together, me reading, him writing, both of us sipping our tea.

Chapter SIX

DREO was gone when I got up in the morning, and I really wasn't surprised. What did surprise me was Michael, asleep on the flokati rug that I had in front of the fireplace. He had one of my sofa pillows, and one of the many afghans that Becky had crocheted me over the top of him. He had not left for the guest room, happy, it seemed, to be there in close proximity to me.

I woke him up, told him to grab his laptop, and sent him off to change and get his ass to school. He was a little bleary but awake and thanked me for the night before.

"You're welcome."

"So your date is tonight, huh?" He waggled his eyebrows.

I pointed at the door.

"Are you gonna make breakfast?"

"For myself," I told him. "Bye."

He whimpered and whined himself out my front door. But I had seen the food Dreo kept in their house—just the different kinds of cereal was daunting.

The knocking kept me from the coffee pot, which was annoying. I threw open the door without even looking and was surprised not to find myself looking at Michael Fiore.

"Nathan Qells? Dr. Nathan Qells?"

"Yes." I studied the two men in the hall.

"I'm Detective Lee, and this is Detective Haddock, Chicago PD. May we come in and speak to you, please? It's a matter of some urgency."

Both men pulled badges from the inside breast pockets of their suits, but I barely glanced at them. The trench coats, the crisp tone the first guy was using, it all sounded cop to me, and I had some experience with the breed, having dated one for two years. I stepped aside so they could come in.

"We have some crime scene personnel with us. May they enter as well?"

"Crime scene for what? Where?"

"Your fire escape."

"What happened on my fire escape?"

"We believe someone fell from it."

But there was no way. I would have heard something. "Sure, I guess." I sighed, motioning them in, stepping aside to make room for the parade of people. I closed the door seconds later, turning to face the two detectives hovering close to me.

"Dr. Qells, do you know an Alfred Mangino?"

"No," I answered before turning toward the kitchen, shuffling away. I needed coffee.

"Dr. Qells, do you—"

"You guys can sit down." I yawned, rubbing my eyes as they began to water. I had read into the wee small hours and was now paying for it. Amazing how much things changed. In college I would have been up until dawn, taken a nap, and been ready to go. Or just not slept for three days, either/or. "I need coffee."

They were silent a few minutes, and I knew I was probably freaking them out with my ease. Detectives should make people nervous. I should have been asking all kinds of questions about what they were doing there, but my ex was a cop, so I was used to all the cloak and dagger crap.

"Dr. Qells, are you sure you don't know an Alfred Mangino?"

"Yes," I said, squinting at the detectives.

Detective Lee was tall, dark, and very handsome except for the scowl he was trying for. It distracted from the hot. He was probably working on cultivating it to look scarier. I understood there had to be some kind of intimidation factor when you were a detective. His partner was a little older but alluring in a different way. He had the lifer look about him, a serious squint and something more. There was hardness in his eyes, but there were laugh lines around them.

"Dr. Qells, are you awake?"

It was an excellent question. The more I looked at Detective Lee, who was trying to look mad and failing miserably, and then at Detective Haddock, who looked like he needed coffee more than I did, the more comfortable I got.

"Sorry." I sighed deeply. "I'll try and focus."

"Excellent," Detective Lee said quickly. "Now, again, did you know Mr. Mangino?"

"No. Who is he?"

"We believe he fell to his death from your fire escape last night."

"It's not possible," I assured him.

"And why's that?"

I pointed with both hands outside. "I would have heard him if he was on my fire escape. It's a really small space out there."

"Were you home all night?"

"No."

"Well, then it's big enough, Dr. Qells. It was very windy yesterday, and if he was there, say, for some time… I mean, if he climbed up while you were out and stayed quiet until after you went to bed, it's quite possible that you never had a clue."

There was that.

"You went out last night?"

"Yes."

"May I ask from when to when?"

So I explained that I had been at the opera until after ten and then stopped for dessert and come home. It was easily eleven by the time I had changed, and maybe eleven fifteen by the time Michael was pounding on my door.

"We found him in the dumpster this morning."

"Sorry?"

"The guy, Mr. Mangino, that's where we found him."

"Oh." I had been talking about Michael and thinking about Dreo and had not been listening at all.

"Dr. Qells?"

"I'm sorry, did you say that he fell from my fire escape into the dumpster?"

"Yes."

I had to wrap my brain around that. "Amazing."

"How so?"

"No, nothing, it's just… tidy." I shrugged. "I mean, of all the places he could fall, right? "

He looked at me like I was nuts.

But it was tidy, no matter how both detectives were looking at me.

I coughed. "Why do you think he fell from my fire escape?"

"The medical examiner did a quick calculation of how far he would have had to have fallen to account for his injuries."

"But he could have just as easily fallen from the fourth floor."

"Perhaps, but—"

"Detective Lee."

All three of us turned and looked at the CSI tech holding a baggie with a gun that had a silencer attached to it.

"Okay, so that answers that question," Detective Haddock said as I turned to look at him. "Unless that weapon is yours, Dr. Qells."

"No, it's not."

"Didn't think so."

There had been a man with a gun on my fire escape. It was just so strange.

“Did he slip?” I asked because it was all I could think of.

“We believe so, yes.”

“What a crappy way to go.”

No one contradicted me.

“How did you even find him?”

“Apparently Mr. and Mrs. Grace up in 801 had some friends over last night to celebrate a promotion Mrs. Grace got at work. They had a lot of bulk trash to take out this morning that wouldn’t fit down the chute.”

“That’s horrible,” I said, thinking how God-awful it must have been to find a dead man in the trash the morning after.

“They’re both still pretty shaken.”

I bet they were.

The crime scene people were very efficient and confirmed beyond a shadow of a doubt that Alfred Mangino had indeed been on my fire escape the night before. Along with recovering a gun, they had footprints, several cigarette butts, like he’d been waiting awhile outside, and a partially smeared handprint on my window glass that looked, they said, like that was where he had been leaning when he lost his balance.

“How did he lose his balance and fall over the railing?”

“Your guess is as good as ours right this second, Dr. Qells. When we know more, you will too,” Detective Lee told me.

“We’ll have to check the registration on the gun to see who it belongs to, but chances are good that the trace will lead to Mangino,” Haddock chimed in.

I nodded.

“So Mr. Mangino was a stranger to you?”

I had already answered that question one or two or ten million times by then, but that was okay. He was either being thorough or hoping my story would change. “Yes.”

“Well, Dr. Qells, so that you’re aware, Mr. Mangino is in our system. That’s why we were able to ID him so quickly from prints he left behind here.”

"Who was he?"

"Mr. Mangino was a contract killer, and we believe he was here to take your life."

"Why?"

"We were hoping you could supply the reason."

"I can't. I'm not interesting enough for anyone to want to kill. There has to be some mistake."

"And yet he was on your fire escape."

"Huh."

"Pardon me for saying, but you don't seem all that concerned. You should be terrified."

"I haven't had any coffee yet," I said by way of explanation. "I'm barely awake, and I cannot stress enough that there really has to be another explanation because seriously"—I put my hand on my chest—"not hit man fodder. And my life is not a movie, and I haven't received any microfilm or witnessed a mob hit or anything remotely interesting in the least. You need to be looking for something besides me."

"Who the hell is in charge of this clusterfuck?"

My head snapped up as both detectives rose to greet the man walking into my apartment. I had recognized the voice but was waiting for him to see me. He looked good, one of Duncan's oldest friends whom I had once upon a time spent a lot of time with. It made me sad that he didn't even realize he was in my apartment, but why would he? Duncan and I had always gone to his and his wife Lisa's house and not ever invited them over to mine. My ex and I were only supposed to be friends, just buddies hanging out, nothing more. And once Duncan had walked out of my life, I had never seen either Jimmy or Lisa again. It was sad, really, but understandable. Duncan had not even been able to trust his friends with the truth of his homosexuality, though I had a feeling that at least Lisa had known. As it was, I had no doubt that James O'Meara had no clue that he was standing in my apartment.

When I saw Jimmy's eyes scan the room, I waved from where I was in the kitchen. It took him a minute to realize whom he was looking at. I was out of place, so his brain had to wrap around it, make sense of things, and take inventory before he spoke.

"Nate?" he said after a few minutes.

"Detective." I smiled, playing it cool, not wanting to assume we were still friendly after so long.

He came forward fast but stopped himself before he took the fateful last step to hug me hello.

I smiled.

He just stared.

It was awkward.

"Detective O'Meara," I heard Detective Lassiter ask, "you know Dr. Qells?"

A heartbeat of time passed.

"Oh shit." Jimmy caught his breath, suddenly grabbing hold of my shoulder tight, his eyes locked on mine. "Oh God, Nate."

He sounded so startled, having jerked like he was electrocuted. "What's the matter?"

"Nate Qells."

"Yeah, that's my name," I agreed.

His pale-blue eyes absorbed my face, and I realized how tired he looked. He was not a classically handsome man, but with the deep laugh lines, his crooked, lazy smile, and his curling dark-brown hair, he was so adorable that you just wanted to take him home and cook for him. And lots of women wanted to. And lots of women hit on him until they saw his wife. No one messed with Lisa O'Meara. For one, she was gorgeous, all long, brown hair and huge brown eyes, and for another, she was damn scary. She liked to explain that since she was Sicilian, she would cut you as soon as look at you. I had always rolled my eyes. She had pinched my cheek in return. Thinking about her made me smile. I had enjoyed getting to know her and spending time with her.

"Oh fuck me," he groaned, letting his head fall forward.

I snorted out a laugh.

"What's wrong, Detective?"

He let me go before lacing his fingers on the top of his head as he looked at the two younger policemen. "This is Nate Qells, and he's a really good friend of Detective Stiel."

Both heads swiveled to me.

"Oh shit." Detective Lee actually trembled. "Oh fuck me."

"Oh God," Detective Haddock groaned, seconding his partner's reaction. "Sir, your friend, Detective Stiel… he hates me."

"I very much doubt that. He can just be a little intense at times," I explained.

The look I got made me smile wide.

"You don't understand."

They were all standing in my living room because someone, supposedly a contract killer, had tried to kill me and only failed because he'd taken a header off my fire escape. But all that was secondary to the fear that my ex was inspiring in three grown men.

Detective Haddock was possibly going to be sick, Detective Lee as well. Jimmy was massaging the bridge of his nose, groaning. And I got it. Families and friends of policemen in the line of fire were scary for everyone but worse for these guys because of Duncan. My ex-boyfriend was frightening, and there was no nice way to put it. No one wanted to be on his bad side, and now here was Jimmy explaining to the two detectives that Duncan and I were close. They were trying not to pee themselves, and they had been so macho with me. I was trying really hard not to smile.

"I have an idea," I suggested brightly, all three men turning to look at me. "How about we just don't tell him about any of this."

No one made a sound.

"It would be for the best, wouldn't it?"

Jimmy wanted to. I could tell from the tilt of his head, the way he had his eyes all scrunched up, the soft noise that told me he was trying to work it out, rationalize what could be said if he was ever caught.

"I think it's a phenomenal idea," Detective Haddock chimed in. "There's no reason he would be looking into our cases anyway since he's in major crimes now."

I looked at Jimmy. "Duncan moved to major crimes? Why?"

He nodded, forced a smile. "He, um—" He cleared his throat. "—can't do homicide if… you know…. It's just not that easy if you don't have… anyway, he can't do homicide anymore."

"Okay." I had no idea what was going on there, but since it was really none of my business, I let it go.

"So, hey." He brightened. "My daughter Joanna is moving home from Sydney, and we're having a party for her on Sat—"

"Oh good for you, Jimmy," I cut him off but smiled as I did it. "I know her being so far away has been killing you."

He swallowed hard. "It has, but now it's—it's okay. But we're having a coming home party for her, and we'd love it if you came by."

"Well, I have a funeral to go to, so unfortunately, I'm going to have to decline, but thank you for the invitation."

"A funeral." His brows furrowed. "I'm sorry. Who passed, if you don't mind me asking?"

"Friend of mine, his boss and some friends. You guys probably heard about it. Vincent Romelli and some of the men who worked for him. I'm friends with Andreo Fiore."

Beats of time—it was almost like I felt them tick off between us.

"Andreo Fiore…. We knew he lived in this building, but… you know him?"

"Yeah, I know him and his nephew. They were both over here last night, which makes this whole thing, some guy on my fire escape, a little creepier, doesn't it?"

"It does something." Jimmy nodded, back to rubbing the bridge of his nose.

"Uhm—so are we agreed, then?" Detective Haddock interrupted softly. "We're not gonna tell Detective Stiel about this, right?"

He got a resounding no as my front door opened and an officer leaned in.

"We've got a kid out here that wants to come in. Yes or no?"

Jimmy gave him a wave. A second later Michael Fiore tumbled back into my apartment, dressed, backpack slung over his shoulder, and looking terrified.

"What's wrong?"

"Are you all right?"

"I'm fine," I assured him. "Come here."

He was white as a sheet, and I thought maybe I understood. Policemen had probably come to tell him when his mother had died in her car accident.

When he reached me, he took hold of the hem of my T-shirt and looked into my face.

"I'm fine." I gave his cheek a pat. "And I will feed you. Put the bag down and get out the eggs."

He nodded, dumped the backpack on the counter, and started moving around in my kitchen loudly.

"I have to start cooking, if that's okay?"

"Sure, sure," Jimmy told me, offering me his hand. "We've got all we need. The crime scene guys'll be out of here soon as they can, okay? The officers are just here 'cause they gotta be as long as the CSI guys are, but… we're done."

"Thanks." I smiled, accepting the camaraderie for what it was, old time's sake, fingers gripping tight as we shook. "It was nice to see you, Detec—"

"Jimmy," he corrected, shaking my hand hard. "And it was great to see you too, Nate. I just wish the circumstances were the right ones."

"Me too," I agreed.

"He looked good." Jimmy coughed softly. "When you two were hangin' out."

Meaning Duncan, of course—Duncan had looked good. It was a really nice thing for him to say.

He dropped my hand then and turned and yelled, and everyone stated moving around me fast, a swirl of activity. The other two detectives said they would be in touch and let me know about any new developments the second they learned about any. I thanked them for the weirdest morning in a very long time and then pulled my omelet pan from the others hanging on the rack above the island in my kitchen.

People started running back and forth, trying, I was sure, to wrap up and get out of my house.

"I'll pour you some coffee and you can tell me what the hell is going on," Michael told me.

The coffee was the best idea he ever had.

AT WORK, I ran my classes through test reviews and collected papers and heard excuses. I told Ashton what I thought of his novel thus far—I was enjoying it, so it was easy to give good feedback—and told him where I thought some of the plot holes were.

"Plot holes." He was indignant.

"Don't fall in love with your own words or you'll never be able to change them," I cautioned him.

"Yes, but, plot holes?"

I bumped him with my shoulder on the way out of my office.

In my intro classes, we were doing oral reports, and I listened and asked questions and made sure the kids were looking at me instead of the vastness of the room with its stadium seating and a sea of faces. When I was smiling at them and nodding, nerves seemed to settle.

When I had my office hours, I was surprised to see Sanderson Vaughn walk into my office, dressed as always like something out of a Harlequin romance novel, the very ideal of what English professors looked like. Corduroy elbow patches on the tweed sports coat, jeans, loafers, tie, and a blue button-down oxford. Before he could say a word, I put up my hand.

"What?"

I motioned at him. "Tweed?"

He flipped me off.

"Just come on, Sandy," I teased. "Update the damn wardrobe. This is 2012, for crissakes."

"Just cut the crap, Nate. What did you say to—"

"I didn't say anything to anybody, and if you knew me at all, you'd know that."

"So, what you're telling me is that the one year that you don't get to put on the Medieval Feast just so happens to be the same year that Greg Butler decides he wants to give money to the college?"

"That's what I'm telling you."

"Are you kidding?"

"This is actually what you think of me?" I said to him. "That I would, what, call a rich alumnus and hit him up for cash for the school just to make you look bad? Really?"

"What am I supposed to think, Nate?"

"You're supposed to think how lucky you are that—"

The door flying open and banging against the wall made us both gasp, killing all conversation in the room instantly.

"Jesus!" Sanderson yelled as I realized who I was looking at.

"What are you doing here?"

"What the hell?" Sanderson yelled at Duncan Stiel.

"I need the room," he growled at my colleague, his voice low and hard and menacing.

Sanderson moved fast, asking no questions, telling me without any power behind the threat at all that we were not done discussing my obvious attempt to embarrass him. Like I had that kind of time or inclination. Just the idea was ludicrous.

He was annoying, but so was my ex as he slammed the door behind him and whirled around, hands gripping my desk as he stared me down with his dark-gray eyes. Once upon a time, I had found the overcast color romantic, stunning. Now they were just cold.

"Yes, Detective?"

"Don't fuckin' 'yes, Detective' me," he growled, all snarling alpha dog. "What the fuck is going on with you and Vincent Romelli?"

My eyes flicked to the clock, seeing that my office hours were actually done, and so I stood up and started packing my messenger bag, beginning with my laptop.

"Nate!" he yelled, his voice bouncing off the walls in the small space. He straightened up, moving like he was going to come around my desk.

"Don't," I said irritably. "You know, Duncan, this is bullshit. You don't get to ask me questions about my personal life anymore."

"This is not your fucking personal life we're talking about! This is Andreo Fiore and a murdered mob boss and a dead fuckin' hit man in your dumpster!"

I took a breath. "For the record, I never met Vincent Romelli, never saw the deceased hit man, and Andreo Fiore and I are friends and neighbors, and that's it."

"Goddammit, Nate, you—"

"I would not have known Vincent Romelli had I passed him on the street. Like I said, I know Andreo Fiore and I know he worked for Romelli, but that's it. As far as the dead man goes, I'm sure you know more about him than I do."

He was breathing through his nose as he studied me, crossing his arms over the broad chest that I knew from firsthand experience was covered in hard, thickly carved muscle. Really, without his clothes on, Duncan Stiel was a work of art; it was too bad that I was being reminded of what I could no longer have.

"So if this is done, I have a faculty meeting to get to and a date later, so… you know the way out."

"Nate—"

"Just don't worry about it." I sighed as I put the strap over my shoulder and walked around my desk to face him. "I'm fine."

"No, you look like somebody hit you."

I groaned.

"Nate!"

And when he yelled, it felt… normal. I had thought that the first time I talked to the man after our breakup, I would be sad or filled with regret. But I was neither. I was nothing. I was completely over Duncan Stiel.

"I'm fine," I soothed him. "I saved a lady from getting mugged the other day." I grinned, opening the door and gesturing him out. "And the next night, I saved my second-favorite kid from getting hit by an enraged father."

He looked at me like I had just fallen out of the crazy tree, but he moved at my bidding, and as he walked out into the hall, I locked the door behind him. When I turned to face him, he was still scowling.

"All this that you're doing," I told him, "is so unnecessary. Jimmy's got me covered. He'll figure out who the guy was actually there to kill, because we both know it wasn't me. Who would want to kill me? That makes no sense."

"You should be scared."

"Of what? Clumsy hit men?" I raised an eyebrow in question.

He was lost or confused or both.

"Come on, Duncan, think about it. I'm not in any danger, not really."

He was just staring at me.

"So, major crimes, huh?" I shoved my hands down in my pockets. "Jimmy told me. I thought you loved homicide."

"What?"

"Wait, that sounded weird." I thought about it a minute, grinning over my poor choice of words. I was supposed to be good with them.

"Nate."

I looked up into his eyes and waited.

"You need protection."

I shook my head. "No, there's some kind of mistake. I refuse to believe that anyone wants to hurt me. I'm sure Jimmy will figure it out—he's a smart guy."

"Nate—"

"Might be the company I keep," I said thoughtfully, really, finally, running the whole scenario over in my head, worried about the timing. Andreo had been at my house, sleeping in my bed, which was closest to the fire escape. It made way more sense that he would be a target instead of me. "Shit, I have to go," I said suddenly, turning away from him, needing to find Dreo.

"I need to talk to you." He stopped me, grabbing my bicep, holding tight, fingers digging into my arm.

"About what?" I asked impatiently, trying not to sound annoyed, because it was rude, and once upon a time, he had meant the world to me.

He took a step forward, crowding me but releasing me at the same time. "I just want you to know that I—I never… I never wanted to go. I miss the fuck out of you."

"You do?"

"Of course."

I was surprised. "But you left so easily."

"What was I supposed to do, Nate? You wanted something I couldn't give you—still can't. It was either my job or you, and the job is who I am."

"I know that."

"But it doesn't mean I didn't care."

I took a breath. "I know that too."

"And you?"

"I think we're both well aware of what my feelings were."

He cleared his throat. "Were?"

Honesty, right there in the hallway. Maybe it was fitting. "Yeah. It's been over a long time, right? Me and you?"

I got a quick nod of his head.

"So we're both good."

"I," he said, closing back in on me, this time gently taking hold of my elbow, "really miss… you, us. There's been no one who's meant anything since I walked out of your apartment that day."

It was painful to hear but so completely unchangeable. He was in the closet; I had found out the hard way that I could not live my life like that. When we had been together, which, honestly, we never should have been, I hadn't liked myself. I was not the kind of man who hid his feelings or his relationships. That had never been me. I was the guy who draped an arm around a shoulder in public, introduced my man to an acquaintance if I passed one on the street, and definitely brought them to any work function I happened to have because I was happy and proud and excited. I had not been allowed to be any of those things with Duncan, and so the relationship had been doomed to fail from the start. In hindsight it was a ridiculous situation, but at the time, my feelings had drowned my logic. I had not been me for two years, and when it was over, when I knew it was truly done, losing Duncan had been hard, but I got myself back. I got to be me again. And really, truly, the trade-off had been a good one.

"Nate."

"Sorry." I smiled automatically. "I was just thinking about ancient history."

"I was worried." He sucked in a breath. "That's why I came. More than worried, actually, more like terrified. The idea that you could be in trouble or—"

"But I'm not," I assured him, taking a breath, easing free of his tentative hold. "I'm fine. Like I told you, I didn't know Romelli, and Andreo Fiore, for whatever reputation he has, is a good man who loves his nephew. So," I said with a sigh, "thanks for coming; it was actually great to see you. Clearing the air and closure, always appreciated."

The muscles in his jaw corded. "So, you have a date?"

"I do." I chuckled. "And you? Are you see—"

"It's the same as it was before you."

I understood. It meant that spotting him outside the bathhouse on Halstead had not been a fluke; he was back to old habits, one-night stands with a parade of nameless guys. It made sense. Duncan Stiel was gorgeous—any guy would want him. It was keeping him, living with him inside the insulated bubble he insisted on, that was the trick.

"Nate?"

My eyes flicked back to his.

He smiled. "Don't know what to say?"

His eyes were hooded, his smile barely there, and I knew by the sound he made under his breath that he wanted to lean in and take hold of me. I remembered it—his looks, his breathing, his smell—and how much I had wanted it to work so desperately. The man could be addictively sweet, and when I had been there some nights, at his loft, when he got home from work, the joy on his face at finding me had been worth all the secrecy. When he crossed the floor to wrap strong arms around me, just needing everything to stop, just wanting me to hold him as tight as I could… I knew that was real, and those moments had sustained me through the rest. It had been physically painful when I took his house key off my ring because I knew those quiet, tender encounters were over.

"There's nothing to say," I assured him.

He nodded and took a breath. "There is. You look great."

"You too." I smiled, relieved, giving him the sincere compliment before I turned to go.

"Nate."

My head swiveled back.

"If you ever find yourself in need of police protection…." He smiled ruefully.

"First call I make," I promised.

He shoved his hands down in the pockets of his dress pants, and I turned again and walked away. At the end of the hall, I looked back. He was still there, watching me.

"Hey, you know I only wish you the best, right?"

"Yeah, I know," he assured me.

I pushed the panic bar on the door and walked outside into the brisk fall air. I felt good. The cathartic talk was done, and it had not been how I thought it would be, instead lighter. But as I took a deep breath, the roll of memory leveled me and I remembered, like you do in the morning when you first wake up after a breakup before everything comes roaring back, that I needed to talk to Dreo. As I began walking in the opposite direction of my faculty meeting, I pulled out my cell phone and called Michael. I needed to find out where his uncle was.

THE dean let me out of the staff meeting after I explained that I had a family emergency and promised to have someone fill me in on what I missed. After catching a cab, I headed downtown to an Italian restaurant off LaSalle that was a huge place that looked more like a warehouse than a high-end dining experience. Supposedly, though, it was a very trendy new place where all the foodies gathered nightly. As I was there after lunch and well before dinner, it was mostly deserted. At the bar, though, situated in the middle of a vast concrete floor, was where I saw Dreo Fiore, just like Michael had told me when I called to ask if he knew his uncle's whereabouts.

Normally, the younger Fiore didn't get an itinerary from his uncle, but I figured with the unfortunate turn of events that Dreo might have been a little more forthcoming. I was right. Michael told me he had given Dreo an ultimatum: he could either tell him where he would be at certain points during the day or turn the GPS on his phone on. Dreo had given Michael a rundown of where he anticipated being as the idea of being tracked around town was not appealing. At the restaurant, he was with five or six other men, and another was behind the bar, dressed, I thought, much too nicely to be serving drinks.

"Sorry," a young guy, probably the host, said as he stepped in front of me. "We're not serving dinner yet, and I think tonight we're all booked with reser—"

"Oh no." I stopped him, pointing over his shoulder. "I just need to talk to that gentleman there."

"Tommy, what's the problem?" someone called over.

I turned, he turned, both of us toward the voice. It was the man behind the bar, but before I could open my mouth, Dreo called my name.

"Hey." I lifted my hand as I looked back at the guy in front of me. "Can I—is it okay? May I go talk to him?"

"Of course." He stepped back, and it was hard to tell what I was looking at. Concern? Worry? Both? He seemed shaken.

I smiled, trying to reassure him that whatever he was worried about with me was fine before I started across the floor. Dreo slid off his barstool, and I noticed he looked bigger than he did at home, broader, more menacing, the all-black suit with the black dress shirt on underneath adding to the image. I had not thought of him as being as muscular as Duncan, and he wasn't. He was somewhat slighter, leaner, but he was also, I realized, just as tall.

"What's going on? How did you know where I was?" he asked as I closed in.

"I called Michael, and I'm so sorry to bother you," I apologized as I reached him, tipping my head back slightly to meet his gaze, "but have you talked to him today?"

"Michael?"

I nodded.

"Not since early this morning, why?" he wanted to know, putting a hand on the side of my neck.

"Dreo, who's your friend?"

I turned and saw faces I had never seen before.

"Nate Qells. He lives in my building," he told the bartender as his hand slid from my neck to my shoulder. "He's the professor I told you about yesterday… you remember."

There was a nod. "Bring him over here."

"Come on," he told me, turning so I could walk forward, his hand sliding down to the small of my back to propel me forward.

"Professor of what?" the man asked me as we closed in on the bar.

"English lit," I replied. "Beowulf to Milton, Renaissance literature, mainly."

He nodded. "Where at?"

"University of Chicago."

Second nod. "Do you know Alla Strada?"

I smiled. "I do know Alla; she's an excellent professor. Is she your daughter?"

"She's my niece, my brother's daughter." He wiped his hand on the bar towel before leaning forward to offer me his hand. "I'm her uncle, Tony Strada."

I moved forward to take the hand, leaning into the polished wood to shake it. "Nate Qells."

"So," he said, releasing my hand, "you're not by chance one of the professors who sat on the board that hired her, are you?"

"I did have that privilege."

His dark whiskey-colored eyes heated. “She told us that it was between her and another guy who was older and had a lot more experience.”

“Yes, but she had fire,” I told him. “Still does. She isn’t doing it for a paycheck. She wants to teach. Did she tell you about her dream?”

He made a noise in the back of his throat. “Don’t get me started. Goin’ to Iraq. Teaching there because she can speak Arabic and Kurdish—do you have kids, Professor?”

“One, a son, so your brother has my sympathy.”

He nodded. “She just needs to get knocked up.”

I laughed.

“No?”

I shrugged.

“Because you know she has a girlfriend.”

“I do.” I patted his arm. “And her girlfriend wants to save the world too.”

“Aww, fuck,” he grumbled, pointing at a barstool. “Siddown, Professor, I’ll get you some food. What’re you drinkin’?”

“I actually have a date,” I said. “But I appre—”

“Sit, Professor.” He smiled and nodded.

I didn’t want to drink or eat, but every glance, even Dreo’s, carried the same look of wide-eyed, thundering panic, like *hurry up and freakin’ give the man an answer*!

I gave up. “Sam Adams, if you have it.”

“It’s comin’ now.”

“*Ma guarda chi c’è*!”

I looked up, and there was Sal walking into the room, and he was really trying to smile and put it on, his happy face, but I saw it in his eyes, the sorrow.

When he crossed to me, I turned on the barstool and put my hand on his cheek. Normally, I was not a big touchy-feely guy, but it seemed like it would be okay. When he leaned in, his face into my shoulder, I felt the tremble just for a second. How both he and Dreo were not sedated in a dark room I had no idea.

I rubbed the nape of his neck, asked how he was, and was greeted with silence before he took a breath and stepped away, smile back, plastered there.

"We're both gonna be fine, aren't we, D?"

Dreo grunted in agreement.

I turned back to him and found Dreo's deep eyes locked on me. They were really something, those eyes of his, so dark that you couldn't ever see his pupils. The brown was so close to black, only the way the light caught them sometimes, making them glint and fire, let you know you were looking at a color and not the absence of it. Being fringed in long, thick black lashes only added to their allure.

"So what are you doing here?" Dreo finally got to ask me.

"I came to tell you that the police were at my apartment this morning after you left."

He leaned close, lowering his voice, though with Sal behind him being loud and entertaining, no one was listening to us anyway. "Tell me from the beginning."

So I went over it: the hit man, Alfred Mangino, who had died after he slipped and fell into the dumpster, how interested the police had been in Dreo, and the fact that Detective O'Meara as well as my ex were worried about him and me.

"I told everyone that you're a good guy, but they're all worried about—"

"What did you say?" he asked, cutting me off, leaning even closer, only inches separating us.

"About what?" My voice lowered as it did whenever my pulse sped up. No longer did my fluster ever show outwardly; I had mastered that with age.

"About me being a good guy."

"Just that you are and you're trying to take care of Michael and that he's the most important thing to you."

He nodded, still crowding me. "Your ex is a cop?"

"That needs to stay between us, all right? It was a secret at the time, and it's still a secret now."

"How long did you date him?"

"Couple of years."

"When?"

"We ended it a little over a year and a half ago now."

He squinted at me. "I never saw anyone; Michael didn't mention anything to me."

"That's because my ex never came to my place, so Michael never met him."

"Why didn't he come to your apartment?"

"Because it was a secret, like I said," I explained. "He was in the closet—still is. It's because of his job."

The way he was looking at me was almost sad. "So he never stepped up and said you guys were together?"

"He couldn't."

"Or wouldn't."

"Don't pass judgment; it doesn't become you."

He tipped his head like maybe not and then leaned back, letting me breathe, giving me space.

"How are you today?"

"Who cares?"

"I care."

He shrugged. "*Non importa.*"

"Dreo?"

"You came to find me because you thought that hit man was after me and you wanted to warn me, yes?"

"Yes." I nodded. "And now I have, so… I should go."

"You need to sit and drink your beer and eat whatever he makes," he told me. "Tony is cooking for you, and he don't cook for nobody."

"Okay," I agreed, lifting the strap of my messenger bag, which had been slung across my chest, over my head and gently putting it down beside me on the empty stool on my left.

He gave his attention to the others, looking away from me, and as he did, as he stood there between me and Sal and the other guys, I had a nearly overwhelming urge to touch him, to soothe the hurt that was right there on the surface.

"Did you sleep at all?" I asked instead.

No answer.

"Dreo."

He turned his head slowly back to me, eyes narrowed, so I noticed again how long and thick his lashes were, the shiny black striking against his pale cheek as he closed them for just a second.

"You're exhausted."

"It's been a long day—we all just got back from going to the funeral home."

"Will there be separate funerals?"

"Yes."

"Is Mr. Romelli's still on Saturday?"

He nodded. "I need you and Michael there with me. There will be a lot of out of town people, and they need to see my family."

I didn't get the chance to ask him what he meant before a bowl that smelled heavenly was put down in front of me.

"Here you are, Professor."

I looked up as Tony Strada put a tall bar glass down in front of me beside the bowl of linguini and clams. It smelled amazing.

"Thank you," I said with a smile. "I can't tell you the last time I had this."

He nodded, clearly pleased, and passed me a spoon, fork, and a napkin.

"Nate, let me introduce you to the others."

So I met guys I could tell Dreo didn't know well. He wasn't warm with them, not like he had been with the men that both he and Sal, from what he said, had grown up with. I asked Sal, when he was done with the introductions, if he and Dreo would be taking some time off.

"What for?" he asked me.

It wasn't my place to tell him that he and Dreo and Tony all needed some group therapy and a vacation to Fiji.

I scarfed down my food, leaving nothing, and drained my beer. I gushed over my meal, and how fast I had eaten it gave honest testament to how great it was. When Tony wanted to give me more, I told him I had a date later and would be expected to eat something. He agreed, smiled, and told me to get the hell out. I liked him a lot.

"I'll see you all Saturday at the funeral," I said as I got up, thanking Tony again.

"*A presto*," Tony said softly.

I gave Dreo's arm a gentle squeeze and headed for the door.

"Wait."

Turning, I watched Dreo jog over to me and stop close.

"Thank you for coming here to talk to me. I'm going to tell them all once you leave so they'll know."

"Why does it matter that they know?"

"It matters."

"Okay." I smiled. "I'm glad you're okay; I was worried."

He nodded before he turned and left me.

Outside, I realized how full I was and told myself that it was okay. Wherever I was going with Sean, there had to be salad on the menu.

Chapter SEVEN

SUSHI was even better than salad. You could order big or small and whatever you ate would be enough. I ordered small, and Sean was worried that it wouldn't fill me up.

"I had a big lunch." I smiled across the table at him.

He took a breath. "You look great. Did I tell you that already?"

"Yes." I chuckled. "But you can keep saying it."

When I had opened the door, the man had caught his breath, and I had been completely charmed. And Dockers and a dress shirt and sweater vest didn't seem like much to me, but he thought I looked good, and that was what was important.

"I—"

His phone buzzed, cutting him off, and he apologized as he pulled it from the breast pocket of his suit jacket, not even looking at it.

"You should check, huh, Doctor?"

He shook his head. "I'm not on call tonight." His eyes zeroed in on my mouth. "You're all mine."

"What?"

"I mean," he said with a flash of smile, "I'm all yours."

I pointed at the phone. "Better check."

Heavy sigh before he looked down at the phone to check the display. The way his face contorted, I was *so* glad I had done the right thing.

"Jesus," he gasped, head snapping up to me. "Shit, Nate, I'm so sorry, but one of my patients, he.... I have to go."

"Go, go. I'll take care of this."

He didn't argue because he didn't have time; he just got up, turned, and left. When the server returned, she was surprised but understanding.

On my way home in the cab, my phone rang, and it was Sean on the other end.

"Hey." I smiled because it was him.

"God, don't be nice to me. I screwed up for the second time in the same week."

"You're a doctor. I get it."

"But it's not—I want you to get that you're important."

"I appreciate the fact that you're calling just to tell me."

"You do?"

"Very much."

"Okay, so tomorrow for sure, let's—"

"Just call me and we can meet somewhere and take it from there, all right? Or tonight when you're done, call me and maybe we could go get dessert, or I could make you some."

Silence.

"Sean?"

"Are you serious? Is that all you think this is?"

So. Lost.

"You think all I'm looking for is some hookup after work?"

"You did say that you wanted us to go to bed," I reminded him. "But no, I—"

"I also said I wanted to be the one who got to take you out. How did 'I want to date' turn into 'I just want to fuck'?"

"That's not what I—"

"I don't take one-night stands out to dinner, Nate." The condescending tone was annoying.

"This is more than just a hookup for me. I'd like to—"

"Listen." I was suddenly irritable. "I thought maybe you could come over after work, and if you were hungry, I would make you some dinner, and if you just wanted dessert, then I could make that too. It was honestly a nice offer with no sex attached that you turned into something else. So, yes, call me tomorrow and we'll talk."

"I—fuck! I didn't mean to, but I'm walking into the hospital, and—"

"It's fine. Tomorrow," I repeated. "I'll talk to you later."

When I hung up, I took a sharp breath, and when my phone rang again, I could hear it in my voice when I answered that I was annoyed.

"Nate?"

It was a different voice, older, drunker, and confused as to why I was mad.

"Sorry." I softened my tone. "What's going on?"

"I need you."

"Why, what'd you do?" I teased Ben.

"I think—" He took a breath. "—that Mel's cheating on me."

There was no way. I knew my ex-wife, my dearest friend, the mother of my son, and she did not have a cheating bone in her body. The woman was made loyal and no other way. "Not possible," I assured him.

"Then get your ass to the Water Lily right now and I'll prove it to you."

What I had thought was funny was not. The man was on the verge of a nervous breakdown. "Yes, dear, coming," I said to keep things light. I needed to show him that he was being an idiot, and make sure nothing escalated.

I changed my destination with the cabbie and arrived downtown ten minutes later. After getting out, I looked around for him and finally saw the waving hand across the street in front of what looked like a charming little pub packed with people.

Bolting over to him, I saw how flushed he looked, and understood instantly that my on-the-phone analysis was correct and that I was looking at a very drunk man. My hypothesis was further confirmed when he breathed on me.

"Jesus," I groaned, waving my hand in front of my face. "Don't stand near an open flame, Ben, shit."

"She's there," he slurred, pointing across the street to a very fancy, very high-end French restaurant, the Water Lily, so named after Monet's masterpiece.

"Who's she with?"

"Her boss."

"From the art gallery?"

"She only has one goddamn boss, Nate."

"Uh-huh." I crossed my arms over my chest. "How did you find her?"

"I wanted to surprise her when I got in, so I used the GPS on her phone to track her down."

It seemed to me that tracking someone without an explanation could be problematic. I was living through an illustration of it. Instead of just calling, Ben had tailed his wife and, upon finding her, had jumped to the completely wrong conclusion. And I knew he was mistaken, because I knew Melissa. It was not in her to cheat.

Uh-huh. "Can I see your phone, please?"

He looked at me blearily, not steady on his feet at all, wobbly to say the least.

"Please?"

He fished the phone out of his pocket, bobbled it, and ended up tossing it at me in a wild Hacky Sack maneuver. No one was more surprised than me when I caught the damn thing.

"What're you doin'?"

"Shhh," I hushed him, arm around his waist as he started his heavy lean into me. I smiled as soon as I saw what I was looking for. "So, where were you?"

"How d'ya mean?" He belched.

"I mean…." I coughed, walking him away from the front door, leaning him against the red brick exterior of the pub, and straightening his tie and his jacket as I looked at him. "Where were you before you were here?"

"On a plane." He was working really hard to focus on me.

"So you were out of town?"

"Well, yeah, that's why she—oh crap," he groaned, cutting himself off, and I saw, the light come on through the alcoholic stupor. "Oh shit, was I supposed to be there too?"

"Uh-huh." I drew it out, turning his phone to him, letting him know with my condescending tone what a dumbass he was. "As you're well aware, your lovely wife downloads her weekly schedule to you—and, for some ungodly reason, to me—so that both you and I are informed of her whereabouts on a day-to-day basis. Again, why I'm in that loop, I do not know. Maybe because we used to be married; maybe because we share a kid. Your guess is as good as mine, but it's fun to read what she's going to do, and the side notes are funny as hell. However—" I cleared my throat. "—tonight, if you were going to be back from your business trip, you were supposed to join her and her boss"—I pointed at the screen so he could see the calendar reminder—"Milton Horne, at the Water Lily at eight for drinks and dinner."

"Shit," he groaned again.

"Apparently the gallery is hosting a huge charity event and they had to discuss a theme, and she thought it would be nice to have you there too because, and I quote," I said, turning the phone back to me so I could read it, "Ben's ideas are usually so funny I almost pee my pants."

"Oh God." He moaned loudly, bending over.

I clicked off the calendar, returning to the main screen before putting his phone in my pocket and looking at him. "Can I ask, what's with you and thinking your wife is cheating on you all of a sudden? What kind of stupid-ass crisis are you having?"

"I haven't been think—"

"Was it the other day when she said she could be having an affair?"

He whimpered.

"What the hell, Ben?"

He straightened up, taking a deep breath. “Two couples that we know, just this week they announced that they were both getting divorces.”

“So?”

“And she’s already been divorced once and so have I, and—”

“Your ex-wife ran off with the pool boy, Ben,” I reminded him. “Unfortunate, but those are the facts.”

He looked so miserable.

“By the way, the yoga outfits they make, kind of hot,” I assured him.

Instantly, he was scowling. “I will beat you ’til you’re dead.”

“Who knew the pool boy was, like, a marketing guru, huh?”

“Seriously, they’ll never find your body,” he threatened me.

I chuckled. “Anyway, your ex-wife left you, and Mel’s ex-husband”—I grinned, pointing at myself—“he’s gay.” I whispered the last part.

He growled.

“So you have been married now for the last sixteen years and—guess what?—it’s been smooth sailing, calm seas.”

“You’re doing boating metaphors ’cause you know I’m about ready to throw up,” he said, sounding like he was actually going to hurl.

I smiled, moved forward, and took his face in my hands. “Idiot, your wife adores you, and you adore her back, and you’re both lucky to have each other, so could we please call a moratorium on the stupidity?”

“We can.” He took a deep breath, smiling. “You know I really love you.”

“Ohh-kay.” I laughed, pulling him off the wall. “Did you eat?”

“No, just drank.”

“Me neither.”

“Why were you drinking?”

“No, I mean I didn’t get dinner either.”

"Why? Where were you?"

"On a date."

"With who?"

"I'll tell you in a minute." I sighed, arm around the waist of my inebriated friend. "Just come with me, all right?"

"Whatever you want." He sighed. "Just don't lemme go."

"I need to get those demands from gay men, not straight ones."

"Sorry." He hiccupped.

BECAUSE it was the safest thing, I took Ben for breakfast. There was coffee and french toast and more coffee and water, and the longer we sat there, just talking, the better he felt. When his phone rang in the breast pocket of my peacoat, I answered it.

"Hello there, beautiful."

"Nate?"

"It's a long story," I said. The preemptive strike seemed best.

"You're obviously with him somewhere."

"Yes."

"Where?"

"We're at Nonna's."

"In Old Town?"

"Yeah."

"Okay, I'm coming."

"No, don't do that. Let me sober him up first, and then I'll bring him home."

"Oh, did he drink too much on the plane again?"

"Sort of."

"Sort of?"

"Give us another half an hour and we'll be there."

"I'm holding you to that."

"Yes, ma'am."

"Okay," she said, and I could hear the smile in her voice. "I was going to call you anyway."

"Just because, or was there a specific reason?"

"I wanted to bug you about Sean."

"Oh, I have news."

She made a noise. "Eww, why didn't that sound good?"

"I'll tell you when I get there."

"Good. Come now."

"On my way," I promised as I hung up.

"Who was that?" Ben asked me when I got off the phone.

"Your lovely wife."

"Is she mad?"

"Why would she be mad? She has no idea what you did yet."

"Shit. Yet?"

I shrugged, smiling.

Thirty minutes later, as promised, Ben and I walked into their lush home in Oak Park, in the historic part, the Frank Lloyd Wright tour of homes area, and when she charged across the foyer and flung herself at her husband, I heard his deep sigh.

"Jesus, Ben." She sounded disgusted as she pulled back. "Why do you reek of scotch?"

Long story, that, but because I had been the one he called, I got to be the one who translated his rambling into cohesive sentences.

First she was mad—how dare he think so little of her, and since when was she a whore, and blah, blah, blah—and then she was charmed because, dear God, the man must really love her if he could worry this much. He was rich and successful and smart and funny and hot, in that Andy Garcia way, so he had nothing to worry about, but he was worrying nonetheless because he worshipped the ground his wife walked on. And then she was disgusted, because Milton Horne? Really? Eww. The man was so not hot, and if she was going to cheat, it would be with a guy half her age, not double it.

"You're really not helping," I assured her.

When she got up from where she was sitting by me on the couch to get in his lap and wrap herself in his arms, I bailed and left them kissing. They were very cute, but I had never been much for voyeurism even when I lived next door to two guys who liked to have sex on their fire escape every morning.

I had to walk back into the town of Oak Park to get a cab, but once I was there, I saw the train platform and decided on that instead. My phone rang when I reached the station.

"You left?" she asked me breathlessly.

"And the fact that you just now noticed tells you why I left."

"I, we, just got a little carried away."

"And the fact that you did—yeah, didn't need to see it."

"You really are such a prude."

"Am I?"

She laughed, and since I liked the sound so much, I couldn't help my smile.

"Thank you for being the voice of reason in his head. Ben worries, but now he won't anymore."

"Good. Everyone should have a meltdown once in a while, keeps things spicy."

"I think that's the sex after, darling."

"Could be."

"But I want to hear about Sean."

"Lunch? Tomorrow?"

"Oh, I would love to have lunch with you. We have to have the tuition talk anyway."

"No."

"Nate. I can afford to pay Jare's tuition at Yale—just let me."

"No. He's our kid, Mel, ours together. Let it go. Besides, I have a hit man on my fire escape story to tell you."

Long silence while, I was certain, she processed. "I'm sorry, what?"

"I'll tell you tomorrow."

"Nate?"

"Make sure you're there," I taunted her.

"You're lucky I love you."

"I know." I chuckled and hung up.

That night, as I was walking by the vacant lot where normally there were the guys who yelled and sometimes threw bottles, it occurred to me that they were missing. Usually, morning, noon, or night, they were there. And now they weren't. The old Cadillac they normally sat on was missing as well. The telltale aroma of marijuana and their raised voices were all absent. It was almost strange. On many occasions, I had seen the police roust them only to find them back the following day. Sal's words came back to me, that maybe I wouldn't see them anymore. I would have to remember to ask Dreo about it when I saw him next.

MELISSA was there before lunch and demanding to know what the hell I was talking about when I said hit man.

"He fell into the dumpster."

"Could you please just start at the beginning?" She looked pained.

So as we walked across the quad, I explained, and she listened and started to hyperventilate. I told her about Duncan coming for a visit and the detectives in my apartment and how it was all a big misunderstanding because really, could she think of anyone less exciting than me?

"Yeah, I can think of a lot of people."

"Really?"

She rolled her eyes, and it took time for me to convince her that I was safe, no one was going to shoot me, and that if she wanted, she could call Duncan and ask him.

"No, thank you." She made a face. "If I never talk to him again it'll be too soon."

"You really didn't like him." I smiled at her.

"I'm sure he's a very good man," she told me. "Just not for you."

I shrugged. "I would have to agree."

There was still no word from Sean by the time she and I walked into our favorite burger place in Hyde Park to eat lunch, and I was not really surprised. Melissa was and told me so as we sat across the table from each other.

"He seemed very interested to me."

I explained about our last conversation and how it had gone south. “I think our timing is off. It feels off,” I told her. “You know how that is?”

She nodded. “I do. Remember Ted Evans?”

“Yeah.” I smiled at her. “You dated him a year after Jare was born.”

“Yes, and he was fine with us being married. He understood that I was straight and you were gay, so we only ever slept together the once. He got that we had separate bedrooms but we lived together because of Jare, blah, blah, blah—he got it all and he was great about it.”

“He was,” I agreed. “I was surprised when that didn’t get serious.”

“But see, that’s what I mean: he was all the things I was looking for, but we never quite got going. We’d make plans and a lot of times they’d fall through, or he was called away and then I was, and we had a good time, but we never even went to bed.”

“You regret that?”

“I did for a long time, but now I really think that would have complicated things more. Sometimes you want something so badly that you don’t realize that the timing is just crap. I was not in a place where I was ready to be anything but a mother. Jared was everything, still is to some degree, but he has his own life and his own path, so now, at forty-six, I can do whatever the hell I want. And some of my friends are still dealing with third grade and high school and birth control, and thank God I got it done early.”

“You never wanted more kids?”

“I have them. I have Ben’s kids and, well, Ben, right?”

I laughed at her. “Fine.”

She took my hand. “I loved being your wife, and for a while I even thought maybe, just maybe, his orientation will change and he’ll want me as much as I want him.”

“Mel—”

“No.” She put up her hand to shut me up. “I did. I’d see you shuffling across the floor late at night, Jare in your arms, walking to—Bob Marley?”

"Yeah. He loved Bob. I still worry that he'll be out driving late at night and 'No Woman No Cry' will come on and he'll fall asleep at the wheel."

She shook her head. "Stop."

"Just saying."

"Well, I used to watch you putting our kid down or falling asleep on the couch with him on your chest and think how badly I wanted to be the one curled up with you."

"Why are you breaking my heart with this?"

"I don't mean to."

"You know I love you."

"Yes." She nodded. "I know, but that didn't change the ache. Little by little, though, year by year, it changed from 'I'm Nate's for the asking' to 'I deserve more and so does he'."

"We both realized that there was more we wanted."

She stared.

"Oh God, what?"

"But see, here's where it gets tricky. My timing was shitty with Ted and every guy I dated until I was really ready to take the plunge, you know? When I met Ben, I just knew. I was in a different place, and I jumped at the chance to—"

"Jumped him, you mean." I cackled.

"I'm going to smack you."

"Sorry."

"But you…." She trailed off, deep in thought.

"Me? Me what?"

"Your problem is not about timing."

"You just said it was."

"Okay." She took a breath. "I mean this, with Sean, this is about timing, but normally, what's with you and guys is that you've never been in love."

"Again with this?"

"Brian Palmer."

"He moved to San Diego." I snickered.

"And you could have gone too if you wanted, if you cared enough to go."

"I was crazy about Brian."

"If it was convenient, which, with him moving, it no longer was."

"I—"

"Marc Takashima."

"Marc wanted me to move in; I wasn't ready."

"And so because it was all or nothing, you guys were done."

I grunted.

"Emmett Wallace."

"He wanted to move in with me, but you can't rush it, Mel. You're either ready or not."

"Uh-huh."

"You're being ridiculous."

"Duncan."

"Okay, now wait, I loved Duncan. I wanted him to move in. I wanted to do everything with him."

"And yet—" She took a breath. "—you let him say what that relationship was going to be. I watched you skulk around for two years, be the Nate I knew when Duncan wasn't around and turn into this freaky Stepford wife when he was. I hated you with him, and you being like that was just another way that you didn't rock the boat. You went along like you always do so it's easy and comfortable, and you eventually grow so bored that you run for the hills."

"I do not!" I snapped at her.

"You do too! I have yet to see you actually, madly, head-over-heels, what-the-hell-am-I-gonna-do in love."

"I loved Duncan," I assured her, because I had.

"Cared for him, you mean?"

"Don't be snide."

"I'm not, love. You're the one who thinks the words are interchangeable."

I sighed deeply. "I don't, not really."

"I know you don't, not really," she said playfully, giving my words right back to me. "You just like to sound like you do."

"Which is kind of arrogant."

There was quick nodding.

"I did love Duncan."

"I know you did, but you weren't in love with him."

"Another clarification?"

"Yes." She chuckled. "Like I said, I've never seen you in love. Not yet."

"Well, it hurt when he was walking out the door."

"But that was your choice, Nate. You could have stayed in the closet with him."

"So if I had continued to live in the closet with him, that would have proved to you that I really loved him?"

"No, what would have proved you loved him was you finding a way, some way, to make it work. You're a very smart man, and when you want to do something, I mean really want it.... I've seen your willpower in action, and you can do anything."

"You have more faith in me than I do in myself."

"Which is what friends are for."

I nodded.

"You look very nice today, by the way."

I was wearing a thick, brown crewneck fisherman sweater under my peacoat, with jeans. "I look like a frat boy."

"You look yummy." She smiled. "Let's walk to the bookstore after this. I miss doing that with you. We used to go all the time."

"You're busy being a docent now."

"I'm never too busy for you."

I had time, on a Friday, to hang out with my ex-wife between my first class and the late-afternoon one. By the time I got back, Ashton was leaving, telling me that yes, he agreed, he did indeed have plot holes in his novel that needed to be addressed, so I had to cease reading immediately.

"But I finished it already," I told him. "I just have to write up my notes."

"Well, hold off until I send you the revisions."

"I bet Stephen King doesn't treat his beta readers like this."

"What do you want?"

"The pumpkin brownies Levi makes."

He rolled his eyes. "Since when are my boyfriend's cooking skills part of the 'you read what I write' deal?"

"Since now." I grinned.

He grunted and walked away.

"Is that a yes?"

"That's a yes!"

Winning was fun.

I saw Sanderson waiting by my office door, so I turned before he saw me, or thought I did, but when I heard him yell my name, I bolted. I went down the back stairs to Tylah Grey's office—she was one of three new assistant professors that had just joined the department—walked in, and shut the door.

Big brown eyes surveyed me. "Do I even want to know?"

"I'm hiding from Vaughn," I whispered, walking around her desk and ducking down behind it next to her legs, my hands on her thighs.

"Ohmygod!" she squealed. "Nate, you can't—"

The sharp knock on the piece of frosted glass at her door cut her off, and I heard the door bang open a second later.

"Sanderson," she gasped, more because of my beard on her thigh than the fact that he had come barging in.

"Did you see Nate? I saw him duck down the stairs a second ago, and I figured he'd come in here."

"No." She laughed as I blew air up her skirt, then flicked me in the forehead. "Why are you chasing Nate?"

"What's so funny?" he barked at her.

"You? Playing like the jealous husband looking for his cheating wife, throwing open doors and yelling. What's going on?"

"I need to talk to him about the Medieval Feast, and he's not answering my e-mails. We're supposed to meet with this event planner tomorrow morning, and I'm not sure if Saturday is good for him or not."

I traced "no" on her knee with my fingertip.

"I think he has plans on Saturday, so I'd push it to Sunday if I were you."

"How do you know?"

"We're tight like that," she teased and then added, "yo."

"Yo?"

"Word," she said, lowering her voice.

"Oh God," he groaned, and I heard the door close behind him as she dissolved into throaty laughter.

"You're not supposed to laugh," I told her. "God, remind me to never hide from Nazis with you."

"You're giving me goose bumps with your breath on my thighs! Jesus Christ, Nate, are you trying to kill me?"

I waggled my eyebrows up at her. "Remember in *The Breakfast Club*—wait, how old are you?"

"I remember Judd Nelson in *The Breakfast Club* under the desk, and you're very cute." She smiled down at me, hand sliding over my jaw, over my beard. "Now get the hell up and get out of my office!"

"What if he comes back?"

"Then deck him." She beamed as I uncoiled and stood up beside her.

"Let's go eat dinner."

"No pity party table for two. I don't need your charity."

"It's not charity; I kind of like you."

She shook her head. "Yeah, and I kind of like you too, even though you're a pain in the ass and all my students keep saying 'Dr. Qells says' this and 'Dr. Qells says' that—really frickin' tired of it, gotta say."

"Just tell them to shut up."

"Seriously? You think that's good advice, since I'd really like to get tenure someday?"

I shrugged.

"And some of us actually need grad students since our class load is heavy, but they all want to work with you."

"I only have Ashton."

"Yes, I know, and they all keep hoping he falls into Lake Michigan so they can take his place."

But it wasn't true. "C'mon," I pleaded. "Have dinner."

"No." She chuckled. "And besides, I have a date. I found him on It's Just Dinner."

"It's just what," I questioned.

"It's an online dating service like eHarmony and places like that, but this is just for the first two dates. You go to dinner twice and see if there's enough chemistry there to go on."

"Really?"

"Yes, really. You want to do it with me?" She looked very hopeful.

"Sounds like you already started."

"Yes, but you could still apply, and then we could double-date."

"No, thank you." I made a face at her.

"I just don't want to date any more college professors."

"Why not? We're lovely people."

"Most of you guys are married, too freaky for cable, or gay."

"Are you serious?"

"Absolutely."

"And Sanderson?"

"Are you kidding? I bet his girlfriend is a dominatrix or something."

"Or his boyfriend."

"No, he's so not cool enough to be gay."

She was very funny.

"Now go away." She shooed me out. "I have a hot Friday night date to get ready for, so I need to get the hell out of here."

"And you'll report back on Monday?"

"If you tell me how the meeting with Sanderson and the event planner goes on Sunday."

"Deal."

She pointed at the door.

"Going, God."

As I was crossing the quad, I heard my name called, and when I turned, I saw Sanderson Vaughn walking fast toward me. I had a very juvenile urge to run, knowing that I could outdistance him, but held my ground and waited.

"You're such a shit!" he yelled when he was close enough to be heard.

I grunted.

"And it's not just me that thinks so. You have just as many detractors in our department as people who love you."

I believed him. I was not the universally liked guy. I tended to be a bit of a boat-rocker.

"Did you hear me?"

"I did."

He almost growled. "So, Sunday, can we meet with the event planner or not?"

"We can," I assured him. "Where and what time?"

"At the Four Seasons at eleven. We're having brunch."

"Okay."

He was glowering. "Do you want me to pick you up?"

"I'll show up," I said irritably. "I don't need a babysitter. I'll see you at eleven."

"Fine," he snapped before he wheeled around to stalk away. He never made it.

"Dr. Qells!"

I looked over his shoulder and saw Gwen Barnaby, one of my favorite undergrad students, jogging up to us. There was no missing the look of utter infatuation on Sanderson's face as he looked at her. The man was entranced, but he should have been. The girl was a goddess, plain and simple, with her long blonde tresses, huge blue eyes, and curvy Botticelli physique.

"Hey, Gwen." I smiled at her as she reached me and took hold of my jacket like she always did when she spoke to me. It was her way.

"Uhm." She took a breath, biting her bottom lip. "I've decided to attend grad school here, and so I wanted to know if you'd be my, uhm… my—"

"Of course." I grinned at her.

"Oh." Her blue eyes softened. "Thank you, Dr. Qells." She sighed deeply. "Now I know I'll be okay. My mom was worried because of the—you know."

"I know," I soothed her.

Her eyes studied me, my face, really looking at me. "Thank you for forgiving me."

"Nothing to forgive."

She shook her head. "There was."

I chucked. "My ego is not that fragile."

She nodded. "I know, but… my first quarter, when I had you for intro and then again for Shakespeare, I used to tell everyone that you were the worst teacher ever."

I knew she had.

"I gave you a really bad assessment—two, I think."

I knew that too.

"But then when I had other professors, I was, like, why are they berating me and telling me what to do, and it hit me." She smiled suddenly. "You did this weird thing where you suggested something that would help me learn whatever it was, build on it, but without ever coming right out and saying that that's what you wanted me to do. You have this whole sleight of hand misdirection, indirection thing you do. It's very clever and very sneaky."

I waggled my eyebrows at her.

"You taught me things without me knowing."

"Smoke and mirrors."

"Except that it's not a trick. I learned shit—stuff. I meant stuff."

"I know you did."

Her breath caught like she was excited, like everything was settled. "So, okay, then, I'll see you Monday during your office hours?"

"Sounds good."

Her fingers tightened on my coat, squeezing as she exhaled, her eyes searching mine for a moment. "You mean… a lot."

I smiled as her hand dropped away.

"Bye."

I watched her walk away.

"Why would her mother be worried?"

I had forgotten that Sanderson was even there. I turned and frowned at him. "I am not at liberty to discuss a student's personal affairs that she has shared with me."

"You're such an ass."

"Yep," I agreed, walking away from him.

The girl in question had an addiction to prescription pain pills that she had kicked the year before, but she had had a relapse three months ago. After choosing outpatient rehab, she was back on track again. Her parents, who had initially not wanted to pay for her education even though they could more than afford it, had decided that if school was what kept her focused and drug-free, then that was what they were going to help her do. It had been the working two jobs to pay for school and an accident at work that had put her and pain medication together to begin with. She had shared the story when she had to withdraw for one quarter. But she had come back, looking better, and now was asking me to be her mentor and guardian all in one. I was more than happy to help with that challenge.

LATER, as I was walking from the platform where the L let me off, my phone rang.

"Hi." I smiled into my phone.

"I, uhm," Michael hedged on the other end, "wanted to know where you are."

"I'm almost home. Where are you?"

"I'm at Tony Strada's house in Northbrook."

"Okay."

"How was your date with the doctor?"

"He got called away."

"Did you reschedule?"

"What is this, twenty questions with my love life?"

"No, I just—I wanted to know is all."

"Okay."

"Are you mad at me?"

"No, why would I be mad at you?"

"I dunno."

He was the one who sounded weird.

"What's wrong?"

"Is it bad that I don't feel like shit?"

I had to catch up. "You mean about Mr. Romelli and your uncle's friends?"

"Yeah."

"Why would it be bad?"

"Everybody keeps saying how sad it is."

"But you didn't really know them, right? I mean, even Dreo's friends, you guys weren't close."

"No."

I was suddenly sad, thinking about Frank's mother, and that it was Friday, and that I was never going to get the forgotten carbonara we had talked about in my apartment. And it wasn't the food, of course, but the man's good intentions that would never be followed through on.

"I don't know what I'm supposed to say."

"You don't have to say anything."

"How am I supposed to feel?"

"You can feel that it's all terribly regrettable, but you're not going to be torn up like Dreo is, or Sal. They were there. That's the difference."

"I would have been sad about Sal. He comes by sometimes, but he was the only one."

It made sense. They had been Dreo's friends. He had grown up with them, but they were not good enough influences, except Sal, apparently, for Dreo to allow them to be around Michael. There were double standards. It had been the same for me after Jared was born.

People you never judged unworthy were suddenly not allowed near your kid or the life you shared with your child.

"I understand," I assured him. "You're not falling apart, and that's what people are expecting, so you feel like you're sticking out."

"Yeah. Everybody's looking at me like because Dreo's all torn up that I should be too, and I'm like fuck you, I ain't sad."

But he was something, probably angry. "Are you thinking about your mother's funeral?"

"No," he snapped, which told me that of course he was.

"Are you thinking you don't remember all those people being that upset when your mom died?"

"What?" His voice went way up. "Why would you even think that?"

Bravado. I understood. I had been sixteen a hundred years ago too. "I don't know what I'm even talking about. Sorry."

He was quiet on the other end, so I waited. After a long minute he cleared his throat. "What're you gonna do now?"

"I'm going to the gym, then home and shower and change and meet friends out for drinks and dinner."

"Oh."

He sounded very disappointed. "Or I can come there if you want."

"No, that's not what I want." He scoffed.

I was so glad I would never have to be sixteen again. Just thinking about it was exhausting. "Okay, then I'll see you."

"Sure," he said and hung up.

I had just put my messenger bag down and unpacked my laptop when my phone rang again.

"Yes, Michael."

"You don't hafta say it like that." He was so indignant.

"Sorry." I chuckled. "Yes, Michael?"

"Dreo says he doesn't want me to go home alone until we figure out who that guy was on your fire escape."

It was like coming into the middle of a conversation with him sometimes. "Pardon?"

"The guy, on your fire escape."

"Yes, that part I got, but the rest is muddy."

"I wanna come home, but Dreo doesn't want me to be by myself."

"Well, I'm home, so you can come."

"No, he doesn't want you to be alone either."

"Really, since when?"

"Since all of this."

"I was alone last night."

"Yeah, but Dreo said he had guys trailing you."

"That sounds scary, not comforting."

"I told him that's what you'd say."

I laughed, and I heard him sigh.

"But anyway, Dreo's all worried, and he doesn't want me outta his sight."

"That will make school difficult."

"I think he's gonna talk to you about me maybe walking over there to you after school for a while. I mean for sure next week."

"That's not a problem." I smiled into the phone. "But tell him I'm home now, so if someone wants to drive you—"

"Can you come get me?"

I knew it was coming. "Sure, where am I going?"

Deep exhale, and I knew he was happy for the first time since he started talking. All that work just to get to the crux of the matter, that he wanted me to pick him up.

"You ready for the directions?"

"I'm ready."

I LISTENED to him after he gave me the address, but only vaguely, since once it was in the GPS on my phone, I wasn't paying attention to "take this left" or "go until you see the blue house with the really ugly yard." I called my friends to tell them I wouldn't be joining them and then went to take a quick shower.

In the car, from where I was in Lincoln Park, I headed up to Northbrook, where Tony Strada lived. It was dark by the time I got there, around seven thirty, and the street was cluttered with cars. As I walked toward the house, I saw people sitting out on the porch, smoking, bundled up because it was cold.

"*A bello*!"

I heard the call but didn't think it was directed at me.

"Hey, Qells!"

I turned to look for the voice, and I realized I was looking at Alla Strada, Tony Strada's niece and my colleague.

"Hey." I smiled, walking up the steps to reach her.

"You didn't hear me call 'hey, gorgeous'?"

I shook my head as she opened her arms and I filled them. When I pulled back, I squinted at the cigarette.

"Don't tell Jen; she'll kick my ass."

"What are you doing here?"

"My family and the Romellis, we go way back. My uncle worked for Vince Romelli, but you know that, right? He said he met you the other day."

"He did. He cooked for me."

"Are you kidding?"

"No, why?"

"He just up and cooked for you."

"Seemed like his thing."

Her eyes were huge.

"I mean, it had to have been ready because I got it so fast. He didn't just cook for—"

"The fact that he even offered is huge. What did you say to him?"

"We were just talking."

"Uh-huh."

"I'm so sorry about Mr. Romelli."

"Yeah, we all are." She sighed. "But what are you doing here?"

"I came to pick up Michael Fiore."

"I know the Fiores." She smiled. "And Michael, he's Mona's kid, yeah?"

"Yes," I sighed, thinking of her, seeing her in my head from all the pictures Michael had shown me. "She died when he was twelve."

"Yeah, I remember her. She was gorgeous and smart—she was a nurse."

"Yes, she was." I nodded, taking a breath. "So I'm here to pick him up."

"Doesn't he live with his uncle… Andreo, right?"

I nodded.

"Well, come on, I'll help you find Michael."

She opened the screen door and then the front door, and the heat and the smell of food was overwhelming. There were so many people, and it was loud and bright and chaotic, and hopefully what Mr. Romelli's family needed and not the exact opposite.

When I met Mrs. Romelli, in the kitchen, surrounded by her brothers and their wives, she thanked me for coming, said it was nice to see me, and told me to eat. She held my hand the whole time we talked, and she held it tight, covered with her other, not letting me go.

"I'll eat something," I assured her.

"Good." She coughed. "And you'll be at the church, for Dreo and Michael?"

"Yes, ma'am, I will."

She nodded, gave my hand a final squeeze, and told me that Michael was out back or downstairs in the basement.

"Nate." Alla took my hand. "Let's go look for—"

But she was stopped and questions were asked of her.

"*Come andiamo*?"

"*Tutto bene*?"

"*Come stai*?"

"*Bene grazie*," she replied over and over, and I understood that these were just greetings from friends and family.

Sometimes the replies were longer, and I stood and waited, listening to her speak beautiful, lilting Italian until she could extricate herself and we began pushing through the crowd again. I stepped around people, and faces turned to me and then smiled. I did a lot of back patting, shoulder squeezing, and hand shaking. I drifted through the house toward the heavy sliding glass door but found the yard empty of life. It was too cold for people to linger out on the deck. Alla excused herself after that, said she had to find her father and uncle, and pointed toward the stairs that led to the basement.

"Try down there. That's where the kids normally congregate."

I took her advice, but once I was there, I realized that he was not in the huge room. I had no idea where he was. Turning to go back up, I pulled out my phone to try and call him in the sea of people.

"They said you were here."

My head snapped up at the sound of the smoky voice, and there, above me, was Dreo.

"I can't find your nephew," I said while climbing the stairs.

He didn't move, so when I reached the last step under him, I stilled, waiting. His eyes narrowed as he stared down at me.

"Are you going to let me up?"

"Yeah, sorry."

I went to move by him but stopped. He looked tired. "You need to rest." The man looked wiped out.

"Yeah, so?" the snide comment came back, like he was daring me to say something else.

I lifted my hand but thought better of touching him at the last minute. "You should go home and get some sleep."

"I can't."

I shook my head and turned to leave him, but his hand was like a vise on my wrist. I wasn't going anywhere. "Dreo?"

"It's good you came. I need to talk to you."

But he didn't start, he just stared at me.

"Are you all right?"

He coughed softly. "You just came for Michael?"

"And to check on you," I admitted.

He nodded. "So check on me, then."

I was as clueless as the next guy until I wasn't. When what people needed was actually brought to my attention, I could do something about it. At that moment, with no one else in the world caring how the hell Andreo Fiore was doing, he needed it to matter to me just a little.

Reaching out, I took hold of his arm, tugged gently, and led him up the stairs and down the hall, walking until I couldn't hear talking and laughing, finally pulling him into the laundry room and turning to face him. He looked drugged.

"Jesus, you're barely awake."

"I need to talk to you," he said as he closed the door behind him.

"About what?" I asked, putting my hand on the top of the washer.

"About what happened to Vincent Romelli."

"Dreo, it's not any of my business what—"

"The hell it's not," he growled. "You and Michael, you're all I have."

Me and Michael? I got Michael, but…. "Are you sure you're awake? I think you—"

"It turns out," he cut me off again, his hand joining mine on the washer, "that Frank Alberone from the Spinato family, he just took over Romelli's territory."

"I don't know anything about the—"

"In Chicago, it's either the Spinato family or the Cilione family, and everyone else either works for one of them or has ties to one of them."

I nodded.

"Sometimes territories get traded around, some new guy is made and things change."

"And that's what happened with Mr. Romelli?"

"Yeah. Alberone's new, and he's somebody's cousin in the Cilione family, and I guess they had a sit-down and things got swapped around."

"No one told Mr. Romelli?"

"I guess they did. He just wasn't listening."

"So what does all that mean?"

He stepped closer, and his hand slid closer to mine. "It means that because Tony Strada is a smart man, he's not gonna find himself getting shot at or fished out of Lake Michigan next week. He's already working something out with everyone."

"Jesus, Dreo."

"*Non farci caso.*"

"Don't tell me not to worry about it!"

He was grinning suddenly. "Since when do you speak Italian?"

But I didn't, I just…. "I knew what you were going to say."

His head tipped as he really looked at me. "You think you know me?"

"Are you safe?" I asked, ignoring his question.

There was a slight shudder that slid through him, so small a movement that unless you were looking you would never have seen it. The man was amazing at hiding his own feelings under layers of a smooth, polished surface.

"Dreo," I said, not even thinking about it, stepping forward, close, my hands going to his face, sliding over his skin, holding him as I stared into his eyes. "Are you okay?"

He swallowed hard. "None of this matters to me or Sal because… like I told Mr. Romelli a couple days before he died… we're out. We have plans, you know? Together. Tony knows, and now he gets it even more than he used to."

"Of course," I agreed, taking a breath, ready to let him go.

His hands closed over my wrists, keeping me there, making sure I wouldn't move. "I talked to Tony." He took a breath, content, it seemed, to have my hands on him. "And he's gonna let us walk away. He's gonna honor Mr. Romelli's word."

I was really trying to concentrate on something other than the man's melting onyx eyes or the sensual shape of his mouth.

"So me and Sal," he almost whispered, finally releasing my wrists, letting my hands fall away from him, "we're both free and clear."

"Are you happy?"

"I am. We both are."

I cleared my throat. "You and Sal are going into business together?"

He nodded. "We already started, but now we can just work at it full-time."

"And what is your business?'

"We're general contractors, some light construction, drywall, painting, stuff like that. I enjoy it, so does Sal, and no one shoots at us."

"Don't joke about that."

He grunted. "All I ever did, all Sal did, was keep Mr. Romelli safe, be his bodyguards, so we told Tony that now, when they're figuring shit out, like who's gonna do what, that he should just count us out. Mr. Romelli was letting us walk away, and now Tony has too."

"So then everything's all set."

"Yeah." His eyes were locked on mine, staring deep. "I mean, before I can have a life I can be proud of, have who I want in it… I had to change what I did."

"So you've done that."

"*Sì.*"

There was a long silence, and neither of us moved or spoke.

"I should find Michael," I said finally, looking into the dark wells of his eyes.

"Yeah," he agreed.

But I didn't move, and after a minute, I was embarrassed for thinking there was more he wanted to say, maybe even more he wanted from me. "Bye," I said under my breath, ready to leave, brushing by him, reaching the door, my hand on the knob.

He leaned forward, forearm braced there so I couldn't get it open.

"You need to let me out."

"Not yet," he whispered.

"Listen"—I turned around, my back against the door—"I'm getting conflicting signals here, and maybe you don't even know that you're—"

"I know," he said fast.

I took a breath. "And?"

He looked miserable, and I suddenly felt very foolish.

"Dreo," I dived in, "you either need to tell me what you want from me or tell me that there's nothing you need at all."

His exhale. "*Ho voglia di te*."

"In English."

He leaned his head against the forearm he had pressed against the door. "I dunno."

"What did you say?" I asked, staring up at him, into his dark liquid eyes.

"I said I want you, but I don't even know what I mean."

I cleared my throat. "I think you want a family, Dreo, and when it's you and me and Michael, you think you like it. If you're out, out of the life with Mr. Romelli, maybe you'll have time to find the girl you need."

"I've had nothing but time."

"That's crap. You've been taking care of Mr. Romelli all day and Michael at night, and the only person you've had around at all on a regular basis is me, so it makes sense that you would develop some—"

"No, it doesn't," he snapped. "You don't just start having feelings for someone because they're around. Gimme a fuckin' break."

"I just mean that—"

"Could you just shut the fuck up?"

The condescending tone was too much. "Fine, you man up, then."

We stood there, staring, and he was furious—it was there on his face—but also more.

"You're telling me to grow some balls."

"Yeah, that's what I'm telling you."

His eyes narrowed. "Some people are afraid of me, you know."

"Not me. Not ever."

He grunted before putting one hand gently around my throat, tipping my head up with his thumb. "*Tesoro... dammi un bacio....*"

I had no idea that my stomach could still flutter, that my heart could pound so hard that it was all I could hear, and that my knees would actually wobble.

"*Per piacere*," he whispered as he bent and touched his lips to mine.

My breath caught, and I saw the corner of his beautiful mouth tip up wickedly before he tilted his head and kissed me.

I held my breath and everything exploded.

The kiss was hard and bruising, devouring and rough, filled with frantic, pulse-pounding heat. Dreo took what he wanted, and I felt it, his dominance, and moaned deeply into his mouth. I craved him, and even when I had to break the kiss to breathe, I kept my hands on him, not letting him go.

"Are you okay?" I asked, sounding like I was giving him a choice to leave even as I held onto the lapels of his suit jacket.

He nodded, just barely.

"My turn."

"Please," he said under his breath, which undid me.

I eased him down, my eyes closing as our lips met again, my mouth slanting over his, my tongue sliding into the wet heat, tasting him, tangling with his as we rubbed and ground together. It was slow and languid, deep and building, and I moved my hands, one behind his head, stroking the nape of his neck, the other on his chest, sliding over the hard pectorals, gentling him.

The growl in the back of his throat was very low, very sexy, and as I stroked my tongue over his, I felt his hands slide over my ass, his fingers squeezing tight.

It was drugging and sensual, and he swallowed my moan as I wrapped my arms around his neck and kissed harder, feeling my body flush hot and cold, the response in him just as consuming, everything but his sweet mouth forgotten, the desire all that there was.

Four years all alchemized into a single moment of scorching, aching, devouring need. I was overwhelmed. Normally I questioned and analyzed, but I was given no time. The man was not stopping, not letting me go. Instead, when I pulled free, I had only a second before his teeth were back, nibbling, and I heard him take a quick breath before his tongue was again exploring every crevice of my mouth, my palette, the back of my teeth, and the hollows of my cheeks.

His hands pulled my hips into his, and he began rubbing against me, grinding, pushing against my already hardened groin. The feel of his body, the heat.... I was lost.

I broke the kiss because I had to breathe, and instantly he shoved my head back so he could press his lips to my throat. He sucked and bit, and I jolted in his arms as he inhaled me, his hands kneading my ass hard.

"Fuck, Nate," he moaned, his breath quavering. "I don't even know what to—"

I had gulped air, so I lifted my head and pulled him back down to me, recapturing the kiss, plunging my tongue inside his mouth, his lips already parted, ready, wanting.

He lifted me off my feet, and I wrapped my long legs around his waist as he shoved me up against the door. I was higher and ground my mouth down over his, my tongue sliding, pushing, the kiss just as fierce as before, still hungry and carnal.

I whimpered loudly and felt him shudder in response, his big, hard body quivering as he began to thrust against my groin, the inside of my thigh.

My hands were digging into his jacket as I ravaged his mouth, feeling him surrender to me, becoming mine to take, to have—all I wanted.

His hips snapped harder, faster, and I tried to drag my lips from his, but he sucked my bottom lip inside his mouth and bit down, holding me there.

I lost myself in the kiss again, but he pinned me to the door with his chest, lifting his lips from mine, taking a gulp of air as he put me on my feet. We were both panting, our foreheads pressed together, trembling with unsatisfied yearning.

"Nate," he rasped, his hot breath on my face. "Will you let me get in your bed?"

"Yes," I answered honestly, because as hot as things had ever been with Duncan, as much as I wanted Sean Cooper, neither had come close to the combustible heat that I just experienced with the man in my arms.

"You swear?"

"I do," I assured him, unwinding my arms from his neck.

"Don't do that," he mumbled, leaning forward, pushing his mouth against the base of my throat, licking before he sucked the skin into his mouth.

He would leave marks, which I was guessing was his intent.

I held on as he unbuttoned my peacoat, tugged my sweater up, yanked my T-shirt out of my jeans, and slid his hands over my hot skin.

"*Sono pazzo di te*." He spoke the words against my throat.

"What did you—"

"I'm so crazy about—I wanna put my hands all over you."

He could do whatever he wanted. When he murmured something under his breath, for once I asked what the word he used all the time meant.

"I call you *tesoro* all the time," he told me, "and you've never asked before."

"It's not 'pain in the ass' in Italian?"

"No," he breathed out before kissing up my jaw, rubbing his face in my beard. "It means treasure, Nate Qells, and you're mine."

"What are you—"

"You and Michael, you're my home."

I was?

"Yes," he said as though I'd spoken the question aloud.

As he stared at me with his hooded eyes, licked his dark, swollen lips, and I heard how heavily he was breathing, I shivered hard. I would have let him have me right there if he wanted and not thought twice about it. I wanted him desperately. I jolted against him as his hands went to my belt, the buckle jingling as he worked it open, then the button of my pants and the zipper.

"Nate," he moaned as his fingers encircled my leaking cock.

I shuddered hard, willing myself not to come, not to spurt over his hand and onto the front of his pants. I never lost control, but I was teetering on the verge of it. "You have to stop or I'm going to make a mess all over you."

"Go ahead," he said, tugging on my shaft, squeezing. "You're… this is so beautiful."

I gave in for a moment to the feeling, to the sizzling electricity sparking over my skin, up my spine, rushing through my body as I pushed in and out of his fist.

"I wanna suck you so bad—gag myself with this."

I was drowning, and I could not recall the last time it had happened so completely.

"*Voglio fare l'amore con te*," he whispered into my hair.

"I don't—"

"I wanna make love to you."

"Fuck," I growled, reaching for him, hand on his sweater, the other wrapped around his neck, pulling him back down to me so I could shove my tongue down his throat.

He straightened up, releasing my leaking cock, his arms wrapping tight around my waist instead, and he pressed the length of his body to mine. One hand went down the back of my pants and cupped my right cheek.

"You are so hot," he groaned softly in my ear. "I knew you had to be something under all these clothes, but goddamn, Nate. I want you so fuckin' bad."

It was all I could think of.

"I bet you like it deep and hard, don't you?"

I whimpered in the back of my throat. "Oh yes."

He growled as he pressed against me tighter. "I want to feel your skin… all of it."

I feasted on his mouth, and he kneaded my ass, both of us rubbing, grinding, until I got my hands wedged on the carved chest and shoved him away hard.

We stood for a moment, both of us gasping, heaving for breath.

"What the fuck?" he panted.

"If we keep this up, I'll be begging you to fuck me right here in the laundry room."

His brown-black eyes, fringed with the long, thick, feathery lashes, just stared at me.

"Come home with me and get in my bed. Let me show what it can be, and then let me hold you after all night long. Don't go home. Stay with me," I pleaded.

He looked me right in the eye, held my gaze, and studied my face.

"Please."

After a long minute, he nodded. "I'll find Michael and meet you at your car."

Even as I was talking, I never expected him to agree. That he did, that his eyes roamed all over me, hot and possessive, that he gestured me close and when I moved, he took my face in his hands and bent to kiss me again.... I was overwhelmed. He was so young and yet not afraid of what he wanted, willing to see what passion would bring.

I went boneless and pliant in his arms, letting him control the kiss, suck on my lips, tangle his tongue with mine, and hold me in his arms.

"You are so beautiful." He spoke the words against my mouth. "Please don't change your mind; please don't say no to me when we get home."

The word *no* never entered my mind.

Chapter NINE

I LOOKED the other way when Michael got in the car, and only turned back when he closed the door and the light went off. I had gone out the back door and around the side of the house because I knew what I must have looked like.

Clothes rumpled, hair tousled, lips dark and red and swollen, I looked like I'd been ravished. Dreo looked the same, but I was flushed, and when I got to the car and checked the mirror, my pupils were dilated like I was on drugs. Anyone older than eighteen would know exactly what they were looking at. Luckily for me, Michael, still young and virginal, had no clue.

"You all right?" he asked, worried. "You look all hot."

I cleared my throat. "I'm fine."

"I thought Dreo was coming with—oh, here he comes."

Michael opened the car door, and I felt like the spotlight was back, but I watched Dreo coming toward the car anyway. And he was ready to give his uncle the front seat, but Dreo waved at him to stay put. He climbed in the back, and Michael closed the door at the same time.

"Let's go home," Michael said. "I'm ready for Friday night Kung Fu Theater."

"No homework?" I asked.

"Homework is for Sunday night, not Friday night," Dreo informed me. "Give the kid a break."

"Yeah, Nate, gimme a break."

"Okay." I sighed deeply.

"Besides, we all have to be up early for the funeral tomorrow. It's going to be a long day."

The thought was sobering.

"So," Dreo said softly, leaning forward between the seats. "I think maybe until the cops figure out what's goin' on with everything that I'd like you and Nate in the same place, where I know you're both safe."

Michael turned to look at him. "Does that mean we're gonna stay with Nate tonight?"

"If he'll have us," Dreo said softly.

"I'll have you," I said, my eyes flicking to the rearview mirror. The dark eyes were there, the gaze hot and unwavering, and even though I wasn't even touching him, I was suddenly breathless.

"Hey, let's stop at the store for Red Vines and popcorn and stuff. Nate puts M&M's in his just like you, Dreo."

I chuckled and turned my head for a second to look at Dreo, only to find him looking at me. "You like M&M's in your popcorn too?"

He nodded, and his smile, curving those beautiful lips of his, made my stomach flip over. "I do, but only the plain ones."

"Of course."

He shrugged.

"That's funny."

"It's good."

At the store, I was down the wine aisle looking for a red to go with the roast I had just told Dreo and Michael I would make on Sunday night.

"It's stupid."

"It's not."

I looked sideways, and there was a very cute couple, perky little brunette with a button nose and a guy holding her hand who, from the eye rolling, thought his girlfriend was nuts but was still enchanted with her.

"You don't have wine with mac and cheese, it's just dumb."

"Excuse me," she said, hand closing on my bicep.

"Kate," he warned her, eyes flicking to mine as he smiled.

"Yes?"

"If you were having wine with mac and cheese, what would you serve?"

"I'm not an expert," I assured her.

"Yeah, but you have a bottle in your hand already, so you've obviously picked something. I wouldn't even know where to start."

Since she was asking.... "Well, with mac and cheese, you'd probably want something light, so I would probably go with a Chablis, because the minerality of the wine goes well with both pasta and cheese."

They were both looking at me.

"See." The girl turned to her fiancé; I saw the diamond then. "Told you."

"Okay." He smiled, throwing up the hand not in his fiancée's in defeat. "Apparently you can have wine with it, so which one, if you don't mind picking?"

I didn't realize we had been overheard by another couple, but when I handed them a Chablis I liked and they thanked me, another man leaned in and asked me to suggest a strong red to go with the steaks he was making for friends. I told him I didn't work at the grocery store, but he asked me to humor him, and his wife's eyes behind him were huge, like *dear God, please*.

"I picked this wine last time, and my wife said it was really tannic. It was a cabernet or a cabernet merlot blend, I don't remember, but no one liked it."

I nodded, and his wife fluttered her eyelids. "It was terrible."

The man groaned, I chuckled, and his wife threw up her hands.

"Should I lie, Ed?"

He looked back at me for help.

"Well, you can't go wrong with a Côtes du Rhône," I suggested, walking over to where they were. "It won't be heavy, you know?"

"Thank you." He smiled, taking the bottle I passed him. His wife squeezed my elbow, and they left.

"Nate?"

Turning, I found Sean Cooper and a man I had never seen before in my life. It took a minute for me to understand what was going on.

"Who's this, Seanie?"

Seanie? Why not shorten his last name? Coop would have made more sense than Seanie.

"This is my old English professor from college, Dr. Nathan Qells."

Old? *Old* had to be thrown in?

"Hi there, English professor." The very attractive man smiled and leaned forward, offering me his hand. "It's a pleasure to meet you. I'm Bryce, Bryce Easter."

"Pleasure, Bryce," I assured him, taking his hand.

"So, English professor, huh?" He chuckled, smiling at Sean before turning back to me. "So tell me, how many classes did you have this guy in?" he asked, wrapping his arms around Sean's neck.

"Just English 101." I smiled, surveying them. They made a nice-looking couple and I wondered if this one was the same man from the restaurant a few nights ago. If he wasn't, then the good doctor certainly made the rounds. Sean would have had more dates in one week then I had in three. But really, there was nothing wrong with it if he was or wasn't. Just as I had told Michael and Danielle that night we saw him out, you had to date many to make an informed decision on whom you wanted in your life.

"May I speak to you a minute?" Sean said, taking hold of my bicep and leading me halfway down the aisle, away from Bryce.

I turned and looked at him.

"I thought I would give you a couple of days to cool down. You seemed very upset the last time we spoke."

I found that I didn't even have anything to say. It wasn't necessary. We were not going forward—it was done, and we both knew it. Our schedules and lifestyles—neither were compatible, but it had nothing to do with age and everything to do with priorities. Michael, and now suddenly Dreo, were bigger priorities in my life than dating, and medicine was more important to him than I was. I completely understood.

"I think our timing is off," I told him, smiling. "Don't you?"

He stared at my face, and I could tell he appreciated the honesty. "I do." He sighed heavily. "I feel like I'm pushing something that just doesn't want to go."

"Me too," I agreed, "but thank you, it was so very flattering."

There was a quick shake of his head. "You just don't even get it."

I didn't even care enough to delve—would have, in fact, just squeezed his shoulder and walked away.

"You done playing wine connoisseur back here?" Dreo teased me, his voice carrying down the aisle.

I turned and found myself admiring his stride as he closed in on me, the confidence, the breadth of his shoulders, and the curve of the smile on his lips. Funny that I had never really looked at him before the last week. I had completely missed the man.

"What are you—"

"We're ready to go," Dreo said gruffly, taking hold of my arm. "Come on, we're going home."

He sounded very possessive, very matter-of-fact, and I found that despite a lifetime of thinking that I would hate it, the exact opposite was true. In all my relationships, the men I had been in them with had espoused partnerships and balance and equality. No one belonged to anyone, no one was the leader, and while I appreciated it, having someone manhandle me just a little was nice too. Even big alpha dog Duncan Stiel had never told me how things were going to be anywhere but in bed. He was never demonstrative in public, and I had no idea that I had been missing anything until then. Dreo Fiore, who was younger than me, was letting me know from the timbre of his voice, the look in his eyes, and the pressure of his grip on my bicep that if I didn't move, he would move me.

It was hard to concentrate with him so close to me. I got that almost queasy feeling in my stomach.

"Nate?" I heard Sean say my name.

"Who's this?" Bryce asked as he joined us.

"Hi," Dreo said cheerfully, turning to look at the two men as he let me go only to put an arm around my shoulders and pull me in close against him. "We met at the hospital that night Nate was there," he told Sean and, in turn, Bryce.

"Yeah," Sean said hesitantly. "I… wasn't…."

"Nice to meet you," he said to Bryce. I tried to smile even as the delicious heat from Dreo's body flooded my senses.

"And you," Bryce said with awe in his voice, staring almost openmouthed at Dreo. I understood; the man really was just stunning. And Sean was gorgeous, and Bryce himself was very attractive, but Dreo was sexy and dangerous, and that, added to the beautiful that he already was, made him absolutely breathtaking.

"You're together?" Sean asked, giving me a look.

"'Course." Dreo smiled lazily, tightening his grip on my shoulders.

"Are you guys exclusive?" Bryce asked, looking at us both.

Dreo laughed, kissing my ear before letting me go. "*Sì, lui è mio*," he finished before walking away to go look at something.

"What did he say?" Bryce asked brightly.

"Something like 'he's mine'," I said, because even though I wasn't exactly sure of the translation, I knew possessiveness when I heard it.

"How long have you been dating the mobster?" Sean asked snidely.

"It's not important," I assured him, offering Bryce my hand. "It was good to meet you, and to catch up with an old student."

"Wonderful to meet you as well, Nate. I wish my English professor had looked like you."

It was nice of him to say, but I didn't even have time to care. I had to find Dreo.

He was on coffee aisle looking for something, and when he turned to look at me, I realized I was getting a very wicked smile.

"What?" he asked as he dropped chicory coffee into the basket I was holding.

"You like chicory?"

"Since you made it that time for me, yeah, I like it. What's wrong?"

"Nothing," I said, rubbing my eyes. "You were very charming back there."

"I can be." He grinned, taking hold of the lapel of my peacoat and pulling me after him.

We walked down another aisle, and I got portabella mushroom soup. He chuckled and moved in close to me, bumping me with his shoulder.

"What?"

"Nothing. You didn't get freaked out, did you?"

"No."

He nodded, took a quick breath. "That's good."

"What's wrong?"

"Unlike that man back there, I don't date many, only one at a time. So if I'm in your bed, then I'm the only one who is and you're the only one in mine. Are we clear?"

"We are. But for the record, Sean Cooper and I never went to bed, and—"

"I don't care about then," he told me. "I only care about now. Are we gonna do this?"

I looked at him. He'd asked the question so matter-of-factly, but the look on his face, how steady his gaze was, betrayed something else. I answered honestly. "I'd like to. You?"

He nodded. "Okay, then."

"But we should, you know, have sex before we move in together, huh?" I teased. "I mean, what if you hate it?"

His eyes flicked to mine, and I knew right then that I was playing with fire even before he stepped in close to me so I had to tip my head back to see his face. "I have thought of nothing for over four years but putting your legs over my shoulders and being buried inside of you," he said, his voice husky and low, sending tendrils of heat through me. "I don't think me hating it will be the problem."

I had to breathe. And when he smiled… the new development that he was gifting me with, from hard, cold man to mischievous, eye-sparkling lover, was overwhelming.

"Come on." He grabbed me, arm around my neck, pulling me close. "I wanna get home and go to bed."

My heart stopped.

"I can't wait to find out what you taste like."

"You shouldn't say things like—"

"I should," he whispered, leaning in, his breath hot and moist on my ear before he sucked the lobe into his mouth, biting lightly before moving. His lips moved behind my ear, so quick, the motion finished before we cleared the end of the aisle and met Michael.

"You still look all red," the younger Fiore told me, tipping his head to the side. "Are you sure you're okay?"

I was, in fact, covered in goose bumps from head to toe.

"He's fine," Dreo told him, hand on the small of my back, pushing me forward. "Come on."

Everything was whirling around, so when I came out of the store and turned left, I crashed right into the guy standing there because I wasn't looking where I was going. There was only Dreo in my head.

"Oh, sorry," I apologized, moving around him.

"What the fuck do you think you're doing?" he snapped, shoving me back hard.

There were three guys, and they were all suddenly too close, yelling, threatening, and I was wondering what the hell was going on when I was yanked back and Dreo was in front of me.

"Let it go," he told them.

"Fuck you!"

Dreo didn't say anything, and because I had been defending myself since I was ten years old, fighting my own battles, I moved around him in time to see the first guy come at him. He was fast, though, my champion, and before his attacker could land a punch, Dreo kicked him in the knee. The man fell forward onto the sidewalk, and as soon as he went down, Dreo kicked him hard in the ribs to make sure he stayed there. With the noise the guy made, I was guessing that getting up was not going to be an option.

The other two guys lunged at Dreo, but before I could even help, he had punched one guy hard in the side and followed that instantly with first an uppercut and then a fist in his face. I heard the crunch followed by the roar of pain as Dreo whirled on the third guy. He threw a roundhouse punch, but Dreo grabbed his arm and flipped him over flat on his back with that sound of smacking flesh on cement.

"Holy shit," Michael breathed, staring at Dreo as he stepped over the guy sprawled on the ground to rejoin us.

"C'mon, let's go home," Dreo said, grabbing us both and pulling us after him.

In the car, Michael, now in the back, was staring at his uncle.

"Dreo, that was amazing," he said in awe. "Really."

"That was regrettable," he told him. "But listen, if you're ever facing three guys, like Nate was, just kick the first guy in the side of the knee as hard as you can, okay?"

"Side of the knee?"

"Yeah," Dreo assured him. "You kick him there, he ain't gettin' back up. A shot in the balls you can get over if the adrenaline's pumping hard enough."

Michael nodded like he understood, and I smiled. He was having a little bout of hero worship, I could tell. It was not every day that someone actually rescued you from scary people. "Just make sure you're aware of your surroundings. Most fights can be avoided, and if you can, you do that. If Nate had been watching where he was going instead of thinking about other stuff, he never would have walked into those guys."

"Dreo," I began, "I—"

"You need to be more careful," he told me, hand on the back of my neck.

I didn't want to move, didn't want him to take away the hand that was now rubbing, kneading away the tension.

"You're not even bleeding," Michael said to Dreo.

"Why would I be bleeding?" he asked, like his nephew was nuts.

"That was so cool," Michael told him.

Dreo's fingers pushed up into my hair, and it took everything I had not to let my head fall back against the sensuous petting.

"So," Michael said after a minute, clearing his throat. "You're touching Nate."

I stiffened, but Dreo didn't move his hand.

"I am," he said to his nephew.

"So, uhm, I'm gonna sleep in Nate's guest room tonight, right?"

"You are."

"Where are you going to sleep?"

Dreo looked over his shoulder at Michael. "With Nate, if that's okay. Is it okay?"

There was silence, and I held my breath, because liking me was one thing. Liking me with his uncle was a whole other ballgame.

"What if you and Nate fight? What happens then?"

"Nothing happens to you and Nate, *ragazzo*."

I felt a hand on my left shoulder. "Nate?"

"I promise," I said, patting his hand. "You and I won't change, no matter what."

He took a breath; I heard him draw it in. "Okay, then."

"Okay." Dreo exhaled deeply and moved his hand from behind my head and put it on my thigh. "Okay."

When we got home, the three of us piled out of the car and rode up the elevator together in silence. They went back to their apartment, and I went to mine. Once inside, everything sort of fell in on me.

Forty-five-year-old men did not start relationships with twenty-eight-year-olds, and definitely not twenty-eight-year-olds who were probably still mob muscle no matter what they said, and certainly not twenty-eight-year-olds with sixteen-year-old nephews living with them and counting on them to be the grown-up. Jesus, how shredded did I want my heart to be?

My phone rang and startled me.

"Hello?"

"So we're all on for Kung Fu Theater, right?" Dreo asked, his voice a husky whisper.

I nodded, not thinking that he couldn't see me.

"*Caro*?"

"Yes." I cleared my throat. "What is, uhm—"

"Like, dear. *Caro* is dear."

I was such a sap, but his voice, how deep it was, almost breathless, and the endearment, I was just—it was ridiculous. Since when had I become so needy?

"*Voglio fare l'amore con te*."

"You've said that before. What—"

"I want… you know what I want."

I had not been nervous and flustered with my stomach twisting into knots since I was fifteen years old. Jesus! He was stripping me of years of smooth, cool, suave lover. I had been complimented many a time on my seduction skills. There was a pattern, almost a checklist, and when I wanted someone, I did those things, followed a formula—dinner, kissing, the suggestive banter—it was the arc of my conquest, but with Dreo… with Dreo I was floundering without control. Normally, I was the one with the agenda. I said when and where, and sometimes men missed it, thinking that because I was the bottom I was not the one making the rules, running the show.

"We're coming over soon. Is that fine?"

"Yeah, I'll leave the door unlocked. I need to take a shower."

"Okay."

I hung up and walked to the front door, unlocked the bottom and the deadbolt, and went to my bedroom, stripped, and then walked naked into my connecting bathroom. Under the hot water, after I scrubbed myself and washed my hair, I let my head roll back on my shoulders and concentrated on letting the tension run out of my body. I closed my eyes and just breathed. I had no idea how long I stood under the spray.

"Are you ever coming out?"

I turned off the water and opened the frosted shower door. Through the steam, I saw Dreo standing with his hand on the doorknob. Stepping out, I reached for my towel only to find it missing.

"I have it," he whispered, closing the door behind him.

I watched him come close, saw the tenting in the front of his sweats, watched his eyes sweep over me from head to toe, and when I lifted my hand, gesturing him forward, I heard the whimper in the back of his throat.

Nothing quite so incendiary as knowing, beyond a shadow of a doubt, that the person you wanted craved you right back. When his hands closed on the sides of my neck, lifting my head up as his mouth came down over mine, the hoarse moan that came out of me made him smile against my lips.

"*Dammi un bacio.*" He breathed over my face before his mouth slanted down over mine and he kissed me.

There was the same drugging effect as the first time, except now, naked, there was no way for him not to know, not to see, what he was doing to me. I trembled under his hands as his tongue got reacquainted with mine, stroking, tangling, tasting. He sucked hard, and when I couldn't breathe, I broke the kiss, my head back as his lips devoured the skin where my neck met my shoulder. When he bit down, I got my hands on him, in his hair, holding as he leaned me back further so his head could drop to my chest. Then his mouth closed around my pebbled nipples. He suckled and nibbled, and when his fingers wrapped around my shaft, the jolt of electricity was involuntary. I would have fallen, but he had me. Bigger than me, stronger, he eased me down to the floor under him, pinning me there with his weight.

"*Guardami.*"

I could barely breathe.

"I told you to look at me."

It was hard to open my eyes—I was drowning in sensations—but finally they fluttered open in time for me to see him take the crown of my shaft into his hot, wet mouth.

Every impulse I had said to drive up into him, but I stayed still as he slid his lips further down, not far enough to choke himself, his hand still fisted beneath his mouth, stroking me, the other fondling my balls.

I had so many questions, because Dreo really seemed to know what he was doing, and earlier…. He'd been thinking about me since he met me? There were answers I needed to—

"I wanted it to be perfect," he growled before a lubed finger slid inside of me.

I would never forget the look in the man's eyes when I jolted under him. That he had caused the reaction pleased him: his eyes, the way they glinted, told me so, as did the curl of his delectable lips. My lube, opened on the bathroom floor beside him, was a surprise. He would have had to have gotten it out of my nightstand, and the thought of him wanting to find it, searching it out, needing me, made me shiver.

"I never thought—" He caught his breath. "—that you could want me."

"You're so beautiful. Anyone would want you."

"No," he said, his voice a deep rumble in his chest. "When I'm with you, just standing with you, I'm different, lighter, softer…. Your influence, you change me."

"Is that"—I shivered, my body flushing with heat—"good?"

"Oh yes," he said as he stroked my dripping cock.

When he added a second finger in my ass, I groaned loud and hoarse; those deep, dark eyes of his, heavy-lidded and hot, made my heart stop.

"I'm sorry," he said, the pressure of his fist leaving my aching shaft as he reached beside the lube and lifted the condom to his lips. "The bed will have to wait."

"I don't care," I told him, arching under him as he scissored and stretched, swirling his fingers inside me, rubbing and loosening the muscles, relaxing and arousing at the same time.

The rip of foil as his slippery fingers continued to push in and out, the glide easy as he curled them forward, rubbing over my prostate, all of it made me shudder.

"Lift your legs."

What? "Don't you want me on my knees?"

"Fuck no," he said, and his voice rumbled in his chest as he dragged me over the rough bathmat, lifting me at the same time I felt the head of his cock at my entrance. I hadn't even looked. His eyes, they were just too gorgeous to tear my gaze from, but when he nudged me, I had to see.

The man was huge. Long and thick and beautiful. Just seeing him tore the whimper from my throat. "Oh God, please."

"Nate… *ho bisogno di essere dentro di te*… I have to be inside you."

"Yes, please yes."

His fingers didn't meet as he held his cock still and lined it up with my fluttering hole. "I'll go slow."

He would not—I wouldn't let him. I was not some ingénue he was about to fuck. I was a man, and I knew my body well. I had been living in my skin a long time.

I pushed into him at the same time he breached me.

"Nate!" he yelled, surprised and overwhelmed, breath catching as his hips snapped forward.

Instantly, I was impaled on the hard, velvet length of him, and as he pulled out and then plunged back inside, the push took the air from my lungs.

I remembered why I so loved being on the bottom. The feeling of fullness, the delicious drag over my prostate, the stretch that was part pain, part pleasure, the slow burn followed by the building heat—I had missed it all so much. Not that I regretted any of the men I had taken to my bed since Duncan. I didn't, but God… to be held and filled was heaven.

As the man drove into me, hard and deep, I moaned out his name.

"*Sei così bello* … you're so beautiful like this."

I could be handsome in a suit or a tuxedo—I cleaned up nice—but beautiful I had never been. Not ever before, to no one but Dreo Fiore. The words, the husky sound of his sultry voice, the hammering, and his angle pooled heat in the base of my spine. The way his hand stayed fisted on my shaft—tugging, pulling—and how he watched his cock slide in and out of me, all of it was more than I could bear. Every wall came down, and I surrendered.

"Dreo, I can't—"

"Jesus, you're so tight and hot and—fuckin' come!"

His demand, combined with those from my own body, pushed me over the edge. There was no holding back the heaving climax.

My balls tightened, my muscles clenched, and I came over his hand and my stomach, the spasms tearing through me so hard, so long, the orgasm devouring me.

He buried himself deeper, driving inside of me as I shuddered with aftershocks, lifting me, grabbing behind my knees, pistoning fast into my body.

I felt my muscles rippling around him, then fist tight, and he came with a roar, using me, rough and bruising and so very needed. The sounds that came out of me, whimpering, begging, moaning, combined with the catch of his breath as his head fell back and he froze there above me.

He looked as though he had been carved out of marble: the smooth olive skin, chiseled features, sculpted chest and abdomen, and long, hard muscular legs folded beneath him. Not once in four years had I actually seen him, the thick, curling lashes, aquiline nose, and full lips. I wondered at my blindness, how I had not been tongue-tied constantly in his presence.

"*Amo guardarti.*"

I smiled up into his eyes as he gently lowered my legs, placing my feet on the rug as he slowly slid out of my body. "What did you say?"

His eyes were so soft, so dark, and so full of raw possessiveness. I realized that no one had ever looked at me like that before. I could become addicted to it very fast.

"I said I love watching you," he told me, tying off the condom and rising from his knees, pulling up his sweats before he carried it across the room to the wastebasket next to the sink.

I wasn't ready to move, and when he returned, standing over me, I told him to get out so I could wash off.

"That's all? I'm being sent away?"

"What do you want?"

"No, it's your turn to say."

I sat up and reached for his hand, tugging him down to me. His heavy-lidded eyes watched me as I climbed into his lap, straddling his thighs, and locked my arms behind his head. I leaned forward, pressing my chest to his, savoring the feeling.

"How do I say—" I smiled, licking my lips, enjoying the catch of his breath. "—I was made for you in Italian?"

"*Ero fatto per te*," he answered me, his eyes on my mouth.

"You'll have to teach me the pronunciation," I breathed out, tilting close to run my tongue over his bottom lip. "I would love to learn."

He shivered under me and captured my tongue, swallowing my laughter as he kissed me, clutching me tight, arms around me as his mouth slanted possessively over mine. I pushed against him, undulating in his embrace, tightening my thighs around his hips.

Who knew that I could so transfix a man seventeen years my junior?

Our tongues tangled, and his hands ran all over me, finally coming to rest on my ass. He broke the kiss for air.

"*Sei fatto apposta per le mie mani*," he whispered over my skin, his hot mouth on my throat washing heat through me in a scalding wave. "You were made to fit my hands."

God, I hoped so. I wanted them on me all the time.

"Nate?"

"I want this," I told him, because I felt the yearning so deep down that it made my teeth chatter like I was freezing, the emotion welling up, overwhelming. "I want us to try… will you? Can you?"

"How do you mean 'can you'?" he asked, his eyes all over my face. He reached out to trace one of my gold eyebrows, touch my lashes, the mustache and beard.

"Your family and—"

"My family is Michael, and he likes this already. And I don't just have custody of him, you know, he's mine. My sister wanted me to adopt him if anything happened, not just be his guardian. She was very smart, and she knew… she never wanted me to have a problem."

"What did she know?"

His arms wrapped back around me. He was making sure I couldn't leave his lap. "She knew I was gay because I told her."

I brushed silky hair back from his face. It was wavy and had some curl, his thick, glossy hair that I could not seem to keep my fingers from touching. "I only ever caught you with women, Mr. Fiore."

"You can't be gay and be mob muscle, Dr. Qells," he told me, hands sliding over my thighs. "And when Michael talked to his friends and they talked to theirs… it got around that his uncle was a player, and that's what Mr. Romelli liked to hear."

"That's a terrible thing to do with those women, get their hopes up."

"I took them out; they were wined and dined. I promise you, they had a good time. And besides, not getting to sleep with me is no great tragedy."

I shivered slightly. "I beg to disagree."

The grunt was all male, very smug, more a growl than anything else. I had to be careful or I would create a monster.

"I just meant—"

"That you liked what we just did right here on your bathroom floor."

"Yes."

"Me too," he said, moving my legs, wrapping them around his waist, pressing me closer, tighter. "Which is why I don't sleep with women."

I nodded.

"And why," he said with a sigh, tracing his fingers down my spine, "until you tell me to go, you will be the only one I will be doing this with."

I wasn't sure where to go with that. "I wouldn't ask that of you."

"You should."

"I have no right to—"

"Yes, you do," he assured me. "As I will ask it of you… only me."

There were a million things running through my head, the least of all that this was fast, much too fast, but then I took a breath and my brain kicked in.

He wasn't confessing his undying love; he just wanted a chance to see if this could happen. I wanted that too. And we weren't strangers; I'd known the man for four years.

"*Sono pazzo di te*," he whispered, leaning forward, mouth on the hollow of my throat, his tongue licking before he took a bite of me and sucked.

The whipcrack of sizzling heat ran up my back, and I jolted in his arms.

"Tell me you are crazy about me too… *tesoro… caro….*"

His mouth and his hands and the rock-hard thighs under my legs, the silky glide of his skin over mine, the muscles flexing to hold me, all of it was so new and so utterly craved. Normally, because I was older, my lovers looked to me to set the ground rules, but not this time. This was different. It already felt like it was going in a wholly new direction. I was terrified and excited and already invested in the outcome. Because I wasn't just taking a lover, I was broadening an existing friendship and becoming responsible for a child. A sixteen-year-old boy who already counted on me and trusted me was in the mix.

"Nate."

My wandering thoughts returned to the man who held me in his arms.

"I don't need words more than this once, but I—"

"What you need doesn't matter to me," I told him, shifting my angle, rising up, and unlocking my legs. Knees on the rug on both sides of his hips, I pressed my bare chest to his, my hands on his face, tracing over his jaw, captivated by his upper lip and the bridge of his nose. "I will tell you things like that, that we just did, you and me… was amazing, and I can't wait to do it again. I will tell you that I hope you want to sleep in bed with me, because lying beside a lover is one of the great joys of my life. And finally, I would like nothing better than to see what this right here can become. I would love it."

"You would?" He seemed so pleased, his eyes wet and dark and filled with happiness.

"Yes."

His smile did the most amazing things to his face, making him a completely different man.

"I'm glad you're out of the business you were in with Mr. Romelli."

"So am I. So is Sal," he said, his eyes fluttering for a second. "And Sal knows about me and knows what I want with you, so he and I are good."

"You lost me."

His gaze was steady as he stared into my eyes. "I don't like secrets, so I had to tell Sal the truth, that I wanted this with you."

"But you never told me what you wanted."

"Now you know."

I smiled when I felt his hands clutch at my ass.

"Do you know what I want?"

"No."

"I want to come inside of you and see it leaking out." He moaned softly, the sound of his breathing and the look on his face both telling me how badly he wanted that. "I went to get tested, and when I get the results back, when you can see I'm good, can I do that? Will you let me?"

"Maybe I want to fuck you," I said, even as his fingers slid down my crease and I bucked back into his hand.

He laughed, and it was deep and rumbling, warm and sexy. "I think you want me back inside of you bad."

No games, I never played them. "Yes," I confessed, dropping my head forward into his shoulder, loving his scent, his sleek olive skin, the sweat and salt.

He exhaled long and deep and just hugged me, content, it seemed, not to move.

"We should get up," I said finally. "Michael's probably out there absolutely scarred for life. I'm sorry I yelled—I couldn't help it."

"I like that you lost control." He smiled, hands on my face. "And Michael is still at home. I told him I had to talk to you alone for a few minutes and I would call him when we were done."

I stared. "Is this what you had in mind?"

"Actually, no," he said, standing up, dragging me to my feet after him. "I did have things to say."

"Like?" I asked, watching him as he leaned into my shower and turned it on.

"Like, would you consider giving us a chance?"

"But I already said yes to that."

"Yeah, I know. It's a lot easier to get the guts to ask it after sex."

My smile was huge, and he made a sound in the back of his throat before he bent and kissed me. That he had to grab me, crush me against him and ravish my mouth, was hotter than I could have imagined. I would have to get used to bearing marks and bruises and found the idea very appealing. Men were normally careful with me; Dreo was too hungry to care. I loved it.

"Jesus," he snapped, shoving me into the shower and closing the door. "We're never gonna get out of this damn bathroom if I don't leave you alone."

"I don't mind." I chuckled, hearing his growl as I turned under the water and soaped up quickly.

"You will when you're too sore to move."

"I'll take that chance." I sighed, rinsing off and stepping back out, shaking my head, letting the drops of water hit him.

He reached for me, hand in my wet hair, made a fist, and dragged me close for another kiss. The sound I made pleased him, as was evident from his mouth slanting down over mine.

Getting out of the bathroom didn't seem to be in the cards.

MICHAEL got tired of waiting, walked over to my apartment, and told us to get the hell out to the living room and watch TV with him. He was demanding and loud. I was charmed completely.

He sat between us, much to Dreo's annoyance, as the flannel pajama bottoms and long-sleeved T-shirt I was wearing were, he said, the sexiest things he had ever seen in his life.

"You need to get out more," I whispered before I got up to make hot chocolate.

He followed me into the kitchen, leaning against the counter as he watched me get out a small saucepan to heat the milk.

"You don't just put some water in the microwave?"

I looked at him over my shoulder. "Real hot chocolate isn't made that way."

"What way?"

"With water."

He nodded, his eyes raking over me from head to toe.

"Seriously," I teased. "Flannel pajamas are not hot."

"Says you."

I swallowed down my heart, concentrating on the task at hand instead of the blood rushing to my groin. How had I ever missed that the man was drop-dead gorgeous? I wanted to lick him all over.

"You're all flushed."

Because I was about to go up in flames.

"It's adorable."

"I'd prefer it was sexy."

"Oh, it's that too."

Jesus.

Once I was done and sprinkling the cinnamon on top of the whipped cream that I knew Michael loved, I told Dreo to carry the mug into the living room for me.

"I want to talk about what clothes you think are a turn-on instead," he murmured, his breath on the back of my neck giving me goose bumps.

"I just… there's leather chaps and thongs and all kinds of things out there, Mr. Fiore."

His hand smoothing down my ass made me lean forward and close my eyes. It had only been three weeks since my last nameless encounter with a guy I picked up at a friend's party, but I had topped, as the guy expected me to, as I normally did because I was not comfortable being dominated by a stranger. As I had not been the one submitting, the one trusting, it had been okay but not great. I had not bottomed since Duncan.

I had to know a man, be comfortable and confident, before I let someone inside of me. Even though I loved it, craved it, being filled and stretched, I just didn't have the faith that my friends did to offer that gift to a stranger. All of my relationships had started the same way, with me in control, me being the one dominating another man. Even Duncan and I had begun with him facedown on his bed. But this… this was already different. It already felt closer because of the foundation of friendship that was there to begin with. And Dreo was so confident, so passionate, so utterly secure, that saying no never even entered my mind. He wouldn't hurt me. Not physically, not mentally, not emotionally. He saw me, amazing as it seemed, like a treasure that he could not believe his good fortune in getting a chance to have. The look in his eyes was carnal heat and awe all rolled up together. There was no doubt in my mind that the man wanted me and more. He was dying to see where it could go.

So because there had been the domination I craved, what I enjoyed most in bed, about bed, when the man slid his hand over my ass, I lost it just a little.

I let out a hiss of breath and pushed back against him.

"Come get in your bed with me," he pleaded, sliding his hardening cock against the crease of my ass.

"We have Michael."

"Michael will be fine on the couch alone."

The man just annihilated me.

"*Mi piaci da morire*," he whispered against my ear, his breath warm and his lips soft and wet as they grazed my skin.

"What did you say?" I asked. I felt twenty-five instead of forty-five whenever Dreo had his hands on me.

"I said I like you a little." He chuckled, his voice husky and low.

"You're lying," I accused him, my body calming down. I eased free of his hands, walking backward into the refrigerator. It was a testament to how big and solid it was that it didn't rattle when he pinned me against it seconds later. "You said you're crazy about me."

He didn't contradict the statement, came after me instead, hand splayed beside me on the stainless steel surface, making sure I couldn't move again.

"What are you doing?" I asked.

"Fuck if I know," he said, eyes fixed on mine. "I just—I love my nephew, but I really wish he would go to bed. I need to talk to you."

"You don't want to talk to me." I chuckled, seeing the way he was looking down my body before he leaned forward, wedging his thigh between mine.

"No," he growled, his voice thick. "Not really."

"Hey."

His eyes flicked back to mine.

"We're going to try, right?" I asked, smiling. "Isn't that what we said?"

He nodded.

"We don't have to talk," I assured him. "We'll just start and hope for the best."

"Not hope. We'll work hard at it."

I put a hand on his chest, and he covered it with his own. "Yes. Now take that cup to Michael."

We joined the teenager on the couch as an old favorite, *The 36th Chamber of Shaolin,* came on.

"Is this a good one?" Dreo asked.

Both Michael and I did the slow pan to him like he was insane.

"Jesus." His eyes got big. "What did I say?"

"You've never seen this?" Michael was flabbergasted.

"Seriously?" I asked.

"There are good kung fu movies besides *Enter The Dragon*?"

"For starters," Michael said, indignantly, "*Enter The Dragon* is *not* a kung fu movie. It completely transcends that label. You understand that without *Enter The Dragon* there would be no *Mortal Kombat* or *Tekken* or—"

"Yes, Christ, I get it," Dreo groaned. "But we're not talking about that." He gestured at the TV. "What is this?"

"You're serious." I looked at him in mock wonder. "You've never seen *The 36th Chamber of Shaolin*?"

"I think I'll live."

I grunted.

He made a noise in the back of his throat as the three of us settled to watch one of the greatest kung fu movies ever made.

"You know the two of you are completely—"

"Shhh," we both hushed him at the same time.

It was obvious he thought we were being ridiculous.

I must have dropped off at some point, because when I woke up, I had my head on Dreo's chest and his hand was in my hair, massaging my scalp.

"Hey," he said softly, sighing deeply.

"Where's Michael?" I asked, groggy with sleep, lifting up only to realize that I was basically in his lap, draped over him.

He tipped his head, and I saw that his nephew was asleep on the other end of the couch. Dreo and I were cuddled up together on the right.

I leaned away from him, rubbing my eyes as he smiled. “I’m sorry. We both passed out after we told you how good the movie was.

“It doesn’t matter; the movie wasn’t the important part.”

I just looked at him, still half-asleep.

“I enjoyed being here with you both more than anything,” he told me, his hand sliding around the nape of my neck and easing me back to him. He tipped my chin up with his other hand. “This was right; it felt right.”

He wasn’t making any sense, but when he drew me forward, his lips sliding over mine, our mouths notching together so perfectly, I forgot what I was going to say.

“Stay—” He kissed me. “—here. Stop moving away.”

“Should I get in your lap?” I teased, still groggy.

“Oh yeah.”

His voice, the rumble in it, the break it did, all hoarse and wicked, was so hot I could not stifle the moan.

His hands on my skin, up under the T-shirt, sliding over my stomach, my hips, down inside my pajamas, on my ass, made me whine into his mouth. The kiss was wet and hard and deep, and our lips slid together, mashed and mauled, sucked and nibbled with breathing occurring only in hurried gasps. The mewling sound that came from way down in my chest made his breath catch. Only when Michael stirred did we push apart, both of us panting, staring at each other.

I got up and went to stand by the mantle as he woke his nephew enough to steer him to the guest bedroom. Watching Michael stagger away with Dreo’s hands on his shoulders was very sweet. I tried to focus on that to calm my racing heart.

In minutes he was back, wrapping his arms around me, one gently draped around my neck, the other across my chest.

“Come on, let me take you to bed,” he said after he squeezed me tight.

It was nice, the way he stepped back and took my hand and gently pulled me after him. He left me to turn off the lights, told me he had to do a quick walk-around like he did in his own loft before he went to bed.

I was lying facedown when he came back. I heard him close the door behind him before I felt his hand on my ass, pulling down pajamas and underwear at the same time.

"Dreo," I whispered as I felt his mouth on my right butt cheek.

"Sorry," he said quickly, and I had a moment of panic that he was going to leave me, that he had taken his name for an admonishment when it was instead an invitation.

I lifted up to turn my head only to find the man shoving his sweats down to his knees and flipping open a bottle of lube, a wrapped condom between his teeth.

"You can't sleep yet."

I shivered, lying back down, my hand sliding under my hip, fingers wrapping around my cock as he straddled me from behind.

"Say yes to me, Nate," he ordered, and I heard the sound of ripping foil.

"Oh fuck yes."

The sound he made, part grunt, part growl, all sex and approval, made me breathless.

I lifted my ass so I could get him inside of me quicker, then gasped as I felt the long, thick, hard shaft sliding between my cheeks, parting them and pressing against my entrance.

I had missed it so much, the claiming, the desire, and now the physical marks on my body, evidence that I had been taken, were added to that. It was primal and was not something I shared with anyone outside my bedroom, my need to be dominated. I had begged Duncan to use his handcuffs on me, but he had never believed that I wanted my power stripped away, that I would allow that. He had never trusted me enough to take me at my word.

There was the burn, the stretch, and then his weight over me, pinning me to the mattress as he pushed and shoved inside my body. The tears were involuntary, the pleasure overwhelming, and I shuddered beneath him and cried out.

"I want to tie you down," Dreo whispered as his hand covered my mouth so my howl of pleasure was muffled. "And I wanna gag you. Will you let me?"

I nodded, barely able to answer, to breathe, squirming and writhing under him, wanting him deeper, loving the rhythm he was setting, the slow, sensual thrust and retreat, as he sucked and bit my shoulder.

"You wanna be mine so badly," he groaned, grasping my jaw firmly, his middle finger slipping between my lips.

I sucked on his finger as he filled my ass, thrust hard and retreated, over and over. The man was huge, and I felt every inch of him inside me.

"Nate. Say yes… you wanna be mine."

"Yours. Yes," I barely whispered the words.

And it was just insane. I wasn't in love; I had barely spoken to the man in the four years I'd known him. His motivations, his thoughts, these were all unknowns, but what I did know of him, of his heart, I was crazy about. He was always there, so close, taken for granted and yet utterly depended on.

"Lift up," he ordered and pulled out at the same time.

I sucked in my breath, the emptiness almost physically painful as I teetered on the edge of my shattering orgasm.

Rough hands were on my hips as he wrenched me backward to the edge of the bed, the tops of my feet falling over the side as my face was forced down between my bent knees. I felt like a compressed accordion before I felt the nudge at my opening and he pressed inside of me, burying himself to the hilt in one long, smooth forward thrust.

"Dreo!"

My ass was slapped hard, and I felt it hot and stinging on my cheek as his other hand fisted in my hair, yanking my head up and sideways so he could ravish my mouth as he pounded into my body.

"I can't—I, Dreo." I moaned out the man's name as my balls tightened, as my muscles fisted around his cock, clamping down with the force of my release.

He hammered me through my shuddering climax and the aftershocks that tore through me. I felt him swell inside of me, but there was no release, no wet and silken heat filling me, flooding me, and I wanted it, missed it.

"You need to get those test results," I told him when my teeth stopped chattering.

"Why?" he asked as he nibbled on my ear, on the skin behind it and down the side of my neck. His soft lips, warm breath, and gravelly voice made me shiver anew.

"Because," I whispered, "I want the same thing you do, for you to fill my ass with cum."

He jolted behind me, and I knew that the idea of coating my insides was way more than appealing. It was a deep, throbbing need. "I'll have them next week. I'll bring them to you as soon as I can."

I smiled and he collapsed over me, arms wrapped around my chest, squeezing, pressing, holding me so tight.

He was still buried inside of me, and that, along with his sweat-slick skin plastered to mine, his mouth open on my shoulder, his heart beating against my back, let me surrender. I finally, completely, let my walls down and took a breath.

"That's it, trust me," he growled, nuzzling my hair.

I had forgotten how much I loved to just be held tight.

"*Tesoro*."

I closed my eyes.

TEN

DREO'S sigh as he looked both of us over made me smile.

"What?" Michael asked him as he fiddled with his iPod.

"You both clean up real nice."

He shrugged, taking the compliment like it meant nothing even though the slight curve of his mouth said different.

Dreo's hand went around the back of my neck, and he dragged his thumb along the newly shaved line of my jaw. "Especially you, *piccolo*."

Having risen early, I had attacked my beard first with my electric shaver and then the straight razor that my father had given me years before. I had taken my time, been meticulous, and, after showering, emerged from the bathroom in time to watch Dreo wake up.

"Who the fuck are you?" He had tipped his head at me.

I grinned wide, and his catch of breath was worth all the effort.

"Dimples?" he said, clutching his heart. "I had no idea you were so pretty."

My eyebrow lifted, and he motioned me toward the bed.

"Get your ass up and get over to your place and shower and change into your suit."

"*Un bacino, per favore*," he growled.

I walked to my bed, which he looked heartstoppingly good in, and bent down to kiss him.

"You're learning Italian," he whispered.

"No," I said huskily, "I just know what I want."

His hands were on my face as he parted his lips for me. I had a second to take in the thick eyelashes that grazed his cheek, the long, straight nose, and the sexy curve of his mouth before I took what I wanted and kissed him until he was breathless.

"Jesus, Nate," he panted when I pulled back, his dark eyes staring up at me.

I waggled my eyebrows. "With the beard gone, I don't look so old, right?"

"You never looked old," he told me, reaching out again only to have me step back beyond his reach. "And I love the beard, always have."

"Yes but without it I for sure don't look old." I grinned slyly, admiring the flush on his smooth skin, his shallow breaths, and his swollen lips.

"Come here," he rasped, and I saw the way the sheet was now tented over his groin.

I shook my head. "Get up. We have to grab coffee and a donut or something on the way."

Walking to my closet, I was surprised when I was grabbed from behind and shoved face-first into the wall. And I understood the action for more than what it seemed. This thing between us was brand new. He wanted me, I wanted him back, and we were combustible at present, flaring at impossible times because we were both hungry for the other. But more than that, he needed the connection, like putting on armor, before he faced the outside world. The hard hands on my hips meant more than simply that he wanted to fuck.

"Tell me what you want," I ordered hoarsely.

He slid his hard, twitching cock over my crease and I moaned softly.

"You used me kind of hard last night," I told him, turning in his embrace to face him. "But I can suck you."

That he went instantly to his knees was a surprise. His eyes as he looked up at me, easing my sweats down so that my own hard cock bobbed free, were enough to pull a groan up from my diaphragm. The man was simply the sexiest thing I had ever seen.

"I'm gonna come just putting this in my mouth," he told me, and I saw that he was already stroking himself as his lips parted and slid over the end of my leaking shaft.

The whine was involuntary as he took my dick down the back of his throat and swallowed around me. My head fell back, knocking against the wall, and his chuckle, more than anything, made me jolt.

We could have fun, we could laugh and joke, and sex didn't need to be this serious business every time. It was such a gift. I shivered with happiness.

There was no way to last, the sucking, the laving, the swirl of his tongue, the sounds he made, his moan when I put my hand in his hair, his urging of me to fuck his mouth.

"I can't… we need to be tested, and—"

"Just me, not you…. You probably have a piece of paper you can show me right now."

I did too. "Yes."

"Nate," he whimpered. "Please."

I was too close, the suction, the heat, the slide—it was all too much. I warned him, tried to pull out, but his hand on my ass flexed and held, and I was gone.

As he drank me down, I watched him, the muscles in his throat, his eyes as they screwed shut with pleasure, and the way he pumped in and out of his own hand as he came. As he licked me clean, I yanked on his hair to get him to stand.

His eyes were slits of heat when he rose over me.

"Kiss me." I lifted for it.

He bent but didn't give me what I wanted.

"I wanna taste me on your tongue."

His lips pressed down over mine in an openmouthed kiss so my tongue could slide over his, tangle and suck. My arms around his neck were tight and claiming, and when I felt his hand on the back of my head, cradling it, between the tenderness and the passion, I was undone.

Jesus, whatever the hell he wanted, he just had to ask. But the sum of his desire seemed to be kissing me until my mind went blank, and stroking my ass over and over and over.

And now, an hour later, at the front door, he was looking at me like just me being there, going with him to the funeral, was the best gift I could have given him.

"You look weird without your beard," Michael told me. "Just sayin'."

I rolled my eyes and opened the door so the three of us could head out.

Dreo wanted to drive, so we took his Mercedes with the black limousine tinted windows and headed downtown. It was raining and dark, and the closer we got, the more somber the feeling in the car was.

The church was awash in enormous elaborate floral arrangements, and Dreo left us to go sit with Sal and Mr. Romelli's family up front while Michael and I took seats on the side toward the back. We both had our overcoats in our laps as mass began. Having not been raised Catholic, Methodist instead, I let Michael be my guide for what was happening and what I was supposed to do. There was no way not to be impressed by the size and grandeur of the cathedral, the pomp of the processional, and the distinguished, regal-looking priest. Just the spectacle was amazing.

Mass was beautiful, and then Father Ross invited people to come up and speak about Mr. Romelli. His wife and daughters took the podium and then other friends, people from the community, and finally his son, Joseph. Michael started leaning against me, and I knew that all of it was getting to him. He had not been to a funeral since his mother's, and it was beginning to hurt. I moved my arm, draped it around the back of the pew, and he pressed his knee to mine. It was nice that he allowed himself to take comfort from me.

The priest retook the podium then and spoke for a bit about the kind of man Mr. Romelli was and his charitable activities and donations to the church. The end was nice: there was singing, and then the priest invited everyone to stay for refreshments provided by the family before everyone drove to the cemetery. After the burial, there was a late lunch at the Romelli home for friends and family, and I wondered if Dreo was invited to that or not.

Since he had to ride in one of the limousines, Dreo walked back to us when everyone was dismissed for refreshments before the trip to the cemetery.

"Here," he said, passing me his keys before putting one hand on the back of my neck and draping his other arm around Michael's shoulders. "How're you two holding up?"

"We're fine." Michael smiled, leaning into him. "Are you okay?"

"I will be." He nodded, smiling. "Come with me."

He gestured us both forward, and before I really understood where we were going, he started steering us toward Tony Strada where he stood across the room, talking to the priest.

"Dreo! Come!"

We had to detour because Joseph Romelli, Vincent Romelli's son, was calling him. He thought, Dreo had told us, that he was going to be the one taking over things now that his father had passed. But what was really going to happen was that the power was moving to Vincent Romelli's strong second-in-command, Tony Strada.

"Joey." Dreo smiled even though there was a sharp edge to his voice. "This is Dr. Nathan Qells and my nephew, Michael."

"I told you I didn't want you here," he practically snarled at Dreo. "How dare you show your—"

"I have every right to be here," Dreo snapped back. "Don't make a scene."

The man looked at me and watched Dreo take my hand in his and pull Michael close to him. His eyes narrowed angrily.

"I don't need to have this shit thrown up in my face—it wasn't enough that you told my father?" His voice was cold and hard. "It wasn't enough that you made him a party to how sick and depraved and—"

"I just wanted to come and pay my respects to your father," Dreo said sharply. "And give my condolences to your mother and sisters."

"If you wanted to show him respect, you would have never said a goddamn word about being a filthy faggot!" Joseph said under his breath.

Sal was suddenly on my right, standing still but close, his shoulder brushing mine. Joseph looked at him, clearly stunned by the obvious show of solidarity.

"You don't care?" Joseph asked. "You don't give a fuck what he is?"

He shook his head.

"It's a sin," Joseph hissed.

"It's not," Dreo told Joseph, pulling the other man's focus back from Sal. "You're just too ignorant to understand."

"This man," he asked Dreo, tipping his head to me, "is what to you?"

"*Lui è il mio fidanzato*," he told him softly, the whisper husky.

Joseph blanched, as did one of the men with him. The other looked stunned but didn't even breathe.

I had a moment to wonder what *fidanzato* was before Sal leaned close and said "boyfriend" in my ear. There was no way not to clutch Dreo's hand as I stared at his profile.

Two years with Duncan Stiel and I was just some guy he hung out with. One day with Dreo Fiore and I was being acknowledged as the one he slept with, spent time with, and wanted at his side. It was overwhelming.

And there were consequences if Duncan came out of the closet, but those didn't include death. I wasn't stupid; I knew what other men thought of homosexuality in Dreo's world. That he would still, with the balance of real-life penalties hanging over his head, tell the truth about me, about who I was to him, was staggering. The honesty undid me.

"I—" Joseph gasped, his eyes back and forth between my lover and me, hard when they finally flicked to Dreo's face. "I can't stand to look at you! Better that you were dead then to bring this shame on me and my family or on your own."

Dreo took a breath. "Your own father let us out. Tony agreed as well. I just wanted to be up-front and have you meet the most important people in my life."

"Tony's not fuckin' in charge, Fiore, I am!"

"Lower your voice" came the fierce whisper.

We all turned as Tony Strada stepped into the circle, two men behind him, both tall and huge and silent.

"What's going on?"

Joseph rounded on him. "You've got no right to let Fiore or Polo out of—"

"The fuck I don't," he told Joseph, reaching out and putting his hand on the younger man's shoulder. "Here's the thing: you work for me, not the other way around."

"You're out of your fuckin' mind!"

"Lower," Tony began icily, squeezing tighter on the shoulder, "your fuckin' voice."

It was tense, and I was surprised that the guys I thought were Joseph's muscle did nothing.

"I know it, my men know it, and your men know it. Wrap your brain around the situation, and if you need more help, ask your mother."

"You leave my—"

"We talked," he told him softly, moving closer, his voice dropping lower. "She and I. She understands what Frazzi's people told her. Everyone knows what's goin' on except you, *figliolo*."

"I am not your son," he snarled at Tony. "I—"

Tony gripped the back of the younger man's neck hard. "You work for me or you can be out. But I made the peace with Frazzi; I'm the broker of the new understanding between the families. Don't fuck with me, and don't fuck with him," he finished, tipping his head at the two men standing behind Joseph. "Take him to his mother and then come back. I have something for you both to do."

"Yes, Mr. Strada," the first man said, and the other nodded.

Joseph was humiliated and furious, and the only thing I could think of that was good in the situation was that his entire focus had moved from Dreo to Tony.

As Joseph was walked away, Tony stepped close to us, reaching out to put a hand on Michael's cheek. "You look like your mother, *ragazzo*." He smiled.

"Thank you, sir." Michael sighed.

Tony then turned to me. "Let the beard grow back, Professor; this ain't you."

I smiled because he was either perceptive or bossy, and I wasn't sure which. I really didn't even know why I had shaved it that morning.

He faced Dreo then. "You could stay. This"—and he shrugged—"means nothing to me."

"But your life is not what I want or what Sal wants," Dreo said, his voice confident, speaking for both himself and his friend. "I started because I needed to take care of Michael, and Sal introduced me to Mr. Romelli. But after the old man's death—come on, no one wants bodyguards that let a man die."

Tony grabbed Dreo's face. "You saved me, you saved Sal, and you saved that piece of shit that just walked away from us. If you weren't there, Dreo, we'd all be dead."

Michael caught his breath.

"You were amazing, Andreo Fiore."

Dreo nodded and eased the older man's hands from his face. "I just wanted to get you all out of there, that's all. And now I just want out of all of this."

He nodded and slapped Dreo's face gently, his smile wide. "People won't understand."

"*Non me ne frega un cazzo*," Dreo told him.

The older man chuckled. "Oh, I know you don't give a fuck; you don't have to tell me."

Dreo shrugged and smiled.

"Well, I did my part and let everyone know you and Sal are out. You should have no trouble, but come see me if you do."

"*Grazie molto*," Sal told him.

"*Prego*," he exhaled. "And if either of you ever change your mind and want to come back, my door is always open."

Dreo reached for the man's hand, lifted it to his lips, and kissed the back of it. "*Mille grazie*," he murmured.

Tony smiled and patted Dreo's face before he turned, the two men trailing after him, and walked away.

"Fuck," Sal grunted. "Can it really be this easy?"

Dreo's smile was huge as he draped one arm around me and another around Michael. "I know, right? I feel bad being so happy at a funeral."

Sal shook his head and was about to turn when Joseph was suddenly back in front of us.

"Listen," he barked at Dreo, finger pointing at him. "Once everyone knows that you're a goddamn faggot, *finocchio*, you'll be lucky to—"

"*Taci*!"

We all turned to Sal, who had yelled.

"*Ma sta zitto che è meglio*!" Sal continued, moving fast, walking behind Michael and covering his ears. "You don't talk to him anymore, you worthless piece of shit!"

"You—"

"Fuck off," he snarled at Joseph. "If you don't want your mother to know you screw whores along with your wife, shut up and walk the fuck away. Just let us go to the cemetery and pay our respects, visit your mother at her house, and then we'll leave and you never have to see us again."

"I—"

"Whatever you think of him, or me, we protected your old man until he made that impossible for us. And the only reason you're not dead is that when the shooting started and you froze like a child, Dreo got your ass out of the club and never told anyone you were even fuckin' there."

Joseph looked back and forth between the two men as Sal moved his hands, allowing Michael to hear again.

"Now." Sal took a breath. "Tony's already telling people we're out. You do the same. Monday you go to work and we'll go to ours. *Sì?*"

After a minute, Joseph nodded.

"*Buono?*"

"*Sì, buono.*"

He turned then and walked away, and then there was just the four of us again as Sal started smiling.

"Fuck, I wanna go home." Dreo sighed deeply.

"Me too," Sal agreed, smiling. "And start living away from all this bullshit."

"Amen," Dreo said, lifting my hand he was holding to his lips and kissing my knuckles.

"Who knew that telling the truth actually would make me free?"

"And not dead." Sal snickered. "Both of us." He smacked me in the arm. "He's gay, I'm the friend of the gay man, of the *finocchio.*" He squinted at Dreo. "Who even uses that word anymore?"

He shrugged. "Joey, apparently."

Sal cackled. "What a fuck. Who gives a damn what a man does in his bed? It only matters what the man does in the world, for the people he loves."

Dreo nodded. "*Sì.*"

"*Lascialo perdere,*" he told him.

"I won't. I don't give a shit what he thinks of me. I cared for his father, just like you, but the son is a piece of shit, and if he's not careful and keeps running his mouth about Tony and not listening to him…."

"*Sì.*" Sal agreed to the unspoken prophecy.

"We may still have some trouble," Dreo told him.

Sal nodded. "We will. We just have to ride it out."

"Dreo?" I asked.

His smile was warm. "Being gay in our business is more than frowned upon."

"You could get hurt," I said.

"Yeah, but it helps that you came by that day to see me and warn me about the guy on your fire escape. It helps that Tony knows you, that his niece knows you, and that she's gay as well. Lots of that is good, but there are still those who will care about the gay part. My father." He shrugged. "He will not understand."

My heart hurt for him.

He leaned in, gently pressing his forehead to mine. "Michael and I will have to spend the holidays with you, Nate; we will have nowhere else to go."

I leaned into him, arms around his neck, squeezing tight. "Wherever I am, you're welcome. I want you both with me."

His face was pressed to the side of my neck, and his arms around me were like iron bands as he held me.

"My father is different," I heard Sal say as I held the man who was becoming more and more important to me with every passing minute that I spent with him. "Salvatore Polo Sr. believes that once you're family, that never changes."

"Meaning what?" Michael asked as Dreo and I parted.

"You're all welcome at my house," he told us. "My parents don't give a crap, and when I told them I was out because you were—" Sal chuckled. "—my mother said you were always her favorite."

"She's such a liar." Dreo laughed softly, taking my hand, unable, it seemed, to keep from touching me.

"You got her son out of a job she hated," Sal told him. "You are golden in my house, Dreo Fiore."

And Dreo liked hearing that if the smile was any indication.

Normally, the trip from downtown Chicago out to Hillside would have taken a half an hour or less, depending on traffic, but the procession of cars was long, and so the trip dragged into an hour. Queen of Heaven cemetery was huge, with a mausoleum as well, and in the cold and damp, the wind whipping around and the dark-gray overcast sky, it was a very fitting day for a burial. I had been to other

Italian funerals in my life, and normally, they were open casket for viewing and people kissed the deceased on the forehead. But Sal had told me there was not much left of Vincent Romelli to bury, let alone view.

Michael and I finally parked and got out, and as we were walking, I heard my name called. I saw Alla Strada, then, with her partner Jennifer St. James, and diverted toward them. Jen had a big hug and kiss for me and immediately asked if I had seen Alla smoking lately.

"Yes, ma'am," I said, and Alla smacked my arm, after which Jen smacked her and made her promise to stop cold turkey… again.

She rolled her eyes but agreed.

"He's a narc," Michael told both the women. "But you gotta figure that," he said pointedly to Alla. "He's a parent, ya know."

She shrugged like she had forgotten that, put an arm around Michael's shoulders, and walked with him as Jen and I followed, arm in arm.

The graveside ceremony took longer than the church service. Michael and I were standing, and after a while, he moved so he was beside me instead of between Alla and Jen. When his head clunked down on my shoulder, I understood that however hard he was trying to hold up, this was slowly killing him. I put an arm around him and held him tight.

Dreo was in the first standing row behind the family who were all seated, and when we had walked up, I saw Mrs. Romelli holding onto his hand for dear life. No matter what Joseph felt now, it was obvious that both Dreo and Sal had been very close to his father and mother.

People again went up and spoke, a string quartet played, and the priest gave the final blessing before he concluded. Everyone then followed Mrs. Romelli and her daughters and her son as they placed roses on the casket. I had never seen so many enormous wreaths, each more stunning than the last. Everyone filed passed the Romellis, and since I didn't think it was a good idea for me and Michael, I stayed in the back and didn't move.

"What are you doing?" Alla asked me when she saw we weren't following her and Jen.

"I don't want to cause anyone any—"

"Oh for crissakes, Nate," she sniped, grabbing my arm and pulling me forward.

The daughters were all kind and shook my hand and Michael's, but when we reached Joseph, he wouldn't touch either of us.

"Joe?" Mrs. Romelli was watching him; her raw red-rimmed eyes were puffy and watering.

"I told you Dreo was leaving, and Sal, and this is why—I told you why."

Her eyes were back on me and then Michael, and then she reached for me, was in my arms, holding me tight. "So good to see you again, Nate. Please take care of Dreo. Love him hard. He saved my son, he nearly died trying to save my husband.... He's a good boy, the best boy... *per piacere*."

"Yes, ma'am," I said, hugging her, rubbing circles on her back. "I'll take good care of him."

She leaned back, nodding, and Michael was suddenly there, hugging her, telling her how sorry he was. He told her he knew how she felt, as he too understood the loss of a loved one. Michael said that it would be hard, but that every day it would get a little better. He promised her.

Mrs. Romelli grabbed him back and was sobbing, her daughters looking at Michael like he was the most beautiful thing on the planet. Two of them took my hands and held them, and the third told me how much they all loved Dreo. They went on to say that I should not be a stranger and neither should Dreo or Michael. They expected to see us at the house.

My eyes flicked to Joseph, and I could see the fury as well as the resignation. In the tide of acceptance and love that was the women in his family, he was drowned. Looking over at Dreo, I saw his gentle smile and warm brown-black eyes. The way he was looking at me, proudly, possessively... I felt my chest tighten just seeing it. We really needed to talk.

THE drive to the house in La Grange took forever, but there was no way we couldn't go. We were expected, and our absence would have been noted. Alla and Jen left her parents' car to ride with Michael and me, and the company was nice. I caught Alla up on my brunch date with Sanderson the following day, and she asked if I was doing penance from God.

"The man's a pig," she told me.

"Is that the one who hit on you at that faculty mixer?" Jen asked.

She nodded fast. "Yeah, even after I told him I was not only in a relationship but gay as well."

Jen chuckled. "Gonna go with 'wow' there."

"You should have seen the shit fit he threw over Nate being in charge of the Medieval Feast this year."

"But now he's in charge," I told her.

"That's not what I heard."

"May I say that you all are a bunch of big geeks?" Jen snickered.

"But we dress up like fictional characters," I told her. "And it's super fun."

"Oh, we do not," Alla laughed. "Don't make it any worse than it already is."

"But we will at my Yule Ball, and you're both invited."

They looked at me, so frightened that I was telling the truth. I nodded to let them know that I was.

As I drove, I checked on Michael in the rearview mirror. He had given up the passenger seat to Alla, insisting that she sit up front with me.

"I'm fine," he told me when he noticed my regard. "I'm just tired. I don't know why."

"Funerals are exhausting, that's why," Jen told him, patting his knee. "I need a nap too."

The Romelli house was a mansion, complete with a long circular drive that still couldn't hold all the cars. We had to park a block away. I was surprised to see the same news trucks, the same gaggle of reporters, and the same squad cars that had been constant for the entire day. It would have been nice for Mr. Romelli's family to be given some semblance of privacy, but it was not to be.

Once we passed the end of the drive, it was private property, and no reporters or police could pass. It grew quiet as crowds of people trailed over the cobblestones toward the front door. There were a couple of maids there to take coats, and then a huge foyer that opened up into an enormous great room, where a buffet was laid out.

"Oh shit," Michael gasped.

"What?"

"Those are my grandparents."

I looked to where he was pointing, and standing with Dreo was an older man who looked just like him and Michael and a gorgeous woman who had the whole Sophia Loren thing going on. Her hair fell to her shoulders, thick and chestnut with dyed blonde streaks in it, and she had the same dark eyes that her son did. Dreo had inherited his broad shoulders and height from his father, who stood just an inch or so shorter than his son. Stunning man, and I had an idea of how beautiful Dreo would be when he too hit sixty. Instantly, I moved to the side of the room.

"What're you doing?" Michael asked, having followed me.

"Go see your grandparents."

"You too, come on."

I shook my head. "Not here. It's not a good idea."

"Why not?"

"It's not fair to them. We already know they're going to hate me, Dreo said. But I don't want to make a scene."

"They won't, just come on."

"You go," I told him. "I'll be right here."

"Nate—"

"Go," I ordered him.

He left me, and I stood there beside one of the huge windows that looked out at the front drive. When Michael closed in on them, Mrs. Fiore reached for her grandson and pulled him into a hug. I watched them talk, looked at Dreo and his father as well. They stood side by side, talking but not looking at each other as Mrs. Fiore spoke looking right at Michael, both of her hands on his shoulders. Whatever she was saying was urgent.

My phone rang as I watched them, and I answered without checking the caller ID.

"Hello?"

"Hey, Dad."

"Hey Jare." I smiled, feeling like the vise my heart was in fell away. My kid, my life, everything righted.

"You got a second?"

"Always for you."

"Okay" was all he said.

I waited a minute. And another. "Jare?"

He cleared his throat. "You can't get mad."

My grunt was loud. "That's not fair. I might get mad; depending on what it is, I might even lose my mind. You can't tell me how to be. Just spill it."

"Shit."

"Jare?"

He took a breath. "Me and Gillian are getting married."

I was confused. "Why would I be mad about that?"

"Really?"

Was he kidding? "Yeah, why?"

"Mom was mad."

"You called her first?"

"So now you're mad?"

"Not mad," I assured him.

"Ohmygod, you can't be hurt 'cause I called her first."

"Fine."

He chuckled. "God, I love you."

It was not that his confession was any kind of revelation. I never doubted he loved me; I was his father, after all. "What?"

"No, I just mean… you always say how you feel, and I never have to dig."

"I hate digging."

"I know, me too, and since you raised me, I always think everyone is just like us."

"Nope."

"Yeah, not at all. So far the human race has been a great big disappointment in that department. No one just says how they feel, you have to excavate."

I snickered. "Not your mother."

"No, she was pissed."

All at once I realized why his mother would have been mad. "You're getting married for a reason, right? Is Gillian pregnant?"

Silence.

"Jare?"

"Yeah," he said softly.

I couldn't breathe. "I'm going to be a grandfather?"

"Yeah." He sounded like he was wincing.

"Really? You're not screwing with me?"

He chuckled. "No."

"Oh. Oh, shit. Oh—where are you going to—what is your—"

"We, uhm—" He cleared his throat. "—were thinking of moving back to Chicago, if that would be—"

"That would be fantastic! You can stay with me!"

He let out a deep breath. "We really don't want to do that. I mean, I love ya, you know I do, but—"

"I'm pretty sure that there are three available lofts in my building," I rushed out the words. "I mean I know for sure there are two, one on my floor even, but that might be too close, so we could talk to—"

"On your floor would be great." He caught his breath.

"It would?"

"Yeah, it—I mean, I would love to be that close, and Gillian has been madly in love with you since the moment she met you, so I know she'd be thrilled too."

"Are you sure, Jare? You want to move home?"

"Yeah, I really do."

I was getting excited. My son would be back in Chicago, close to me where I could see him whenever I wanted, whenever he wanted, whenever he needed me. "I do too. God, it would be a dream to have you back home, to be close to the baby so he or—"

"She."

"She?" My voice quavered. "A little girl?"

"Yeah."

I felt the tears behind my eyes as I nodded.

"You're cryin', aren't you?"

"Not yet," I managed to get out.

"God, Dad, are you serious? You want us that close to you? I mean right there? You just got rid of me not too long ago."

"Yes." I was smiling so big I knew I was probably glowing.

"Ohmygod, that would be so perfect. That would be… amazing."

"Okay." I was shaking. "Then I'll get to work on it first thing Monday morning and give you a progress report later that day."

I could hear him breathing, but no words were coming.

"Jare? Honey?"

"Jesus, you're just so—" He sucked in air. "—I can always count on you."

"That's what fathers are for, love," I promised him. "You must know that."

"Some fathers, Dad, not all."

"I know you'll be like that. You'll be a wonderful father."

"'Cause I have you to… you…."

"Nate?"

"Gillian." I was surprised my kid was gone but happy to hear her at the same time. "What happened to Jare?"

"He's fine. He's just a little… it's been a weird day, but—" She took a shaky breath herself. "He just needs a minute."

"Okay." I smiled into the phone. "How are you, sweetheart? How do you feel?"

"What," she said, sniffling, and only then did I realize that she was upset, "did you say to Jare? He's all smiling and crying and—"

"Oh, I told him that there's a couple of open lofts in my building, one down the hall from me and one two floors down, because maybe you guys don't want to be quite that close and—"

"No, I'd love to be on the same floor as you."

Amazing. They both liked me. I was doing something right, that was for sure. "Well." I cleared my throat. "I was telling him that first thing Monday morning, I'll call my Realtor and she'll find out who owns them, and we'll get started on purchasing—"

"Ohmygod!" she gasped, cutting me off, squealing. "You're the only one who… my parents just disowned me, and Jare's mother was so…." She inhaled like she could barely breathe. "Nate… it means… oh God!"

"Gillian," I soothed her, "love, your parents will come around. And I know Melissa. You guys just shocked her. She'll be around too, you'll see."

"But you… you were just wonderful right from the start, first words out of your mouth were just—perfect and supportive and let's do this and…." She had to stop, to cry for a second and get herself back under control. "I mean the baby, our baby… this is my child that everyone is angry about, and you, you're actually happy to be a grandfather, aren't you? Like really, completely happy?"

"I'm over the moon," I told her honestly. "I would give you a happy whoop, but that would be in very poor taste at the moment since I'm at a funeral. When are you coming?"

"When can you make arrangements?"

"Sweetheart, you guys can come today. I have room at my place. You know that; you've been here."

"Yes, I have. Some of my favorite holidays are the ones I spent with you and Jare."

"There, see. We can put your things in storage for a couple of weeks and then move it all right in. Don't wait, just show up. Everything will be fine. We'll have a place for you guys certainly well before Christmas."

"Ohmygod!" She squeaked, and there were muffled sounds, and then my boy was back.

"Dad," he said, his voice a throaty whisper.

"Jare," I said back with the same über-serious tone.

His laughter was loud and boisterous, and since I loved it so, I couldn't stop smiling.

"When can we seriously come?"

"Come now, come today, come before Thanksgiving. I was sick that I wouldn't get to see you. I would love it if you could make it. I'll cook a huge turkey."

"I don't know if we can get things together that fast, but we'll so try. I didn't want to be away from you for Thanksgiving either. It doesn't feel like anything special if I'm not with you."

My kid was trying to kill me. "I feel the same exact way."

He sucked in his breath.

"I'll talk to my Realtor like I said, get things rolling on the place, and I'll find Gillian a top OB and have the appointment made when you guys get here if she wants."

Muffled sound again, he had his hand over his cell phone.

"Yeah," he said after a second. "That would ease her mind."

"Okay, good."

He was quiet.

"Jare?"

"I… this is my family now, you know? I mean, how everyone was, they only get one shot at that. I'll remember this for the rest of my life. I may forgive what they said, but I'll never forget it. Not ever."

"Your mother doesn't do change well," I reminded him. "You know that. Give her a second chance, love."

"I don't know if I… this is my baby."

"Please," I pleaded. "One more chance for Mom."

He took another breath. "I love you."

"I love you too," I told him. "Call me."

"Oh I will, very soon."

"Okay."

"Okay." He sighed and hung up.

"Who do you love?"

I looked up and Dreo was there, looking unsure, brows furrowed, eyes cloudy.

"My kid."

He brightened, nodded.

I grabbed his arm and pulled him back behind a crowd of talking people, next to the drapes, before I put a hand on his face.

"My son and the woman he loves, the soon-to-be mother of his child, they're going to need to move in with me for a while, but I don't want you to think that I want this, us, to stop because of—"

"Why're they moving in with you?"

"Because they need a new home until I can find them one."

"Why don't they just move into my place?"

I wasn't sure I had heard him correctly. "I'm sorry?"

"My place," he reiterated, "is right across from your place. Me and Michael could move in with you, and your son and his girl could move into my place. It's nice, just not as nice as yours, but I'll sell it cheap."

It couldn't be that easy. And Jesus, I was not prepared to move in with.... What the hell kind of slow start to a relationship was that? We were just beginning. You didn't move in a minute after you said "ready, set, go." Nothing fell into place like that, not without somersaults and cartwheels and everything else.

"So?"

"Dreo, you don't just—"

"I think you do."

"I think we need to talk about this some more."

I could see the worry. "You don't wanna live with me?"

"No, I do, I mean, maybe I do, I just… this is fast, right?"

"Four years is fast?"

"Dreo, we have not been having a relationship for four years."

"Haven't we?" And he looked honest to God confused.

Was there a chance that what I had thought so little of, he had taken as a foundation? Had we been building something without me knowing? Had we been dancing slowly toward each other since we first met?

I thought about him then, about Dreo Fiore. What had I considered him? When I used to look at him, when I explained who he was to others, what had I said? What had I thought?

Friend? More than friend? What was he to me?

He raked his fingers through his thick hair. "You know, never mind, I was being stupid. You're right, just—forget I said anything. Me and Michael, we'll be waiting until you're ready, whenever that is. And take as long as you want to and don't feel like—"

"No," I cut him off, because there was Dreo, all set to start his whole life over, new job, new plans, and new relationship with me, and if I wasn't ready to dive in…. But why wouldn't I be? Normally, I contorted myself into whatever a new partner wanted, and that was for people who I could just maybe, possibly imagine a future with. But Dreo… at that moment he was all I could see, all I wanted to. What kind of an idiot did I have to be to turn him down?

"Nate?"

I grabbed his hand and squeezed tight. "Move in with me. I want you to."

He shook his head. "No, I got ahead of myself there, and—"

"Please."

"I don't wanna force you."

I arched an eyebrow for him. "You really think you can make me do anything I don't want to? Me?"

He was searching my eyes.

"Dreo?"

He finally chuckled. "Maybe not."

"I just hadn't thought that far down the road. Forgive me."

His face infused with light, and I smiled.

"If it doesn't work out—"

"Fuck that," he cut me off, leaning close, pining me to the wall behind me, hands on my hips, mouth close to my ear. "This is gonna work; I know it is. When you want us to move in?"

"Next week?"

"But starting from now, we're gonna stay with you?" he asked, leaning back, his eyes meeting mine.

It was hopeful, the look I was getting, and I was stunned. Where was all this longing coming from? It was like he had been carrying around feelings and plans and he was ready to unload it on me, cover me, if I would just let him.

"I would love that."

"Are you sure?"

I nodded.

"Everything is new with me, and I just want a chance with you too."

"You have it."

He took a breath. "It won't be easy. My parents just told me that they don't wanna see me for Thanksgiving but that Michael is welcome, and he told them to—"

"Try not to worry about that," I assured him, cutting him off because I didn't need to hear poison when I was on top of the world. "You and Sal are going forward with your business, you're moving in with me, and Michael supports all your decisions. Your parents can feel however they want because, big picture, I'm going to take care of you both. I have a wonderful family that I would love to share with you if you'll let me."

He put his arms around me and held me close, his mouth open on the side of my neck, kissing hard before he sucked on the skin. "I went a little crazy there hearing you tell someone you loved them."

"Why?"

“You know why.”

I sighed deeply. “That’s a very nice thing to say.”

“My plan is to get you to really see me.”

“I already do.”

He gave me a final hug and then stepped back from me. “You’ve made me very happy.”

“Well, that goes both ways,” I assured him.

“We should go,” he told me. “It’s hard to keep my hands off you.”

I smiled wide. “Is it?”

He grunted and reached out and took my hand. It was nice when he squeezed tighter before he let go to walk back across the floor to get Michael. He was done, I could tell from his stride, from the way he moved, the way he barked at his nephew, who perked up immediately, nodded, and, after saying goodbye to his grandparents, started across the floor to me. We were all ready to go home. When Michael reached me, his smile was huge.

“What did Dreo say to you?”

“He said ‘Get your ass over there to Nate, ’cause we’re going home.’”

I put my hand on his cheek. “It was very sweet, what you said to Mrs. Romelli.”

He shrugged and moved so he was standing beside me. “It was no big deal.”

I nodded. “So your uncle said that he’s not welcome for Thanksgiving this year but that you still are.”

He scoffed. “Like I would go anywhere either of you guys wasn’t welcome. Screw that.”

“I hope they come around.”

“I don’t care; I don’t wanna go over there anyway.”

“They’re still your grandparents.”

“If they decide to change their minds, they can come visit you and me and Dreo.”

"What do you mean by that?"

"We're movin' in, right?"

"What?"

"You want him, I know you do. I'm not blind. I can see how you look at him, and I can see how he looks at you."

"How do I look at him?"

"You've got this dopey look on your face, and you're smiling and shit, and he can't seem to look at anything but your ass."

"Michael!"

He cackled. "Shit, he told me this morning that he was gonna ask you to move in with us, but I told him to ask if we could move in with you instead 'cause your place is bigger and nicer."

"He told you this morning?"

He nodded. "He likes you a lot."

"I like him too," I told Michael. "You have to tell me if you have trouble at school, okay? I don't want anyone to hassle you."

"Danielle already knows," he told me. "I mean, she doesn't know about you and Dreo, but she knows about you, and my best friends know too. And my friend Tatum, she's gay, and my friend Garret, he's gay…. Nobody hassles them; it ain't like that at my school. Dreo pays like a small fortune to send me, ya know?"

"Well, I just want to make sure you're okay."

"Was your son okay about you being gay?"

"He was," I told him. "But he had great friends."

"So do I," he assured me, his smile wide.

"You should tell them that you value them."

He scoffed. "Yeah, right."

Boys.

ELEVEN

IT WAS after three when we got home, and the day that had started out dark and cold and gray got darker and more charcoal, and the sky just opened up and dumped down rain. I sent Dreo and Michael back to their apartment to change and was making sandwiches for them when my front door was flung open and Melissa charged through it.

"I'm going to kill you!" she roared.

"But I'm making sandwiches." I sighed, making a sad face for her.

She growled and stomped across the room, driving her purse down into my counter, tearing her trench coat off and hurling it at my couch.

I tried not to snicker too loudly.

"He's too young!"

"And you would have them do what?"

"Nate!"

I lifted my shoulders. "Love, I'm just saying, the ship has sailed, you know? I would have preferred they waited as well. He's not the same twenty-seven that either of us was. I mean, hell, I think we were both more mature at eighteen and seventeen than he is now, but really, what are you going to do?"

Arms crossed, scowling, she was standing next to the opening into my kitchen when the door opened again and Ben and Dreo and Michael came through it.

"I just…." She caught her breath. "You always look better than I do because you think first and then you talk, and I really hate it!"

I smiled at her. "Love."

"No!" she snapped as I moved over to her. "When we were married, I could count on you to make sure I didn't put my foot in my mouth!"

Gently, slowly, I put a hand in her thick, blonde hair and pushed it out of her face.

"And now he hates me!"

"He doesn't hate you," I assured her, sliding my arm around her shoulders. "He loves you; he's just hurt that you weren't excited."

She turned to look at me. "I was excited. I just think he's too young!"

"Which he is." I smiled wider, taking her into my arms as the floodgates opened and she began to sob.

She was shuddering in my arms, crying all over me (the woman was not a delicate, movie-star heroine crier), when the three men, her husband and the two staying with me, joined us.

"Ben," I said brightly over his wife's howling, "did you meet Dreo and Michael?"

He nodded. "I did, outside."

Dreo looked concerned, Michael confused.

"Maybe we should call him now, huh?" I offered my distraught ex-wife.

The frantic nodding made me smile.

She ended up hiccupping and, as she calmed down, was very pleased to meet Dreo and Michael. Even though she looked like someone had punched her in the face, really not a pretty sight, both men were enchanted with her. I put Jared on speakerphone when I called him back.

"Dad?"

"Tell your mother you love her because she's sorry already."

He started chuckling. "Shit, Mom, that was fast."

She took a shuddering breath. "I just think you're too young. I never said I didn't want a grandbaby!"

"Oh for crissakes, woman, don't cry. I know you love me and Gill and the baby. And you might have to help me make lease payments on the loft Dad's putting us in, so just quit already."

It sounded like both of them, mother and son, had experienced a reality check. She realized there was no changing what was, and he realized that his mother had been surprised only, nothing more judgmental than that.

"You still love me?" Melissa whimpered.

"Dad!" Jared yelled for me, wanting me to make her stop. It went that way. She crumbled; he looked to me to fix it.

I was laughing and she was crying again, and he was swearing because, goddammit, when had he ever said that didn't love his mother, before Gillian got on the phone and Melissa started gushing.

"I'm so sorry," she told the mother of her son's child.

"Oh Mel, it's okay."

"When are you two getting married?"

"Oh." Gillian sucked in her breath.

"Oh for the love of God, what did you say now?" Jared was back on the phone, and I asked when he was planning to make an honest woman of his girlfriend.

"Dad!"

I noticed then that Dreo was smiling. "What?"

He nodded. "You have a nice family, Nate. Really nice."

I shrugged. "They're all nuts. Wait'll you meet my mother."

Mel looked over at Dreo and nodded. "Oh, I so wasn't upset about letting that relationship go. Good luck with that."

"Mom, are you talking about Nana?" Jared cackled on the other end of the line.

"What? No!"

"Dad!"

Ben talked to Jared then, and told him we'd all be there, ready, willing, and able to help them both. Jared appreciated it, told us all he loved us, said they'd be there in a week, and hung up. Melissa grabbed me again, and I squeezed her really tight.

"You see what we did there," I said, hands smoothing her hair out of her face, wiping tears away with my thumbs. "We distinguished ourselves from Gillian's folks forever. They're moving here, not to Connecticut."

Her eyes got huge. "Ohmygod, that's right."

I nodded, smiling smugly. "We got the grandkid."

Her smile lit up her face.

"High five." I grinned at her.

She lifted her hand to hit mine and was beaming a second later before she took direction and left to wash her face in my bathroom.

"I hate it that she only listens to you," Ben grunted, eying my sandwich.

"Do you want one?"

He smiled at me. "Since you're asking, yes, please."

We were all eating when she came back, and she moved over next to me and picked up the untouched other half of my sandwich off my plate without asking.

"Who are you?" she asked Dreo.

"Andreo Fiore, and this is my nephew, Michael," he introduced himself.

She smiled around the sandwich she was eating. "You live across the hall?"

"*Sì*, your son is going to move into my loft."

"And you'll move where, Andreo?"

"Dreo."

She nodded, one eyebrow lifting evilly. "Dreo."

"Here," he told her. "Michael's getting the guest room; I'm sleeping with your ex."

Her lips curved as she turned to look at me before nudging me with her elbow. “You’ve been holding out on me.”

“No, this is new.”

She waggled her eyebrows. “Me likey.”

I groaned, and she laughed, and Ben sighed deeply as we all turned to him.

“What?” she asked her husband, the sound muffled because she was talking with her mouth full.

“You’re exhausting.”

“So what?”

Only then did it dawn on me that she’d eaten half my sandwich and I was starving.

I could tell that Dreo and Michael were both absolutely enchanted with Melissa Ortiz. But I understood: she was an easy woman to love.

“Why did you shave?”

I turned to look at her as she straightened up, picked up my beer glass, and took a long swig. “I dunno.”

Her eyes narrowed. “I think you thought, he’s so young, and I’m old, but if I look younger, if I shave off the beard, people won’t think I’m robbing the cradle.”

“He’s not old,” Dreo told her.

“Oh, honey, you’re preaching to the choir.” She shrugged before returning her eyes to mine. “And while it is nice to see the hot dimples again, you can let the beard grow back and people will still think you and pretty boy here belong together.”

There was throat clearing.

We all turned to Dreo.

“I’m not,” he assured her, “pretty.”

One of her perfectly shaped golden brows rose. “Maybe you need to go look in the mirror, Mr. Fiore.”

“I’m considered kind of scary, you know.”

“By who? My husband’s scarier than you are.”

“What is that supposed to mean?” Ben asked her.

She just shrugged.

Ben and Michael took up residence on my couch to watch *SportsCenter* on ESPN, catching up on the all the college football that had been played that day, the scores and highlights captivating them both. Later, poor Dreo was grilled by the woman he found so charming, answering question after question she fired at him as they sat together at the kitchen table drinking oolong tea, which apparently they both liked. The buzzer that connected to the outside security door went off a couple of hours later, and when I asked who it was, a familiar growl answered me back.

"I need to talk to you," Duncan said.

"I'll be right down," I told him and cut him off before he could argue.

I went out in jeans and a T-shirt, socks, and a fleece hoodie, all of which I had changed into when I got home. Opening the security door, I found him safe out of the rain in the small foyer where the mailboxes were.

"Come in." I smiled, holding the door so he could slip by me. When I turned, I was surprised how close he was to me, and took a step back. "You're working on the weekend."

He looked me up and down but said nothing.

"How may I help you, Detective?"

"Can we go up?" he asked, taking a step closer to me even as I took one back.

"No. I've got company, and you've got news about something, right?"

He nodded, walking around me to take a seat on the couch that was in the lobby. "Come here."

I joined him, taking a seat in the chair across from him, not beside him, and waited.

"What the fuck, Nate?"

I blinked. "What?"

"You can't even stand to sit close to me?"

"Duncan, why are you here?"

He took a breath. "I've never seen you without the beard. You look great."

"Thank you." I forced a smile. "Did you guys find out something about my hit man?"

"No." He took a breath. "The organized crime guys aren't buying that the shooter was there for Fiore. It makes no sense."

"But it makes no sense that he wanted to kill me, either."

"Unless he wasn't there for you or Fiore."

But who else was… Michael. My eyes met his. "You guys think that the hit man was there to hurt Dreo's nephew?"

"We're exploring all the possibilities, but the fact is that the kid spent a lot of time with you and—"

"How do you know that?"

"We interviewed people in the building."

I nodded.

"So if someone was trying to get to Fiore—to hurt him—they might have gone through his nephew or…."

I knew what he was fishing for. "Sure," I agreed, instead of telling him more than he needed to know. "So is Michael safe, or—"

"He's safe as long as that was the only guy someone sends."

"But why would they? I mean, Dreo's out of that business now, so I wouldn't expect to see anyone else."

"Oh? How do you know that?"

I took a breath. "Because he and his nephew are moving in with me, so I kind of have to know what's going on with him."

"I'm sorry, what?"

I stood up, shoving my hands into the big pocket at the front of the hoodie. "Duncan, I don't want to have a whole thing. We don't need to, and we're so past the time that it should matter to either one of us. You have your life, I have mine, we're done."

He stared at me, and after a minute, I started toward the elevator.

"Nate!"

I stopped and turned and waited while he caught up to me.

"How are you just so ready to let this be over?"

"Because it's been over for a year and a half already." I sighed deeply. "What happened?"

"What do you mean?"

"I mean something changed to remind you of us, and that's why you care all of a sudden."

"Oh for fuck's sake, Nate, I always cared." He smiled suddenly, his dark-gray eyes glinting. "I didn't want anything to change."

"Duncan, you're in the closet. I'm not. I need a partner in every sense of the word. You can't be that guy, and I'm so sorry, but when we broke up, I worked through things and realized what I wanted."

He frowned. "You could have made it work."

And it was so true that for a moment, I was dumbstruck, because God, who knew that Melissa Ortiz was the damn Oracle at Delphi? Hadn't she said almost the exact thing? Because if I put my heart and soul into something, I could make anything work. But it took concentrated effort, and instead of doing that, I had given up on Duncan Stiel.

"Nate?"

My head snapped back, and I looked at him.

"You didn't want to put in the work to make us happen."

It was true. I had been so captivated by Duncan, so enamored, so infatuated, that I let his life drown mine for two years. I went along, and when I got tired of it, tired of it just being easy and comfortable and convenient but not love, I ended it. And that was why I had the man in my lobby looking at me like there were still places for us to go. I had let him believe that he was my whole world, let him be everything, and then one day just stopped loving him and walked away. It was something I did, something I had always done—poured on the charm, made myself into the ideal partner, lover, friend, indispensable and irreplaceable, and then, when I got bored or tired or tapped out, instead of fighting, I just quit. It was wildly unfair, and the only people I didn't do it with were my family. Even my friends complained that I was always around and then just gone. The only reason I was constant with Ben was because he was attached to Mel and she was, even though she was my ex-wife, still my family.

"Nate?"

"Jesus, Duncan, I'm sorry," I told him, reaching out, putting a hand on his bicep. "I'm really so sorry. I don't know why I… and with us, I mean—I saw things weren't going to change, but I just gave you the ultimatum that I knew you couldn't change, and then when you said that was it, I just let you walk out."

He was staring at me, and I saw all the pain there and felt even worse.

"That was my scene, my ending, and I blamed you," I told him as he put his hands on my face, tipping my head up as he stepped close to me. "God, I'm so sorry. I let you believe that what we had, what we were doing, was enough and then one day just pulled the rug out from under you and told you it wasn't. Forgive me, please."

He took a breath and bent toward me at the same time I eased free and stepped back.

"Nate?"

I shook my head. "The fact remains that we're in two completely different places in our lives. And now, finally, I'm ready to take the leap, the big one, the real one, and not run and not turn myself inside out and make myself into something I'm not." There were no tricks needed, no midair trapeze work, no acrobatics without a net to impress and keep Dreo Fiore. I could do it without theatrics, with just me and my heart. "You need to find a guy who can live with what you can give him, and that's not me."

"I want you back," he said softly, reaching for me again.

I moved further away, too far for him to touch. "I need more than you can do, Duncan, and the time where we could have maybe worked at it is over. You know that."

The muscles in his jaw were clenching.

"You went from having what resembled a home life with me to screwing guys in bathhouses again, so I totally get that you're grieving for that piece that we had. You don't wanna do the nameless, faceless fucking anymore," I advised. "I understand it, but don't confuse the little life we were sharing with the big romantic Hollywood blockbuster that you could have."

He let out a quick breath, and suddenly he was smiling.

"Move, start a life, get out of Chicago. There's nothing keeping you here. Go and find a place where you can be a cop and come home every night to the guy of your dreams. It's not me, and you know that just as well as I do, but it was as close to good as it's ever been for you when you were with me, so that's where this is all getting screwed up in your head."

Long, heavy sigh as he looked at me with his gorgeous charcoal eyes.

"If I had loved you more than I loved myself, I wouldn't have been able to let you walk away. If you loved me more than yourself, you would have never left," I clarified for him.

His eyes locked on mine for long moments before he turned away. He didn't look back, didn't turn around before he went out the door. Before, when he had gone, I had always thought that our paths would cross again. This time the parting felt permanent. We were two very different people, and it hurt and it was sad, but both of us made sense, which was why neither of us could give in. I couldn't thrive in his world; he couldn't be himself in mine.

When I got back upstairs, I slipped in and realized that no one had even noticed I was gone. Walking to my bedroom, I sat down on my bed and stared outside at the pouring rain.

"Hey."

I turned toward the door, and there was Dreo, leaning on the doorframe.

"You were talking to that detective for a long time downstairs."

"How did you know?"

He levered off the frame and crossed the floor toward me. "I went to check on you and saw you guys talking. Melissa filled me in on him when I got back. She recognized his SUV parked outside."

"Oh."

"So, what?"

I shook my head. "Nothing, just same old stuff."

He nodded, reaching me and sitting down beside me. "So what did he want?"

"Just to talk about the hit man on the fire escape."

"And?"

"Nothing else. They just still don't think he was there for you."

"That makes no sense."

I shrugged.

"Then who?"

"Maybe Michael."

"Michael?" he echoed.

"Yes. They think the hit man might have been after someone close to you."

"As a warning?"

"Maybe."

"A warning for what?"

"I don't think they know, or Duncan would have told me."

"So then it could have been you," he suggested.

"But no one knew you thought I was pretty," I teased.

His eyes were hot and wet. "Anyone who really knows me, knew."

"Yeah?"

His eyes searched mine. "Yes."

"I like that," I murmured.

There was a quick shrug of his broad shoulders. "Except that obviously someone was paying better attention than I thought, and I don't want you hurt."

"But like I told Duncan, there's no reason for any of it now."

"Unless the point is to just hurt me by hurting you or Michael."

"Who would do that? How is that logical now?"

"It's not anymore."

"So we have nothing to worry about," I said before wondering, "I wonder if anyone went after anyone that Sal cares about?"

"I dunno. He never said anything, and when I told him that day after you left, told him and Tony, neither one of them remembered seeing anybody around."

I thought about that for a moment. "That's strange, right? Why you and not Tony? Why you and not Sal?"

"And why after Mr. Romelli was killed? It would make more sense before he died to threaten us or him."

"None of this makes any sense."

He smiled. "So what are you thinking?"

"I just wonder, maybe someone wanted to hurt just you?"

"Like who?"

I turned to look at him. "I don't know. Maybe Mr. Romelli's son?"

"Joey?"

"Why not? He hates you, he hates the fact that you told his father you were gay… it makes sense that it would be him."

"Nate—"

"He was horrible today. The things he said to you were obscene."

"Yeah, but you don't think that's a huge jump from hating that I'm gay to sending someone to kill you or Michael?"

"Putting out a hit on you, you mean?"

"Oh, look at you sounding all made man over here."

I bumped him with my shoulder. "I'm worried. It doesn't make sense, and I hate things that make no sense."

He nodded. "So, your ex, huh?"

"Yeah."

"And all he wanted you for was to talk about the hit man?"

I turned to look at him. "There was a little more."

"How much more?"

"I promise it's not important."

His eyes searched mine.

"Tell me what you're thinking," I requested.

"Okay, what are you doing with him?"

"I'm not doing anything with him," I said, smiling at the man I was planning on being around. "I'm doing everything with you, Mr. Fiore, if that's what you want."

He took my hand in his, and as I stared down at our entwined fingers, I noticed, as I had on many occasions, how strong they were. The veins that ran from his fingers, corded wrists, and sinewy forearms—the man was powerful everywhere but able to be gentle at the same time.

"What are you thinking?"

I smiled before I lifted my head to look into the deep, dark brown eyes. "That you're just gorgeous all over."

His grin was wicked as he reached over and slid his knuckles up the column of my throat. It was so nice to be petted; I let my eyes flutter shut to savor the feeling of his skin stroking over mine.

"Here's the thing, I want us to do this for real. I wanna be here, and I want you all in, 100 percent. Mel says I have to demand it if I really want you."

My eyes drifted open. "Is that what she said?"

"Yeah."

"Well, I can suddenly see my life with you in it, Mr. Fiore, so all the tricks I've done in the past to impress people, I'm going to give that up and concentrate my efforts on making this work."

He leaned close, kissing me softly, tenderly, sucking at my bottom lip just enough to send a throb of heat through my body. "Don't stop doing all your tricks… *tesoro*… I have many positions I plan to put you in."

I chuckled, my eyes drifting closed again as I parted my lips for his kiss.

"You submit to me so beautifully," he whispered before he claimed my mouth.

The kiss was drugging, and he tasted and explored, licking, nibbling, biting, making sure he missed nothing as he pressed me back down onto the bed.

"Nate," he gasped, panting for breath as he lifted off me, his mouth still hovering over mine. "You have to tell me if you want my ass."

I chuckled. "Crudely put, Fiore."

"But you got my point." He smiled back.

I licked my lips and saw the ripple in the corded muscles in his neck, heard the low sound in his chest, and watched his eyes narrow. The thrill of being desired was almost too much to bear. "If you want that, I'll do it for you. But if not, then submitting to you… that's so good."

He looked like he was in pain. "Is it?"

"It's—we all have what we like best."

"Yes, we do," he agreed, his lips hovering over mine. "I'm gonna kiss you before we go back out there."

"Please," I whispered.

And he bent and took me in his arms.

TWELVE

I WAS surprised when I showed up at the Four Seasons hotel the following day that Sanderson was actually stunned to see me.

"You actually thought I wasn't going to show." I rolled my eyes.

"Yes. To make me look bad. I see no end to your machinations."

Who had that kind of time? "Where are we going?" I asked, the irritation filling my voice.

"We're supposed to go to the front desk and have the hotel catering manager paged. She will be with Greg Butler's event coordinator."

I lifted my hand like I would follow him. Halfway there, I heard my name called. Turning, I saw Gregory Butler and at least twelve other people walking toward me.

He looked the same as he had five years ago, when he was in my class.

"What're you, like, all of twenty-five?" I called over to him.

"Twenty-six, actually." He smiled, stopping close, extending his hand. "It's really good to see you, Dr. Qells."

Same brown hair, same blue eyes, same ordinary, handsome, all-American goodness face. Even the freckles across the bridge of his nose added to the apple pie image. I took the hand and squinted. "Tell Professor Vaughn here that I didn't put you up to this."

He squeezed my hand tight, not letting go as he turned to Sanderson. "I took over from my father just this year, Professor, and when I did, I got control of all the charitable dollars at my company's disposal. I'm building a homeless shelter downtown in March of next year, and we made a lot of other donations, but on top of my list was my alma mater, even though I barely made it out."

I grunted as he finally released my hand.

His smile was huge. "Dr. Qells took me in his office one day and told me that if I didn't do some work damn soon he was going to flunk my lazy ass."

Listening to everyone gasp at once was fun. I scoffed; Gregory's smile lit his eyes.

"I reported him to the dean," he told the entourage and Sanderson while he kept his gaze locked with mine. "And the dean told me that I must have misheard, because that kind of behavior was completely foreign to Dr. Qells."

I waggled my eyebrows for him.

He nodded, tipping his head to the side. "When I went back to class the next day, I asked Dr. Qells if he knew who my father was, and he told me that the only use he had for my father was if he knew anything more about Milton than I did so maybe he could tutor me."

I laughed softly at the memory.

"God, I hated you." He shook his head.

"You weren't my favorite either." I snickered. "If we're keeping score."

His sigh was heavy. "First time anyone ever stood up to me, told me where to go, and gave me an ultimatum. I had no idea I could be treated like everybody else."

I grinned.

"I never worked so hard in my life."

"It was strong C at the end," I told him.

"It was a bitch to get," he told me.

"But it was earned," I assured him. "If you hadn't screwed around at the beginning, you probably would have gotten an A. You had quite the grasp of Chaucer especially."

He reached out and took hold of my shoulder. "Walk with me."

The hotel was beautiful, the atrium, the chandeliers, the marble floors, the staircases—and the grand ballroom where the feast would be held was breathtaking. There, waiting for us, was Katherine Abrams, Greg's fiancée.

"Oh, Dr. Qells." Her smile was dazzling, as was she. "Such a pleasure to meet the man who made such a difference in Greg's life."

"I had no idea I had." I smiled back.

She took my arm after we shook hands, holding on. "You did. He always tells me it was you. His father will be here the night of the party, and he'd like a word as well."

"Of course." I patted her hand in the crook of my arm.

"You see"—Greg was smiling—"I was going to be a trust fund baby or what I am now. Everybody likes the after, Dr. Qells. Before you, I guess I was kind of a malcontent."

"You were a slacker."

"I am better now for having known you."

I chuckled. "Who knew I was a saint?"

"You're an ass," Greg assured me.

"Greg!"

"Oh, he is." He made a face at Kate. "And he knows it."

"I am," I agreed with him, grinning at her. "I know it. Ask Sanderson."

"Who?"

I pointed behind me, and the introductions began. The thing was, she didn't care. She had absolutely no interest in Sanderson Vaughn at all, and she was one of those women who was insanely sweet and proper, but still, you knew it. She really cared about finding out if I was bringing anyone with me to the party.

"My boyfriend, Dreo," I told her, and I couldn't help beaming because the sound of it, *my boyfriend*, was really nice.

"Oh," she whimpered. "I can't wait to meet him."

And she really couldn't. Both she and Greg walked me over to the event coordinator. It was nice, Kate sitting beside me, Greg leaning, hand on my shoulder the whole time. Who knew he really liked me that much?

As I was leaving, after an amazing lunch with Greg and Kate and Daniel Kramer, whom I had met that day in the dean's office, and Sophia Petrovich, Greg's event coordinator, Greg actually wanted to hug me. Kate found it enough to tear up over, and I hugged her too. I told them all that I had no doubt that this year the Medieval Feast would be something no one at the College of the Humanities had ever dreamed it would be. They were all happy to hear it. Before I could make a clean getaway afterward, though, Sanderson called my name.

"God, what?" I grumbled, looking, I was certain, as pained as I felt.

"Must you be such a colossal prick all the time?"

"Yes, I must," I assured him, "especially to you."

He growled. "Are you going to e-mail Ms. Petrovich with the list or—"

"I already e-mailed Gwen, and she'll take care of it when she gets into the office tomorrow," I told him, turning to go.

He stepped in front of me.

I threw up my hands.

"Do you have any idea what it's like to be in that department with you?"

I crossed my arms and waited.

"Everybody loves you. The students think you walk on water. The faculty—I mean, those that don't really know you—still respect your scholarly accomplishments. But what gets me the most is the women. I don't get that at all."

I huffed. "I have no idea where you're going with this."

"Oh, I know," he said, so very annoyed. "Every woman that meets you is just smitten, and you're gay, so what the hell."

"You shouldn't care about women at the university," I told him. "You shouldn't shit where you eat, Sanderson."

He stared at me.

"Bye," I said, and I left him sputtering in front of the Four Seasons.

As I walked toward the train station, I thought about what he had said. If he knew that every relationship I had with my colleagues, had been worked on and cultivated, his thinking about me would change. It looked easy to him because most of those friendships had been cemented years before he showed up. The difference was that he was a jerk. And not just to me. In his race for tenure, he came off like a brown-nosing prick, and he had alienated more than half his fellow professors with his one-upmanship. No one wanted to coauthor papers with him to help with his publishing credentials, no one wanted to go to conferences with him and present papers, and his teaching evaluations all stunk. I knew they did because the kids made sure to show them to me. Even if I said no, I still got them e-mailed to me, or stuffed under my office door, or slid between pages of my books. They knew it made me crazy, so they went out of their way to plague me with them. The affection was there in the harassment, and I was sure that Sanderson got none of that. He was so far from getting what he wanted, and he had no idea.

He overloaded the few grad students who had made the mistake of working for him, and had overpromised and underdelivered almost from day one. It was not that I was so great; he was just so universally loathed by professors and students alike that to him it appeared that way. There was a small part of me that felt bad for him, but it got squashed down a little more each day by his negativity and hubris.

Since I was thinking about Sanderson, I didn't notice the man on my right until I turned the corner, heading for the raised platform. I had decided to take the L since I still had things to pick up for dinner. But I was stopped by a hand on my chest, and a stranger was there, in my face, so close. We could have kissed.

I couldn't catch my breath suddenly, and I had no idea why.

"Dr. Qells," he whispered as my knees went weak.

I looked down my body and saw his hand on the hilt of the knife that had been buried in my abdomen.

He had shoved it through my peacoat, thick cable-knit sweater, and T-shirt before it punctured my skin. I felt the heat as he twisted it and tore it free. I crumpled down hard onto the sidewalk, the sky a giant raincloud ready to burst above me.

"Tell Dreo Fiore that Joey Romelli sends his regards."

I had no voice, and I barely heard him over my own heartbeat, suddenly so loud in my ears. I felt like I was drowning even before it started to drizzle. I was so hot, I wanted to tear off my peacoat, but everything, my whole body, was limp.

He spit on me, on my chest, and then I watched him, as I lay on my side, get into a car before it was gone.

"Jesus, Nate, what the fuck?"

And of course it was Sanderson Vaughn who was there, which was just the cherry on the cake of my day.

He pulled off his scarf, wadded it up, and pressed it to my diaphragm as he had his cell phone to his ear. I watched him, never having realized before that he had a dimple in his chin, that his nose was small and upturned, or even that his eyes were a pale China blue.

"Not," I gasped, "going to be nice to you."

"I know." He nodded even as he talked on his phone, barked out the address, and yelled at whoever was on the other end to hurry the hell up.

"Charming." I smiled up at him, noticing that it was getting harder to see him. "You have to start being nicer, gentler. Not such a prick. Sugar… not vinegar."

"Okay," he agreed, placating me, his phone hitting my chest as it fell from his ear, both hands now on the scarf on my abdomen.

"Stop pushing," I ordered him. "It hurts."

"I'm sure it does."

"Your eyes are kind of pretty."

"I will remind you that you said that." He took a breath and bit his lower lip.

And I thought that for a guy who hated me, he looked sort of concerned. When he yelled my name, I wanted to tell him to stop, but nothing worked, not even my eyes.

THE whispering woke me. It took a minute of focusing, but finally the room took shape, and then the lovely face looking down at me solidified so I could see who it was.

"Nate," she gasped, and I smiled up at Melissa.

"Oh, thank God." Her eyes welled fast, and there were tears running down her cheeks seconds later.

"Hey," I managed to get out, my voice a gravelly whisper. "What's going on?"

She was shaking, and I felt her squeezing my hand then, so tight in hers.

"Mel?"

She cleared her throat. "Somebody stabbed you."

"Yeah, I know."

"So you know, since I'm the emergency contact on the back of your license, they called me."

"Oh shit, I'm sorry."

"No!" she snapped. "Thank God you never changed it, and don't ever do it in the future. I always want to be first."

"That's not even reasonable." I chuckled, but there was suddenly so much pressure that I froze, having to suck in my breath.

"Yeah, don't do that, don't laugh. Just lie there, okay?"

"It doesn't hurt exactly," I told her, looking down but only seeing blanket. "Can you lift this up so I can see?"

"No." She scowled. "There's nothing to see. There's a bandage over a stitched-up wound. You're going to have one hell of a scar."

"Awesome." I grinned.

"I'm going to beat you when you're well," she gasped before her voice cracked and she started to sob, facedown on my forearm.

Oh crap. I had scared her. "Honey," I soothed her, trying to pull my hand away so I could touch her head.

"Just lay there!" she roared, sitting up straight.

"Yes, ma'am," I said softly.

She cried, and I was still and quiet, and when I finally told her I was thirsty, she got me some ice water to sip.

"What happened?" I asked her.

"You know what happened."

"I mean after."

She sniffled, letting my hand go so she could blow her nose, brush her hair back from her face, and wipe at her wet cheeks with a tissue. She was adorable with her red nose and puffy eyes, her breathing finally under control. "The man who did it, he just left you in the street, and I know you hate that guy Sanderson, but I'm sending him a fruit basket and flowers and whatever else he wants for a week. He wants to get laid, the escort is on me."

"Gross," I grumbled, squirming to sit up.

"Don't move or you'll tear your stitches!"

I grunted. "So when can I go home?"

"Tomorrow or the next day. They have to make sure there's no infection and make sure the antibiotics work and that your insides are okay."

"The guy who did this," I told her, "he wasn't trying to scare me. He was trying to scare Dreo."

She nodded. "I know. You were saying that when they brought you in. You were talking about Dreo."

"Where is he? Is he here?"

"He was here earlier, but he left."

"Oh." I was disappointed.

"He stayed until we all knew you were going to be fine. He promised to be back later."

I squinted at her. "What?"

She sighed deeply. "He left, and right after that, Duncan did."

"Duncan was here?"

"Oh yeah."

I didn't like the sound of that. "Mel?"

She stood up and started pacing. "Jesus, Nate, it was a mess. I got here and the police were here, and it looked like Duncan and Dreo went at it and beat the shit out of each other. Dreo was bleeding, Duncan broke his own wrist when he hit Dreo… I mean, do they both know what's going on with you?"

"How do you mean?"

"I mean, who do you love?"

Jesus, what kind of question was that? "I just woke up from being stabbed!" I rasped.

"Nathan James Qells! Who do you love?"

"Mel—"

"Just answer the—"

"I'm hurt and—"

"Nate! Who do you love?"

"I—Dreo!"

Silence.

I looked at her.

She stared back with huge eyes.

"Shit."

Her smile spilt her face. "Really?"

"I… shit."

Her laughter was warm and rich and bubbling with happiness. "Ohmygod, Nate!"

Leave it to her to extract the truth.

"Oh honey, finally. You're finally in love."

How in the world it had happened so fast I had no idea, but I was just… blindsided.

"I'm going to call him and tell him to get his ass back here right now."

I nodded. "Yeah, tell him that," I said as a monitor started to sound.

"Nate?"

She was blurring suddenly. "Call the OB, Mel, and the Realtor. Don't forget, Jare needs a status update, okay? Tomorrow. You have to make those calls."

"Nate!"

Her face, the way it contorted, I knew she was screaming, I just couldn't hear it. And then everything faded to nothing.

I ROLLED my head, and there was a stunning woman sitting at my bedside. I knew who she was, it just made no sense. Maybe I was still asleep.

She smiled.

I decided to speak to my hallucination. "Mrs. Fiore."

Her smile was really something. It changed her face from cold, hard matriarch to gorgeous Hollywood icon. I understood that her son had inherited the transformative power of a simple smile from his mother. Her eyes were just absolutely pools of warm chocolate and… oh man, I was stoned.

"Hi." I smiled at her.

"*Buonasera*," she greeted me.

"Oh, I love that song," I told her, laughing softly, unable not to.

Her brows lifted. "I do too."

I cleared my throat. "Where is everyone?"

"They had to eat. My son, my grandson, his girlfriend Danielle, that woman—yours—she is… *bellissima*." She smiled.

"Yes, she is," I agreed, knowing we were talking about Melissa.

"Her husband is very handsome as well. They are lovely together."

I nodded.

"But they have to eat. My husband, he took them, he knows a place close to here."

"And you stayed with me?"

"*Sì*."

"Why?"

"Because, Nathan—may I call you Nathan?"

"Yes, ma'am."

She leaned forward. "You see, Nathan, I have lost one of my daughters already. Michael's mother. You know about this."

"Yes."

"So I will not lose my son."

I just stared at her and waited.

"My son," she told me, "is stubborn. He has always been this way. He makes his mind up and acts. I said, I know your sister wants you to be the one to raise Michael, but she never meant for you to do it alone, *ragazzo*. Move home, I said."

Her hair, her eyes: really, really beautiful woman.

"But no, Dreo, he goes to see his friend Sal instead and takes a job working for the worst kind of man, a man my father would have forbade him from even speaking to."

"Is your father still alive?"

"No, he died shortly after I moved here from Palermo."

"I'm sorry."

"It was a long time ago."

I smiled as she lifted a cup of water off the table for me, angling the straw to my lips so I could drink.

"It was beautiful there, in Palermo. I still miss it."

"When did you move here to Chicago?"

"I met Mr. Fiore on holiday in Rome. My father, he didn't like Anthony, but me, I liked him." She grinned wickedly, her eyes shining.

"It was a love affair."

"*Sì*," she agreed, sighing deeply. "Still is, so I came with him to America."

I was enjoying listening to her talk even though I did need to find out things. Like the date, for starters.

"I have been in Chicago many years, and Dreo's father and I have raised a family, and I was always very happy, but… when my daughter died, I would have followed her into the grave if not for the others, my daughters—I have three—and Dreo, and especially for Michael, her son."

"He's a great kid."

"*Sì*, but you know this more than I, as you are the one Michael loves. You are the parent he chose after his mother passed."

"Dreo's his parent."

"Dreo is more like a big brother than a parent. I can see this for myself."

"What happened to his father?" I said to try to change the subject.

"His father is from a rich family. He left Mona as soon as he knew she was pregnant."

"What a dick," I said without thinking, because the stop block between *think it* and *say it* was not working at present. Whatever was dripping into my veins from the IV hanging above me was fabulous.

"I agree." She laughed. "And you are qualified to say, Nathan, as I have recently learned that when you got a woman pregnant you married her even though you are gay."

I grunted.

"You are a good man to put your own needs behind those of your child. One cannot help but be impressed with you."

"Oh yeah?" I beamed up at her.

Her hand slid over my cheek as she looked down at me. "*Sì*."

"So you, uhm, like me?"

The soft laughter was even better than the smile. "I do, and though I do not understand my son loving a man, I cannot fault his choice."

Loving?

I coughed and hacked, and as she patted my knee and gave me more water, I heard the lilting words but didn't understand.

"*Caro*," she soothed, "rest. You love him, my son. I know you do."

"How do you know?" I asked when I could breathe, sipping the water, breathing hard.

"Because you were the one who figured out that Joey Romelli was trying to hurt Dreo by killing you. It makes sense to me. You don't hurt the man; you make him suffer by taking away that which he lives for. This is how a vendetta begins. But it doesn't end with you dead, because Dreo would make sure that it didn't. And then what? Then Joey comes after my Michael next? No no no, it's good that you are so smart and you figured it out. Dreo is lucky to have you."

I was so lost.

"Go back to sleep, rest. You need your strength."

"Will you tell them all I was awake?"

"*Sì.*"

It was so weird. I should have asked a million questions, but I could not for the life of me. I could only close my eyes again.

"Are you going to let Dreo come over for Thanksgiving?" I asked, even as my eyes dipped closed.

"Yes, and you too, Nathan Qells."

God, how long had I been out?

IT WAS dark when I opened my eyes, but enough light was coming in around the drawn curtain for me to see the room. Enough so that I could see Dreo Fiore asleep in a very uncomfortable-looking chair beside my bed. He was in jeans and a sweat jacket under a black leather motorcycle jacket. The beanie on his head was very cute; the stubble on his cheeks, above his lip, was hot. There were curls sticking out from under the cap, and his socked feet were on the edge of my bed. The man was a vision of exhaustion and hunky male animal. My heart hurt just looking at him.

"Baby," I said instead of his name, and I caught my breath and prayed he hadn't heard it. I needed to let him sleep.

He nearly fell out of his chair.

"Nate," he gasped, feet sliding off the bed, his body jerking forward as he stood suddenly, eyes wide and blinking and no more awake than he had been seconds ago.

"Hey." I offered a small smile.

"Oh." His voice broke, and his hands were on my face as he bent and gave me a kiss.

It slammed through me, that simple, amazing, hot kiss that made my entire body clench and twitch all at the same time. He made love to me with his mouth, his tongue rubbing over mine, letting me taste chocolate and clove and him. I felt him tremble, and my cock jerked under the blanket. The roll of desire as I shivered made him smile as he leaned back, our lips parting slowly, with great effort.

"Oh please no," I whimpered, reaching for him. "Kiss me again."

There were tears in his eyes, and I saw then that they were bruised and so was his face.

"What happened?"

He shook his head, more upset than I had ever seen him, even more than he had been after Mr. Romelli's death.

"Who hit you?"

"It doesn't matter." He sighed, straightening up and letting his head fall back in relief. His hands scrubbed his face as he laughed softly.

I remembered something Mel had said. "Oh God, did Duncan hit you?"

"Yeah," he snapped, "and I hit him too, fuckin' sonofabitch."

He was tense and frustrated and angry and… I had just woken up. That was my excuse for being slow.

"You were fighting over me." I chuckled.

"Why is that funny?"

"Well, for starters, because it's stupid. What the hell were you thinking?"

"I was thinking that we were both pissed."

"Why?"

"Because you scared the shit outta me."

The man was a frustrated, grouchy mess. He was adorable. "You were worried about me," I whispered.

"I was more than worried," he growled to the ceiling, still not looking at me. "Fuck."

"Dreo."

He turned his head, dark eyes locked on mine.

"I'm okay, right?"

He nodded.

"And?"

"And nothing."

"Tell me."

"I don't—"

"Dreo!" I said sharply.

"I just got you!" he barked. "What the fuck, Nate? You just gave me a chance and either you were gonna die or ditch me as soon as—"

"Back up," I soothed him. "You thought I was going to die?"

"You got some kind of infection from the fuckin' knife the bastard used! I mean, they finally get the bleeding stopped and get you all sewn up and then suddenly your heart is enlarged with an infection and… and then you're more hurt then they first thought and—"

"But I'm fine now."

"And Michael is freaking out because he lost his mother, right, and he's pissed at me because I brought this on you, and he—"

"But I'm okay."

"And your fuckin' ex is here yelling at me that it's all my fault and I'm gonna get you killed because—"

"Dreo."

"I've never been that scared!" he howled. "Never!"

I stared at him.

"I just got you," he repeated softly.

"I'm okay," I assured him. "Where's Michael?"

He took a breath. "He's outside. Everyone's outside."

"Who's everyone?"

"Fuck, Nate, everyone."

The man really did look terrible. He was wrung out, and as he stood there, his forehead leaning into his hand, trembling, I got that I had really frightened the holy crap out of him.

"Hey."

No movement.

"Andreo."

His head came up slowly.

"I'm not leaving you. Not going to die on you."

He remained silent.

"And we're not breaking up. You can't get rid of me that easy."

The breath he took was shaky. "You called me baby."

I winced. "Yeah, I'm—"

"You told Mel you loved me."

My eyes didn't flit away from him. I was awake and ready.

"Now tell me."

It was time to jump. Nothing ventured, nothing gained. "I love you, Dreo."

"But that's fast, right?" he asked me skeptically, but I knew why.

"Four years is fast?" I threw his words from days before back at him. Or maybe it was weeks. I had no idea how long I'd been in the hospital, but right this second was not the time to contemplate it. Right now was for Dreo.

He smiled just a little.

"It was friendship for a while, and I do worry that it's changed so fast and that I feel this way already, but—"

"How do you feel?" he asked, moving nearer to the bed until he was close enough that I could have reached up and grabbed his hand.

"Like I want to do everything with you." I sighed, reaching for him.

He sat down in the chair beside the bed, took my hand, and leaned his cheek against it.

"Is that what you want?"

"Nothing's different for me, Nate. I made changes in my life for you and Michael. If I was alone, I could do what I was doing forever, move up and live my life in that world, but if I want you two… I had to be free. If I wanted you at my side, Michael to see the kind of man I want him to be, model it for him, how things should be done, then I had to be out." He exhaled and reached for my cheek, sliding his fingers over days of stubble. "You gotta let this grow back in, all right? I love your beard, and it's hot as hell."

I wrinkled my nose. "I don't want you to ever look at me and think I'm too old for you."

"I don't. That's all in your head."

"Okay."

"*Mi sei mancato molto*," he said, his eyes swimming with tears suddenly.

"I missed you too," I told him.

"How do you always know what I'm saying?"

"I speak Dreo."

Lifting up in one fluid motion, he kissed me hard and long, and I whimpered and whined until he started laughing, which brought Mel and Michael and Ben from outside. It was a madhouse after that.

There was a stream of people in to see me for the rest of the day. Friends in every flavor: personal, work, other faculty, the dean, students, Alla and Jen, Ashton and Levi, Danielle and her parents, and even Sean Cooper, who had a look at my chart just to show off. Ashton was not impressed, and his face, like he'd bitten a lemon, made it obvious. Dreo, on the other hand—my grad student thought my new boyfriend was just yummy.

I had to agree.

Chapter THIRTEEN

JIMMY O'MEARA came by my room the following morning and explained all about Oscar Darra, the guy who had stabbed me on the street. It turned out, upon investigation, that Joseph Romelli had felt that killing me would send Dreo a message that he did not make decisions, men like Joey made them for him. The same message had been sent to Tony Strada. His girlfriend, Geneva Moscone, had been grabbed and stuffed in a car, and the whole thing might have ended badly but for the lady herself. Four-inch platform boots, long acrylic nails, and a fighter attitude had sent the car full of four men careening into the side of a building.

"This woman"—Jimmy made his eyes big over the word—"or force of nature, I should say, is kicking the crap out of one of the guys when we got there, swearing in Italian, and spitting on him. They needed like eight guys, or just two that actually knew that they were doing, if they were going to kidnap her."

"She's a tiger, huh?"

"And then some," Jimmy assured me. "The thing was, Joey had one professional left on his payroll, and he sent him after you, Nate. The guys who went after Geneva were just punks. They're lucky she didn't kill 'em."

"I'm so glad she's all right," I told him, sitting back, squeezing Dreo's hand. "I don't even know her and I'm happy."

"Yeah, us too, because when we caught those guys, they all had a lot to say."

"About Joey Romelli," Dreo said.

"Yes." Jimmy nodded, squinting at Dreo. "I understand you've left the life."

"I have."

"And Sal Polo as well."

He nodded.

"That's good. We all knew the two of you were just muscle, but it was smart to get out. I understand they're restructuring. I don't suppose you'd like to tell me who they settled on, Pearl or Strada?"

"I have no idea, Detective," Dreo lied. "Out is out."

He nodded and looked back at me. "So you know, Nate, they found Joey Romelli in his penthouse this morning with a bullet in the back of his head."

"Oh God, poor Mrs. Romelli, to lose her son and her husband in so short a space of time."

"But that's the life, right, Mr. Fiore?"

"Yes, it is."

"And she and two of her daughters were on a plane for Milan this morning," he told us. "I don't suppose you want to hazard a guess who paid for that trip, do you, Mr. Fiore?"

He shook his head.

"I didn't think so."

"When you're out—"

"Yeah, I got it," Jimmy cut him off. "But you gotta know how this looks. Me being here with you. Guys might think you talked to me."

"If I wasn't out before Nate was stabbed," Dreo corrected him. "Which I was. Now the only thing people think is that fuck Romelli tried to kill Dreo Fiore's boyfriend out of spite even though Dreo saved Joey's life."

Jimmy's eyes widened. "Joey Romelli was there in the restaurant that day when his father and the others were killed?"

"Yeah."

"No one told us."

Dreo shrugged. “It didn’t matter then; it barely matters now.”

He turned and looked at me. “You should be careful, Nate. This life may still come and bite you on the ass.”

I opened my mouth to respond.

“Don’t worry, Detective,” Dreo said. “I might not be in anymore, but after this, I got a lot of guardian angels, you know?”

Jimmy sighed heavily. “All right.” He got up then, walked over to me, bent, gave me a hug, and told me to take care of myself.

Dreo told him that I had him to take care of me now.

He rolled his eyes and turned to leave the room but stopped at the door.

“Yes, Detective?” Dreo asked.

“There were some guys that used to hang out close to that park down off Pearson.”

“And?”

“And they said that some of Romelli’s boys came down there and told them not be out there anymore. Do you know anything about that?”

Dreo shook his head. “No, I have no idea.”

He nodded quickly. “You can come down to the precinct any time and collect your property from us, Mr. Fiore.”

“Thank you, Detective.”

He grunted, lifted a hand for me, and was gone.

I turned to look at Dreo. “What property?”

“My gun.”

“Oh,” I said, studying his face.

“*Caro*?”

“You and Sal took care of those guys that hurt me and attacked that woman, didn’t you?”

He shrugged.

“You did that for me.”

His hand slid over my jaw. “I would do anything to keep you safe, *tesoro*. Anyone who tries to hurt you or Michael should think first.”

Yes, they should. Dreo Fiore was not a man to be tested. I smiled up at him. “You cut me off earlier when I was going to answer Jimmy.”

“’Cause you were gonna tell that nice detective that the only thing you knew that would bite you on the ass was me.”

I laughed. “How did you know?”

“I know you, *caro*.”

I lifted for the kiss that he bent to give me.

“Nate!”

We both looked toward the doorway as Melissa came rushing through it, followed by Ben, Michael, and Danielle.

Dreo stepped back as my ex-wife flung herself down into my arms.

“Shit,” I groaned, because when I was not all whacked out on drugs, that hurt a little.

“I love you so much.”

I hugged her tight. “You saw me yesterday. You know I’m fine.”

“Not the point.”

“Mel—”

“What would I do without you?”

And I got it because it was her, and I was trained, after thirty years—I’d known the woman since I was fifteen—to listen to her.

What would she do without me?

I was necessary to her, but she wasn’t the only one.

To Dreo, to my kid and his girlfriend and the baby they were expecting, to the woman blubbering in my arms, to her husband standing there looking like death warmed over behind her… I was indispensable. To Michael, who was biting his bottom lip as Danielle held his hand and smiled at me, I was crucial. To the students I had helped, like Greg Baylor, to those that still needed me, like Gwen Barnaby, I was vital. And for Sanderson Vaughn, whom I planned to actually make an effort with, even though it would be damn hard, I would be critical to his success. I was not the second coming, but to the people around me, I was irreplaceable. Time that I worked harder and dug in.

"I'm not going anywhere," I told Melissa, leaning her back, pushing the hair out of her eyes. "You look terrible."

"Because I've been haunting this fuckin' hospital!"

I snorted out a laugh. "And Jare?"

"I took care of it," she snapped. "Or, Dreo and I did. We transferred the deed, we're getting him paid out, and the movers are coming tomorrow."

I looked up at the new man in my life. "What about your furniture?"

"This is what you care about?"

I nodded.

He rolled his eyes. "I'm leaving the furniture for Jare because he said he—"

"You talked to Jare?"

"Well, yeah. Mel called to tell him you got stabbed, and he was pissed at me for putting you in danger and—"

"It wasn't your fault! I—"

"He knows that now, but he was mad at first. I would've been too. But we're good, and so I asked about furniture and took some pictures and texted them to him, and he liked what he saw. Gillian really likes the couches."

Did she.

"And so I'm dumping my bed, keeping Michael's, swapping out the one you had in your guest room and giving that one to them for the baby's room, and we're all good. Like Mel said, the movers will be there tomorrow."

"And the OB?" I asked my ex-wife.

"I have one, and they're going to love her. The appointment is made."

"And when will Jare be here?"

"Next Monday."

I looked back at Dreo. “What is today?”

“Friday.”

“So I’ve been here five days?”

He nodded.

“And when do I get to go home?”

“Tomorrow. You can sit on the couch and watch the movers.”

Michael cleared his throat.

“Hey.”

He forced a smile.

I lifted my arms for him. “I’m okay.”

And he was there, harder than Mel had bumped into me, his arms tightening fast as he buried his face in my shoulder. I felt the shudder and held him tight. “It’s okay, honey,” I told him, leaning my head against his. “I’m fine. Don’t worry.”

Dreo stroked Michael’s hair and then mine, and I saw the breath he took.

“What?”

“Just looking at my family.” He smiled. “It’s nice.”

And just like that, the lump in my throat was too big to speak around.

“IF YOU knew my son better,” Mrs. Fiore was telling me later that day when she and Mr. Fiore came to see me, soup and bread in hand, both homemade, “you would know that he loved you for a long time, Nathan. He does not let anyone in his life who he doesn’t.”

The epiphanies just kept coming.

“He thought he should change his life for Michael, but for you, to have you, he had to. I am very grateful.”

I looked at her and then over at Mr. Fiore standing by the window.

“I hope someday that you and I can be friends, sir.”

He grunted, and I knew where Dreo had picked up the now familiar patronizing tone. "We don't have to be friends, we're family. What does *friends* matter?"

I had no idea what to say to that.

"Dreo says your boy will be here for Thanksgiving. You bring him to the house, and his girl and your son's mother and her husband. Them, I will be friends with."

He just made these statements like of course that was how it would be, so certain, this patriarch, that all of us would just fall into line. And of course we all would. I felt it. Like the man said "jump" and the rest of us asked "how high?"

"Yes?" he barked.

"Yessir," I agreed fast.

"*Bene*." He gave me a quick nod.

I looked back at Mrs. Fiore, and she reached out and put a hand on my cheek. "You'll learn. You have to agree fast in our family."

Our.

Amazing.

"I know you wanted a woman for Dreo, grandchildren and—"

"I have enough grandchildren. I have three other daughters that you need to meet, their husbands and their children. You will see." She smiled. "My family is big."

"Yes, ma'am."

"But I will lose no one else, yes?"

I nodded.

"I want to keep my Michael and, more importantly, Dreo. I will see him now more. You, you will bring him. Yes?"

She was expecting me to act as an intermediary between—

"*Sì?*" Mr. Fiore barked at me again.

"*Sì*," I copied him fast.

"*Bene*," he told me for the second time, liking, I could tell, that he was starting to train me.

I realized then that I was soon to have someone else in my life ordering me around. As though my own father was not annoying enough.

Mrs. Fiore took my hand.

"You will make sure Michael sees me more as well?"

"Yes," I agreed quickly.

Mr. Fiore was smiling at me.

I had always been a quick study.

I WAS watching Dreo sleep. He had passed out while I was on the phone with my son, and when I hung up, I started looking at him.

The long line of his throat looked so vulnerable, his hands flopped together on his chest, and his crossed socked feet at the end of my bed were all enough to give me heart failure. He was so at ease with me and so constant and really not about to leave me alone in the hospital. I had told Mel that everything was moving really fast for me, and she had asked me if that mattered.

"Not this time," I had confessed and then noticed she was crying. "What's with you?"

"You." She had smiled through her tears. "I was so worried that you were never going to find anyone to love as hard as you could. I didn't want you to miss feeling how I do when I look at Ben."

I sighed deeply.

"I'm so happy to be wrong."

I was too.

And now as I lay there, looking at Dreo, I wondered what my life would soon be like. When the door opened, I looked up and was surprised to find Duncan Stiel.

"Hey," I said softly, because I didn't want Dreo to wake up.

He moved slowly across the floor to the end of the bed. "I just wanted to come and check on you and talk for a minute."

I nodded, noticing the cast on his right wrist. “I’m sorry you guys fought.”

“I should have been more careful. I’m used to fighting guys who don’t know what they’re doing, thugs on the street, but him”—he tipped his chin at Dreo—“he knows what he’s doing.”

“You guys shouldn’t have even gone at each other. You were both just worried about me.”

He gave me a slight smile before taking a breath. “I’m taking your advice and going on vacation.”

“I said to move.” I grinned.

“Well, I’m not ready to do that yet, but a buddy of mine lives in Colt outside of Eureka, California. Small town. Will be nice to just do nothing for a bit.”

“Good. I hope you enjoy it.”

He sighed deeply. “I hope I never hurt you.”

“No more than I hurt you,” I said, reaching for him.

We held hands for just a moment.

“I keep saying good-bye.”

“Then stop. Say I’ll see ya.”

“Okay. I’ll see ya.”

I nodded, and the man walked out the door.

“So.” Dreo cleared his throat.

Rolling my head to right so I could see, I smiled. “You’re awake.”

“I’m a light sleeper.”

“Something you want to ask, Mr. Fiore?” I smiled to encourage him.

“Yeah. It’s me, right? Not him?”

“It’s you.”

He closed his eyes. “I thought so. I’m hotter.”

And he was, but I would not give the man the satisfaction of a response. Because really, what made him hotter was not so much the outside as what lay underneath. He was ready to tell the world that I was his. Was prepared to walk down the street with me and hold my hand. Had no qualms about being my date to anything, anywhere.

"God, I really love you."

"I know." He yawned and reached out a hand to me.

I took it and held on tight. "Talking to your folks was good."

He grunted.

"I had no idea you had three other sisters. Are you the youngest?"

"Yes," he whimpered. "Please, *caro*, go to sleep. We can talk about the coven later."

"Coven?" I smiled.

"Wait." He exhaled, getting comfortable in the chair. "You'll see."

I was really looking forward to it.

FOURTEEN

BEST intentions aside, I was ready to kill him. Sitting in on one of Sanderson's lectures was giving me a migraine. Ashton, beside me, was scowling as he typed up notes on his laptop of things to improve. He was now at two pages of bullet points.

"Well?" Sanderson asked me when he was done and the classroom had emptied of undergraduates.

"Are you kidding?" Ashton looked surprised.

"What?"

"Do you mean to speak to your students like they're idiots, or is that just what comes out?"

"I don't do that," he snapped defensively.

"Yes, you do," I assured him. "Let's have lunch."

"You know, Nate, just because I saved your—"

"Don't push it," I warned him. "Or we won't be writing that paper together on 'The Squire's Tale' for the Chaucer symposium in March."

He shut up.

"Just let me and Ash help."

And for once, he nodded instead of being combative, and when we got to the bottom of the stairs and a student opened the door for us, he thanked them and put a hand on my shoulder when we got outside.

"How are you feeling?" he asked me.

"Okay, thank you."

"I'll treat you guys to lunch," he told me and Ashton.

I nodded, and Ashton gave him a begrudging thank you. It was small, but it was a start. That his hand went to my back to lead me into the burger place was also nice.

He was trying, and so was I.

For once.

IT WAS scary how organized Dreo was. Already we had a joint bank account that he and I both put money into for the mortgage payment and household expenses. Bills were in both of our names. He changed the address on his driver's license and put in a change of address card with the post office and Michael's school. If he said he would do something, he did it, no reminder needed. Jared and Gillian's place was all ready to go, and even though they had been delayed another week and would miss Thanksgiving, they would be there the week after, and we would all be together for Christmas. It was what Gillian wanted. Being disowned was hard on her. She wanted to sit in my living room with me and Melissa and Ben and was insanely excited to meet Dreo and Michael and Danielle. I had told her all about Michael's now "official girlfriend," much to his begrudging glee. I was looking forward to her and Jared meeting them too. Crazy to think that I suddenly had everything I always wanted.

"Why do you think that is?" Melissa had asked me as we had strolled arm in arm down the Miracle Mile earlier that week.

"'Cause I'm living right," I told her.

"Just you living is good," she assured me, squeezing my arm, sighing deeply.

When I got home a little after seven on that Friday night, I was surprised to find the TV on and Dreo sprawled out on the couch watching soccer. There were five open containers of Chinese food on the coffee table, two paper plates, and two beers.

"Hey," I greeted him.

He grunted. Obviously whatever was happening on screen was more interesting than me.

"Where's Michael?"

Nothing.

"Dreo?"

Another grunt.

"Where is Michael?"

"Spending the night at…."

"Dreo!" I snapped, then laughed.

"Parker's house," he finished, unimpressed with my volume. He didn't even turn around.

I remembered that now. Michael was staying with his friend Parker Barnes until after their track meet the following day. We were to meet him at the park, watch the competition along with Danielle, and then bring her home with us to let Michael shower and change before we all convened at the Fiore house for dinner. Dreo's parents were enjoying the new closeness that Dreo having a partner had given them. They had been disappointed that Jared and Gillian would not be there for Thanksgiving, but were looking forward to seeing Ben and Melissa and their kids. I was too.

The first Sunday night dinner I had spent with the Fiores I had been amazed at the volume and my welcome. Dreo's sisters, Loretta, Felice, and Alisa, their husbands, and their children were all happy to meet me. The coven, as my boyfriend called the women he had grown up with, told him that I was handsome and kind and attentive. I was a hit. In the kitchen drying dishes, Dreo had leaned close and whispered something.

"What did you say?"

"That your eyes are beautiful."

I smiled.

"Until I got close I didn't know they changed color when you were happy."

"Do they?"

He nodded. "Those beautiful hazel eyes of yours become dark green."

"You like that?"

"*Sì*," he murmured, leaning close to kiss me.

I felt a roll of heat run through me just thinking about it until he yelled at the TV. This was definitely not about to become a romantic moment.

"Pull your head out of your ass!"

I snorted out a laugh. "So is that beer for me, and some of the takeout?"

"Yeah."

"Did you have a good day?"

"Yeah."

"Did you discover the meaning of life today?"

"Yeah."

I chuckled and went to change.

Looking around my bedroom, I had to smile. Just seeing the man's watch, wallet, and change on the nightstand on his side of the bed was nice. He slept closest to the door, and under the bed, easily accessible, where he could grab it if he heard a weird noise in the night, was a baseball bat. His gun, the SIG Sauer P250 that he had retrieved from the police station, was in a combination-locked box in the closet on the top shelf. We were having conversations about it. I wanted it gone, but he wanted to keep it. The fact that no one but him could get in there and that no one but the two of us even knew where it was, was a start. I was worried about the baby. He wanted to know how the baby could reach the box or get it open. I knew why he had held onto it. He was still worried about his former life intruding on his present. But as each day passed, he shed another layer of wariness, and I enjoyed seeing him do it. He was confident and content.

After walking back out to the living room in an old pair of faded jeans, a long-sleeved T-shirt, and socks, I took a seat beside him. The beer was still icy cold, so it had not been out long, and the food was hot.

"You just get home?" Another monosyllabic grunt, and I laughed softly. "Who's playing, baby?"

"Milan," he managed to answer before he yelled, "*Passala*!"

It was more fun watching him get mad than keeping an eye on the game.

"*Cazzo, tirala in porta*!"

I ate, drank one beer, then got up to get another and realized that something about just hanging out with him, even though I knew he was focused on the game and not me, was fun. We were together, and this was Friday night. I really liked it.

I was starting on my third beer, bringing him back his second, sprawled out beside him, when his hand went to my thigh. It was sad, but just that much contact made me hard. Ever since I got home from the hospital, he had been careful with me. I got sucked off and jerked off and there was some amazing frottage, but anal had been off the table. Every time I brought up the fact that I was okay, that what I really needed was for him to pound me into the mattress, he gave me a patronizing smile and told me to go to sleep. I was ready to attack him, but he was really good about using Michael as a buffer and our schedules to his advantage.

So the strong hand that was now gripping my thigh was making my dick twitch and weep against the zipper.

"Dreo," I whimpered.

With his left hand, he worked open the top button of my jeans, pulled the zipper down, and slid his hand under my briefs. His fingers wrapped around my steadily leaking cock as I bucked up into his fist.

"Oh God," I moaned, pushing in and out of his firm grip, loving the calluses, the way his skin felt smoothing over my heated flesh, and the possessiveness. I was his, so he could touch me whenever he wanted. It was so hot.

He slid off the couch then, dropped to his knees between my spread legs, and as he yanked my jeans over my ass, bent and swallowed my shaft.

"Dreo!"

He sucked hard, his cheeks hollowed out as he laved and licked, the suction so good, so perfect, saliva rolling down into my crease. I wanted to fuck his mouth, but more, I wanted him.

"I'm fine!" I yelled.

He lifted his mouth from my cock, and I saw it then, in his right hand: lube.

"Where was that?"

"Under the couch," he told me, pulling a piece of paper out of the pocket of his jeans and passing it to me before he popped open the cap.

I unfolded it and saw that I was looking at negative test results. My man was disease-free.

"So you—"

"Yes," he growled, and two lube-slicked fingers were wedged inside of me.

I gasped because the burn was jarring and exquisite at the same time. He was rough with me, and the fact that he was normally infinitely gentle—but couldn't be at that moment—spoke to the depth of his need.

"No more condoms," he told me.

I nodded as he added a third finger, scissoring, stretching, and making me ready even though it was unnecessary. I groaned his name.

He hooked my legs up over his shoulders, lifting, shunting me to the edge of the couch as his hands gripped my ass tight and spread my cheeks.

I arched up toward him as he pressed his swollen head to my entrance.

"What do you want?"

The words were hard to form. Only babbling came out.

He pushed forward a fraction. "Nate?"

"You, Dreo! I want you!"

The plunge inside was hard and fast, and I yelled his name as the long, thick length of him dragged over my prostate. My hand went to my own cock as he thrust deeper with every stroke, his hands locked on my hips, adding to his domination of me.

"Oh fuck," he moaned, and I opened my eyes to see him watching as his cock filled my ass, pounding into me. He was lost now as his head fell back in submission to the sensations roaring through him. "I am so close, Nate, you—*ti amo, tu sei tutta la mia vita*!"

It sounded good, but I hardly cared.

"I love you, Nate. You're my whole world."

God.

His shaft, hammering into me, pounding me down into the couch, driving in and out, was all there was. The crest that was suddenly upon me, the orgasm torn from me, rushing through me, turned my vision white for long seconds.

My body clenched around Dreo's cock, my muscles bearing down on him, rippling and spasming as he pumped cum deep inside my body. I felt the heat, the wet, coating me, running out of me, leaking down the inside of my thighs.

"*Sei così bello….*"

I shivered with my aftershocks, reaching up, pulling him close even though the front of his T-shirt was covered, splattered with my semen.

His mouth covered mine, and I opened for him, tasting and sucking on his tongue, the kiss hot and wet and claiming. Never had a lover made me so crazy, so needy, taken every artifice I had and stripped it away, leaving just me, vulnerable and wanting.

Pulling back, I saw the hooded and dark liquid eyes, clouded with passion, full of heat and seduction. "Jesus, Dreo, I'll be dripping with you for hours."

"Yes," he almost snarled, mouth on my throat, licking, nibbling, sucking as he remained buried and pulsing inside of me. "You belong to me. So beautiful, and you're mine."

"Oh yes," I agreed, loving every word of his promise, trembling with my body's reaction to our lovemaking, the absolute joy of it.

"You know, I'm gonna have you so many times tonight: I want you on your knees, on the bed, in the shower…. I just fuckin' want you."

"Why?"

"Because I love you… *amore mio*… my love…."

"Me too." I smiled up into those gorgeous eyes. "You're my love."

The grin I got was so full of complete and utter happiness that all I could do was kiss him and kiss him and kiss him.

There didn't need to be any more words.

CPSIA information can be obtained at www.ICGtesting.com
Printed in the USA
LVOW071006310512

284074LV00001B/41/P

9 781613 725009